The Wolf's Assassin

Katie Dunn

Titles by Katie Dunn

Ancient Elements

Myth Blessed

Four Horsemen

Sapphire Sparks

The Wolf's Assassin

<u>Skor Stone Trilogy</u>
Pirates from Under
Prince of Shayd
Rebel in Skorval

Chapter 1

Jessie

I like to think of myself as an adventurer. Almost like Indiana Jones. I travel the world, find artifacts, and take them back to headquarters for safe keeping. Some people may call it treasure hunting, but I call it treasure protecting.

Is it my fault people end up dead when I am procuring said treasure?

Well, yes, yes it is.

Unfortunately, my likeness to Indiana Jones only goes as far as finding artifacts, partaking in adventure, and wearing a cool sable fedora because unlike Indiana Jones, I, Jessie no-last-name, am an assassin for the Infinite Order.

And I just received the assignment of a lifetime.

"Shut. Up!" I shout at Dorian. My boss. The head of the Infinite Order.

He sits back in his chair, totally relaxed with a smug smile.

I probably should have accepted this assignment calmly and acted as if he didn't just change my life with a file folder. That's what an elite assassin would have done. But I can't help it. I am so excited. I clutch the folder close to my chest and beam at the man behind the desk.

He is young, either late twenties or early thirties...or maybe forties. No one really knows how old he is. He has got one of those faces that look young, but he has been around long enough that he must be older than he appears. He wears a black suit that matches his long dark locks, and his light blue eyes look haunted despite the crinkle around them from his smile.

"Well, you aren't one yet. You have to bring that item back to me, then we can talk," he says, gesturing with his head to the folder in my hands.

I suck in my excitement with a long inhale, shut down my grin until I am professional again, then bow my head respectfully, trying to show him he is not making a mistake by trusting in me. "It shall be done."

I wait until I am down the hall from Dorian's office to let my excitement burst free once again. I look up and down the hall, making sure no one is around then do a happy dance, complete with a butt wiggle and everything. I know my dance is a little premature, but I am an artifact retrieval expert so whatever it is Dorian is sending me to get can already be considered mine.

I know better than to open the folder here, so I reign in my excitement and force myself to be patient as I make my way out of the office. To anyone else, this building in New Jersey is home to The Dressy Cleaners. Its innocent front makes it less suspicious when the Order carts in items from a van or leaves with large, heavy bags.

I thank the universe when I do not run into anyone as I leave.

My colleagues embody what I always imagine an assassin to be like. Cold. Uncaring. Deadly. I am deadly too, but I go about my work with a little more cheer. I mean, dead bodies are already depressing enough, no need to make it worse by joining in on the doom and gloom, am I right?

I don't have a car since the streets are usually too packed to get anywhere in one so I pick up my Moped scooter from the side of the building and leave The Dressy Cleaners behind, clutching the key to my future tight in my hand.

I make three circles around the block and two false turns before I stop in the alley by my home, parking my scooter behind a dumpster and covering it with a dirty tarp. Call me paranoid. Call me cautious. I just don't trust people and I am always wary of being followed. My home is my safe space and if that were ever to be discovered that would leave me vulnerable. Instead of going through the front door and up the stairs to my apartment, I climb the fire escape to my living room window and enter my home. I glance around and smile at the sparse furnishings and the green plants that add life to the place.

Home sweet home.

No pets greet me. I always wanted a dog, but I would never be able to care for one since I am gone for long periods of time. I run my fingers over the little succulent on the windowsill which is as close as I will ever get to a pet. The only sound in the room is the whirring of the overhead fan which shakes as if it is about to fall off. I ignore it and make my way to the kitchen and open the fridge, looking for food. Of course, there is nothing but carrots and expired milk.

Gross.

Delivery it is then. I make the call to my favorite Chinese food restaurant then sit on the couch to wait. The folder is still clutched in my hand and I stare at it, letting the excitement that usually comes with getting an artifact retrieval assignment rush through me. Hopefully I will not have to kill anyone on this mission. Not that I am opposed to killing, it just gets messy and complicates the mission. I open the folder and lay out the pages inside on the coffee table until I can see every paper at once.

"Oooo, Peru!" I clap happily at the destination I will be flying to tomorrow. There is already a plane ticket with a fake ID and passport next to a map showing me where I need to go. I look at the ID and grin at the name I will be assuming. Marion Ravenwood. The female character in *Raiders of the Lost Ark*. Dorian does not show it often but he has a sense of humor.

I sift through the papers, making sure to read each one carefully until I am familiar with what I need to retrieve and how to go about doing it. When I get these kinds of assignments, it is easy to forget I am an assassin. There should not be anyone in the jungle to get in my way and there is no one I need to kill to get to my destination. Just a simple get in-get out assignment. Easy peasy. I collect all the papers and put them neatly into the folder then get up to pack.

A knock at the door makes me change direction and I open it to see someone holding a take-out bag. I grin and hand the man money before taking the food. He leaves quickly which I am thankful for. I am not particularly good at socializing. I take a quick break to eat before continuing to my room to pack. There is not much to do since I always keep a go-bag in the closet. I add the folder and some extra changes of clothes, not knowing how long I will be there. Ideally, only a couple days, but

I know better than to assume the best. I finish quickly then turn to the last things I need to pack.

My weapons.

I know I will not be able to bring them through a carry on, so I stuff my daggers and gun into the bag alongside a few shuriken. My favorite weapons are those I can throw but I will always turn to my gun when I need a quick kill. Sometimes, for fun, I dabble in poisons, but they are too slow and require proximity, so I do not mess with them often.

With that finished, I plop onto my bed and force myself to fall asleep, knowing the faster I do the faster I can get to the mission which means the faster I will be able to become an elite.

To blend in I must ride in coach even though I know the Order has enough money to spring first-class seats for their assassins and retrieval experts. I don't mind, though I make sure to sit near the aisle where I can keep an eye on my surroundings better and where I can get up faster if I need to.

The other two in my row ignore me. They whisper to each other as they watch their movie on the screen on the back of the seat in front of them. I am tempted to take a quick nap here knowing this might be the last comfortable space I will be in. From here on out I will be sleeping in the jungle as I make my way to the artifact. However, I keep my eyes open, not trusting the people around me even though they are all just tourists excited to see Machu Picchu.

I am dressed as a tourist too, but as soon as I am on my own in the jungle, I will change into my adventure gear. (Yes, I called it adventure gear and not assassin gear. Remember this is a different mission. I will not be killing anyone.)

Once we touch down on the tarmac and are able to get off the plane, I don't hesitate to jump up and leave. I am not bogged down by a carry-on which makes it easier to maneuver around the tourists trying to grab their things from the overhead compartments. I still have to wait behind a line once I reach first class but thankfully, they are quick. I speed through the airport until I reach the carousel where our bags will be dropped off. This part is the longest so I wait against the wall where I can keep my back covered and have an eye on everyone who comes by. Despite me leaving the plane faster than the other passengers they still manage to catch up to me before the carousel begins depositing bags. A few of the people grab their things from the conveyor belt before I finally spot mine. Pleased to see my bag since it means I can finally start my adventure, I don my classic sable fedora, grab my bag, and leave the airport without a backward glance.

It takes only a day to reach the spot on the map. I slept under the cover of a tree with a small fire near me to keep the animals away. I also set up a trigger to alert me if any animals were brave enough to creep closer despite the fire. Now, in the light of day, I move without much caution, confident there is no one this far into the jungle to notice me and the animals will not bother me now that I am awake.

The map is difficult to use when I am in the middle of the jungle since there are no landmarks or signs to point me in the right direction. I have to use the compass I brought with me and a watch to keep me oriented. This is not the first time I have had to go through a jungle or rough terrain to get what I need. I know how to find food and water and how to hide my tracks if necessary. I would have made an awesome Scout leader if my profession did not go the way it did.

A mountain in the distance catches my attention through the canopy of trees. I let out a sigh of relief. I need to find a cave near that mountain, so I know I am close. Thank the universe too, because it is hot, and I need a rest. The only reason I haven't taken a rest yet is because if I want to get back home in a timely manner then I need to get the artifact as quickly as possible. I tuck my map into my bag, confident I know how to get there the rest of the way.

I lose the mountain a couple times when the trees get thick enough to cover the sky, but I keep moving forward and am soon at the base.

So, where is the cave?

I pace along the base looking for an opening, but the mountain is solid and the only thing to do is go up. I sigh. My legs are going to hurt after this. I am going to need a long soak in the tub when I get home. I check the map once more to make sure I am in the right place then begin climbing the mountain, making a zigzag so I can check for a cave as I move upward.

I wonder how Dorian knows of this place. It is so remote and takes a day's journey and a trek up a mountain to get to it. Who put it here and why? There better be booby traps or puzzles to solve. I have never had to deal with more than combination locks or lasers before but the idea of having to avoid traps like Indiana Jones sends a thrill of excitement through me, spurring me onward with renewed energy.

It takes another hour before I finally find what could be considered a cave. It doesn't look big enough for a person to enter comfortably and I am hesitant to go into a darkened cave where wild animals could be hiding. This might not even be the one I am looking for, but it is the only one around, so I have to check it out.

I light a few tactical glowsticks and throw them in, hoping the noise and light will send out any animals inside so I can scare them off. Once I enter, I will be in their domain.

Nothing comes rushing out, so I take a deep breath and shimmy my way inside, throwing my bag ahead of me as I go. Thankfully, the cave widens inside, and I no longer have to crouch or squeeze through. There is no way any sane person would have gone through that hole. Does that mean I am insane or elite worthy?

I take out my flashlight and shine it around. The glowsticks only do so much. The cave is like I would expect. Rough stone walls, darkness in every corner, cooler air which is a relief from the humidity outside. I gather the glow sticks and toss them farther into the cave. I repeat this over and over until I come across what I think is my next obstacle. A rounded stone that is obviously not natural covers an opening. There is a sliver of light on one side which surprises me since the only lights so far have been my glowsticks and flashlight. Taking a deep breath and letting it out slowly to calm my racing heart, I peek through the sliver into the next room.

I can't see much but what I do see makes me gasp. Large crystals stick out of the walls and each one glows with a strange blueish-white light. I peer around as much as I can looking for the artifact, but the stone hinders my attempts. About 80% confident I found the correct cave, I study the stone in front of me. How will I move it? It probably weighs tons, and I may be strong, but I am not Supergirl.

I push against one side of the stone anyway but give up when I know for sure that I cannot move it. I stand back and put my hands on my hips. WWID. What Would Indiana Do?

Look for levers.

I run my fingers along the stone edges then the wall near it searching for levers, switches, or buttons. Anything that can roll the stone out of the way like a door. I sigh in frustration when I do not find anything. Who put this here and how?

A sound from behind me, back near the entrance of the cave, makes me freeze. Was that an animal? Please tell me it is something soft and cuddly and not the poisonous or dangerous variety. As long as I don't disturb it, I should be fine. I focus on the stone door again and begin trying different methods to open it. I cannot go back empty handed. I have to open this door. There is another sound from behind me but this time much closer. Whatever it is, it will find me soon.

Making a last-minute decision, I gather up my glowsticks and shove them in my bag then hide in a shadowed corner away from the stone door, hoping the animal will just come and go. I wait with slow, soft breaths and hope that it will not see, hear, or smell me.

My breath puffs out in a gasp when two men approach the stone door rather than an animal. My hand immediately goes to my bag to grab a weapon. I pull out a dagger and my gun as quietly as possible.

"So, this is where you hid it?" One of them asks with a laughing tone. "How did you know the cave would open up and that you wouldn't get stuck squeezing in through the entrance?"

The other man doesn't stop as he responds. "I didn't but I saw an animal about our size squeeze in here so I assumed it had to be bigger inside."

My eyes widen and I glance around discreetly looking for large animals. Thankfully, there is only me and the intruders. Well, technically I am the intruder, but I was here first, so it doesn't count.

"Help me move this," the second man says.

Ha, good luck with that. It weighs tons. I thought the man would know that since he is the one who supposedly hid the artifact here. I eye him, taking in his tall frame and muscular arms. From what I can see he is handsome. I cannot see much since it is quite dark, but he has lightly colored hair, short on the sides and the longer pieces on top are combed back but strands fall into his face anyway. His voice holds authority, but it is not cruel. They both have an air about them that demands attention.

The first guy who spoke is a little shorter but not by much. He has darker hair and seems to be a bit cheerier and more energetic. He is constantly moving even though I don't think he notices it and while the second guy produces a no-nonsense tone, the first guy sounds excited.

I should have shot them by now, but I want to see if they can open the door first. I have come to the conclusion that I will not be able to do it on my own. Did Dorian know that before he sent me? I shake away that thought. If he knew I could not do it on my own he would have sent backup…right?

The men stand on one side of the stone door and push against it. Their arms strain and they growl with exertion. I am about to shoot them and find another way inside when the stone begins to scrape against the wall and the glowing crystals shine through. I try not to gasp at this show of strength. There is no way two people should be able to move that with their bare hands, but I just witnessed it so I must believe it.

Believe it and be thankful for it.

When the stone is completely removed from the entrance to the crystal room, the light-haired man turns to his companion. "Alright, go outside and keep watch. I will be out soon."

"Aw, but I want to see—"

The leader glares at the protesting man making him grumble and leave the cave. Now is my chance. There is only one of them. I wait for the first guy to leave then wait a couple minutes to make sure he is truly out of the cave before revealing myself. The leader has already gone into the crystal room, so I sidle along the stone wall with my gun raised and peek inside.

The room is amazing. The glowing crystals are everywhere, more than I first thought, making my flashlight and glowsticks inconsequential. In the center of the room is a pedestal with a golden, bejeweled chalice. The man hovers his hand over it before grabbing the artifact and turning to leave. That is when I jump out to block his exit. The man freezes and his eyes widen ever so slightly before hardening into a glare. I am kind of impressed. I thought I warranted a bit more shock than that, but he hides it well.

"I will take that," I say confidently with my gun pointed at him.

"Mmm, no, I don't think you will," he counters.

My eyes flick up to his, wondering what brings on this bravery in the face of a gun. As soon as my eyes meet his, my world seems to slow. I know that sounds cliché but it really feels that way. My heart starts beating faster and my breath catches. My hand slackens and the gun tilts down as I try to make sense of this strange yet exhilarating feeling. His eyes are a crazy beautiful green and gold color. The gold part is surrounded by green in a most mesmerizing way. I could get lost in those eyes for hours.

His glare is replaced with wonder as if he is feeling the same thing I am. I take an involuntary step closer. I want to touch him. I *need* to touch him. To run my hands through his styled, combed back hair. To hold his face in my hands. To feel his lips on mine. He looks like he wants the same thing and steps closer, reaching out with his other hand. My stomach flips when he nears then sends butterflies fluttering around inside at his heated gaze. I have never felt this way after seeing someone for the first time. It is a little scary but also wonderful.

"Who are you?" he asks in awe.

Somehow that snaps me out of my infatuation. The world returns to normal and I raise my gun. Without hesitating, I shoot him. His eyes widen. He looks hurt by my action more than the actual bullet in his body. When he doesn't fall, I shoot him two more times until he finally collapses. The chalice he held clatters against the ground and rolls away. I suck air through my teeth hoping I didn't ruin the artifact. I pick it up and check for marks or damages, but it is fine. I breathe out a sigh of relief.

I spare a glance at the dead body. My heart twists at the sight. I do not usually have such remorse. It is my job to kill. But something about him makes it feel all wrong. I start to bend down to brush the loose strands of hair away from his face, but I stop myself. That other guy will have heard the shots and be here soon.

I straighten and turn my back on the dead body. I race out of the crystal room and through the cave. I hear the man from the entrance running towards me, so I hide in the shadows along the wall and watch smugly as he passes by without a glance in my direction.

I wait until he is far enough away before making my quick exit from the cave and out of the jungle with the artifact in hand.

Chapter 2

I glance around my accommodations with distaste. Everything is cream and yellow. The bed spread, the curtains, the walls, even the dresser and couch. I wonder if it is too late to slip away and go home. I traveled to Canada as summoned, but they don't need me here. My brothers should be good enough. I creep to the window and pull aside the horrifying curtains, peering out at the empty surroundings. I am on the second floor, but the jump will not be difficult. I unlatch the window and begin to open it but a voice from the door freezes me in place.

"Running away already?" My brother laughs. "You just got here!"

Sighing, I close the window, knowing I can't escape now. I turn to see which brother it is that caught me and can't help but smile when I see it is Easton.

"No, I am merely getting some air," I lie and move away from the window to the couch that hurts my eyes.

Easton smirks and shakes his head at me then peers around the room. He winces. "I don't blame you. Mom has got bad taste in décor."

"What does your room look like?" I ask, almost not wanting to know.

Easton grins. "Mine is orange."

We both make a face at the image of an orange room then chuckle at our reactions.

"Are the others here?" I ask.

Easton shrugs then nods toward the door. "Care to find out?"

I nod and follow him out of my room, grateful to get away. Thankfully it is only the rooms that need to be burned. The rest of the house is quite nice and almost reminds me of home. Most of the rooms in the manor are upstairs so we go to each door peeking in and cringe at the awful décor before moving on to the next. Easton's room is only a few doors down from mine so our other two brothers cannot be far off. When we do not see them in any of the upstairs rooms, we do the only other thing we can do.

We shout for them.

With our exceptional hearing they should be able to hear us if they are in the manor. A few seconds later a human-made howl pierces the air coming from downstairs near the kitchen. I should have known that is where they would be. Easton shakes his head and smiles, thinking the same. We race down the stairs and pass the sitting room where we will have to meet Mother in a while then crash into the large kitchen to find our other brothers surrounding a baking sheet of cookies while Chef Donelley stands on the other side of the room over a couple pots of food. I sniff the air and smell chicken though I don't know what he is making with it.

"North, East, you've got to get some of these while they're hot," our youngest brother, Sutton, mumbles through a mouthful of cookie.

The last of the bunch, Wesley, holds up his freshly baked cookie in a calmer and more sophisticated manner and nods his agreement. I cross my arms, declining their offer and stare at them with a soft smile. I haven't seen them in a while. That happens when we all live in different parts of the world, yet they act as if we have never been apart.

Easton steps toward the counter and takes one of the cookies then moans after he takes the first bite. I shake my head at them with a laugh then turn back to the entrance of the kitchen. By now Mother and Father would have heard the howl and our shouts and will be looking for us.

Just as I have the thought, Father walks into the kitchen.

Arthur Kane, King the wolf shifters. His thick, dark hair is tied back today, and his beard and mustache look recently trimmed. At first glance, everyone would think he is no older than forty. In truth, he is at least 200 years old, but he never confirms exactly how old when we ask. Today he is sporting dark blue pants and a white and blue patterned button shirt with the sleeves rolled up.

Father quirks an eyebrow at us and the corners of his lips pull up slightly which is the closest thing to a smile we will get. "Are you boys bothering Chef Donelley?"

We are not boys anymore, haven't been for years, yet our father never ceases to see us that way.

The Chef turns at his voice and waves his hands. "No, no sir, they are fine. I made an extra batch since I knew they would be coming."

"Smart man." Father nods his approval.

He turns his back on us and walks out of the kitchen calling over his shoulder for us to follow him. It is not surprising he would get right to business. Not even a *hello, how are you* or a *welcome back*. Just as good though, I was not about to offer him pleasantries either.

I roll my eyes and turn to my brothers to make sure they come along. We follow him out to the sitting room where our mother waits by a fireplace holding a cup of tea. She grins at us and puts her cup down on the little table beside her.

Aida Kane, Queen of the wolf shifters. Cheery, outgoing, energetic, basically the complete opposite of Arthur Kane. She has her blonde hair in a braid, but strays pop out in random disarray. She must have been busy before this. Today she is wearing a gold jumpsuit and brown sandals, both of which were birthday presents from Wesley.

"My boys! How are you? Did you see your rooms yet? I redecorated."

I hold back my look of disgust and plaster a smile on my face instead. "Yup, it's, uh, interesting."

Easton snorts and I elbow him to make him shut up.

"Oh, I am glad you like it!" Mother claps with excitement. "Maybe I can redecorate your castle and—"

I hold my hands up as if I need to physically stop her. "No! No, that's ok. I think the castle is fine for now."

"O-oh, ok. Well, if you change your mind…" Mother shrugs as if that signifies the rest of the sentence.

Easton smirks at me and I glare.

"Enough." Father says bringing all our attention to him. "I did not bring them here to talk of décor."

Mother nods and her smile drops. I stiffen, knowing it is serious if it causes my mother to stop smiling. She is an all-around sunny person. My youngest brother Sutton takes after her.

"Norden, I need you and one of your brothers to retrieve the Chalice," Father tells me looking grim. He turns to the others. "The other two need to retrieve the Moonstone."

"Why? I would assume we are inducting a new member, but your look tells me it is something else," Wesley says looking between our parents worriedly.

"You are right. We have received word that the Infinite Order has found the location of the Chalice. It is unknown if they know the whereabouts of the Moonstone, but we should move both to be safe."

I breathe out a sigh of relief and sit back. "The Infinite Order? Aren't they the ones who were bothering you fifty years ago? I thought you dealt with them."

My father gives me a stern frown. "Yes, well, apparently I did not."

"They can't actually know where they are right? You hid them so no one could possibly find them," Sutton says looking between me and our father.

It's true. I hid the Chalice in the middle of the Amazon jungle. My father hid the Moonstone and not even I know where. There is no way anyone outside of our packs would be able to find them. My eyes widen and my head jerks up to look at my father.

He nods solemnly and I curse. Someone in our packs betrayed us.

"Who?" I growl.

"Norden," Mother admonishes, looking pointedly at my hands. I glance down and notice my claws are out, gouging my mother's new furniture. I retract them and take a deep breath to calm myself.

"I have already dealt with him," Father answers vaguely. "However, now we need to remove the artifacts and hide them elsewhere. I am sure the Order is already sending someone after the Chalice, so you must leave first thing tomorrow morning."

I purse my lips and nod. This is serious. If someone were to get the Chalice and knew how to use it, then they could become immortal. Our Chalice became known in the Middle Ages when Arthur, not my father but the King of the round table, learned of its existence and that whole story about the Holy Grail came about. My ancestors spent a long time making that story nothing but a legend so no one would go looking for it. Now it seems as if it has become known again.

I glance over at my brothers. "Which one of you wants to go to Peru with me?"

Sutton's hand shoots up and he bounces in his seat. "Me, me, please pick me!"

I laugh and shake my head at his childish antics. "Fine, rest well tonight because tomorrow we will be in the jungle."

Sutton shrugs not bothered by my warning. He travels frequently so I wouldn't be surprised if his travels include jungles and humidity.

"Good, Easton and Wesley, you both go retrieve the Moonstone," Father orders.

Easton and Wesley nod then Easton grins at Father. "Is that a dog joke?"

Father shakes his head and sighs, refusing to respond to Easton's joking question. I elbow him but that only makes him laugh. Sutton joins in but thankfully Wesley is more mature than that. I get up and give my mother a kiss on the cheek and wave at my brothers before heading upstairs to my room. Sutton may be okay with the jungle, but I was going to hate going back there. Especially to that cave. But there is no way around it now. I just have to hope we don't run into anyone.

"We should shift, we will be able to get there faster."

Sutton frowns and looks around. "Won't it be suspicious if wolves are running in the Amazon?"

I shrug and start stripping my clothes off. "Maybe, but there are maned wolves here, plus no one will be around anyway."

"What about..." he looks around again warily, "...other shifters?"

Again, I shake my head. "Last time I checked, there aren't many shifters in Peru." I incline my head. "Other than the lone wolves who of course stick to themselves hence the lone part, there are some Jaguar and Panther shifters but they too are usually alone." I don't mention that the last time I checked was years ago.

Sutton nods though he doesn't look reassured and starts stripping. South America is unusual since there is no official pack under our family's leadership. Because of that it could be dangerous to shift here in case other shifters are in the area, but we should be ok.

Soon we are in our wolf forms holding our clothes in our mouths and racing through the humid jungle. In this form we can hear and see better so we are able to avoid any big predators. Like I thought, we did not come across any humans either. The journey to the mountain where the cave is hiding our Chalice only takes half a day to get to. Normally it would have been a day and a half as a human. I have to hope that puts us ahead of whatever Infinite Order member is heading this way.

I slow when we get to the base of the mountain and drop my clothes. I shift back to my human form and quickly get dressed. I hear my brother shift behind me and put his clothes on.

"Where to now?" he asks when we are both clothed and ready to continue.

I point up the mountain in the general direction of the cave then begin the trek up.

Thinking about the Chalice brings me back to last year when we inducted a new member to our packs. We found him in Brazil. He had terrorized many towns and my father came in to deal with him. He was a lone wolf, meaning not under our jurisdiction, but we are still the Alphas of the world and are in charge of keeping our secret safe as well as humans' lives. My father went in to kill him but noticed he was going mad from his constant changes. Instead of killing him, Father inducted him into the North American pack with the Chalice and the Moonstone and the man has been fine ever since.

Drinking from the Chalice is not necessary, but it does tie the drinker to our packs and it gives them immortality and faster healing abilities. A born shifter does not need to drink from it until they are older since they already have enhanced healing and ties to the pack, but eventually they would drink from it for the immortality. Humans on the other hand who are changed are usually required to drink from the Chalice by the Alphas immediately, which happens to be my family, so we can keep them in line.

The Moonstone gives a shifter control over their shifts and their other half. Without the Moonstone ritual, the shifters would change every full moon and whenever their emotions ran high, and they would not be able to maintain their human mind when they shifted. The Moonstone is the most sacred to us even above the Chalice because it also creates new shifters. It is important we do not let the Chalice or Moonstone fall into the wrong hands.

"Are we almost there?" Sutton asks.

I glance around then point to the cave which is almost out of view. It is so hidden, one would need to be looking for a cave to notice it.

Sutton snorts. "You expect me to squeeze through that?"

I grin at my brother and clap him on the shoulder, pushing him toward the entrance. Sutton stumbles forward and turns back to glare at me but his glare quickly morphs into hesitance. I nod my head at the cave, my smile never faltering. I want him to go first so I can watch him struggle to squeeze through the tiny opening. I know I will have to do the same but at least this way I can enjoy myself first.

Sutton heaves a sigh then steps into the opening, one foot and one arm at a time. He gets halfway in before he stops. I clap a hand over my mouth to stifle my laughter. Sutton's arm that has yet to go inside starts flapping and finally the laughter bursts free. I double over and tears prick my eyes as I watch my brother flail about, trying to squeeze himself the rest of the way in. When I calm down enough to hear him, Sutton's voice comes out muffled and annoyed.

"Really? Could you help me?"

Taking a deep breath to calm myself I rush forward and push my brother. Sutton yelps and crashes through the rest of the way. I wait a moment to hear from him to make sure he is alright.

"Oh, wow! It's much bigger in here."

Satisfied that he is through safely I extend my leg into the small opening, then my head, and an arm. Unlike my brother, I get through relatively easy though it is still a tight fit. Doing this every year has taught me that the key to getting through is to twist the shoulder when I am halfway so I can fit the rest of my body.

Sutton pouts when I am inside the cave and can stand straight once again. "That's not fair."

I grin. "It's not my fault you are a giant of a man." In truth I am taller than my brother, but he has wider shoulders which makes my claim valid.

Sutton looks as if he is about to say something but a strange yet intoxicating smell hits my nose and I hold up a finger to stop him from speaking. I tilt my nose up and take a sniff, but the scent I had previously picked up is gone. Strange.

I wave for my brother to follow me as I lead him further into the cave.

Eventually we come across a large stone in the shape of a circle. Anyone else would think it is the end of the cave, but I know better. It is hard to tell at first, but the stone is a door which is hiding a room with our artifact. It took a long time for me to make that door and it usually takes me a while to move it on my own. Thankfully there are two of us so it shouldn't take as long.

"So, this is where you hid it?" Sutton asks laughingly as he eyes the stone door with interest. "How did you know the cave would open up and that you wouldn't get stuck squeezing in through the entrance?"

I run my fingers over the stone door, looking for the best place to push. "I didn't but I saw an animal about our size squeeze in here, so I assumed it had to be bigger inside." When I find the place for us to roll the stone out of the way I call my brother closer. "Help me move this."

Sutton moves forward with excitement and helps me push the stone. We growl with our exertion and push harder until our arms strain. At first the rock doesn't budge but with our extra strength we are able to slowly move it from the entrance. The stone scrapes against the wall and the inside begins to shine through until there is enough room for one person to enter at a time. I stand back and gaze into the room with a wonder I cannot hide. The crystals shine with an unnatural blueish-white light sending haunting shadows and an almost magical aura around the room. I was astonished to find these crystals when I was looking for a place to hide the Chalice. I took one home for my mother last time. I believe she turned it into a lamp.

I know the Infinite Order may be here any time now so instead of gawking at the light some more I turn to my brother. "Alright, go outside and keep watch. I will be out soon."

"Aw, but I want to see—"

I glare at him, cutting off his protest. He grumbles but does as I say. Despite us both being Alphas I am the oldest, first in line to take over after our father, so I hold more authority.

Once he is gone, I stalk into the room to retrieve our prized possession. The Chalice sits on a pedestal in the middle of the room. I hover my hand over it admiring the jewels and shimmer in the gold from the crystal lights in the cave before snatching it from its resting place and turning to go.

I freeze when I notice I am not alone. My eyes widen slightly at the woman blocking the exit. How did I not sense another presence in here with me? She is wearing what looks to be a safari outfit, complete with tan shorts and tan button shirt with boots. Though her hat is something else, a fedora of some sort. If she were not aiming a gun at me, I would think she was a tourist who had accidentally wandered in from a trek through the jungle, not that the scenario was very likely. I glare at her, realizing she is the Infinite Order assassin come to retrieve the Chalice. How had she gotten passed Sutton? My breath catches as a thought comes to mind. Is my brother de—? No, I refuse to believe it. We don't die that easily.

"I will take that," she says, no hint of hesitation or fear in her voice. In fact, she is a bit overconfident, as if it is already in her hands.

I look down at the Chalice and smile, showing her I am not concerned with her little threat. "Mmm, no, I don't think you will." I look up to see her reaction, but my smile falls when I meet her eyes and my breath freezes in my chest.

There is a snap in my mind, like an instant connection, and my chest tightens both painfully and wonderfully. Like I can't breathe right until she is beside me and my heart yearns to be near her. I sniff the air subtlety and realize that same intoxicating smell I picked up earlier is coming from her. The smell of plants and soil after a rain and a sort of floral scent with a hint of spice. I stare at her in wonder, knowing exactly what this feeling is.

Mate.

She takes a step toward me, heat pooling in her eyes as her eyes dip to my lips. That little movement sends shivers down my arms. I want to reach out and touch her. To see if she is real. This can't be real. *She is my mate.* My eyes involuntarily glance at her lips and I almost growl possessively. *Mine.* I want to hold her. I want to touch her golden hair. Trace her perfect lips. Feel her soft skin.

I take a step toward her and reach out. "Who are you?" I ask in awe.

Something changes in her expression. The dazed look she had when our eyes met is gone and a hard glint replaces it. I am confused at the abrupt change.

Suddenly there is a loud bang and pain blossoms in my chest. My eyes widen. The pain of the bullet is nothing compared to the pain in my heart. My mate just shot me! She shoots me two more times and I cannot stand any longer.

I drop the Chalice.

Well, this is not how I pictured meeting my mate. I want to stop her. To save the Chalice? To talk to her? I don't know. The pain increases until I cannot handle it anymore and my mind shuts down until there is nothing more than darkness and silence.

Chapter 3

Jessie

I place my hand over the messenger bag at my side for the millionth time. I am back in New Jersey, having arrived just a couple hours ago. I only stopped for a quick shower and bite to eat before I headed to The Dressy Cleaners with the artifact.

My palms are sweaty as I open the door and step inside. As usual there is only a front counter but no one to greet me. It is better that way. I don't feel like making small talk and showing fake cheeriness. I am so nervous that my cheeriness may come across as deranged anyway. I move past the counter and turn right. I see a couple of other people down the hall, near the break room. A room no one really uses but it came with the building.

I grip the strap of my bag tight as I make my way toward them. My shoulders tense the closer I get. These are either assassins, retrieval experts, or even the elite that I have heard so much about. I never get along with anyone but Dorian in the Order. Everyone is too cold and always looking out for themselves. I am hesitant to pass the two women, worried I may get stabbed in the back and/or get my artifact stolen by them so one of them could be the one to turn it in. I don't have any proof that things like that happen, but I wouldn't put it past anyone here.

They glance up at my footsteps and scan me from head to toe with their judging stares. I straighten my shoulders and walk with purpose despite my heart beating faster and steps quickening. They scowl, but don't make any remarks. Instead, they just move into the break room and I pass by without any problems. I let out a relieved breath and quickly knock on Dorian's door a few feet down from the break room. At his go ahead, I enter, glancing behind me before I do. The two women are poking their heads out and staring at me, but I can't decipher their expressions. I frown at them then duck inside the office, closing the door behind me.

"Jessie, good to see you," Dorian says with cheer.

My brows rise at that. Was that a hint of surprise I detected? "Um, good to see you too." I pat the bag by my side drawing his eyes to it.

Dorian grins and leans forward eagerly. "You got it?"

Instead of answering verbally, I pull the artifact from my bag and set it on his desk.

Dorian reaches for it but pauses before his fingers make contact. His hands hover over the chalice and his eyes hold an almost reverent look as he gazes at the artifact.

"For so long I have been looking for this." He looks up at me with crazy glee in his eyes. Never have I seen him this excited about an artifact retrieval. "Did you meet any resistance?"

I shrug. "Nothing I couldn't handle."

He laughs loudly and claps his hands together as he sits back in his chair. I startle at the sound and take a step back. I don't think I have ever heard him laugh before. What is so funny? I don't think my response is out of the ordinary and the mission wasn't that difficult, except maybe for the rock door.

"And all without silver," Dorian murmurs to himself.

Silver? Did I hear that correctly? Maybe he was expecting the Chalice to be made of silver?

Dorian takes the Chalice and gently lays it in a drawer in his desk. Then he stands and rounds the desk toward me. He sits on the edge, facing me, and crosses his arms. He studies me while I try not to fidget.

After a few silent moments, he straightens with a smile. "Jessie, I think it is time you meet the elites."

A wide grin breaks out across my face and I leap forward with a squeal to hug my boss. Before I make contact, I halt and stand up straight. I brush my hand over my bag and clear my throat. Breathe, Jessie, breathe. I am professional. Don't make him regret this by acting like a child who just got everything she wanted for Christmas.

"Thank you, sir."

He chuckles and shakes his head. "Follow me."

He leads me into the hallway where I throw a quick glance at the break room to see if those women are still there. They are. I resist sticking my tongue out and push my shoulders back instead. Dorian nods to them as we pass but I keep my eyes straight ahead.

He takes me deeper into The Dressy Cleaners, past our storage area for artifacts that are in between transfers, past a couple of briefing rooms where groups of assassins and retrieval experts meet for more complicated assignments, and through a couple of double doors that say 'Authorized Personnel Only'.

My body is quivering with nerves and excitement, each emotion battling for dominance. I am finally going to be an elite. Just like my mom. A position held in the highest esteem in the Infinite Order, despite no one knowing what they do. My mother never told me any elite secrets, just that I should do everything I could to become an elite so I may know the truth. I have been waiting five years to get to this point. At 18, I will officially be the youngest recruit, thanks mainly to my mother who made sure I was trained since 13 and ready to complete missions by 16. Her death last year was a shock. I was told her mission involved boarding her target's private plane which ended up crashing in the sea. Something about the lack of details always put me on edge.

We stop outside another door where Dorian turns to me with a serious expression. "Are you sure about this?" he says softly, "If you go in there, there is no turning back." A warning, one I am stunned to hear coming from the head of the Infinite Order. Did he give the same courtesy to the other elites? To my mother?

Or is it a threat rather than a cautionary warning? Maybe he means there is no turning back because they will kill me rather than have me walk away with their secrets.

That sounds about right.

Inside I am freaking out at his ominous words but on the outside I show him a calm, confident Jessie. I nod and he gives me one last look before pushing through the door and guiding me inside.

The room looks like any other conference room with a large table in the middle for meetings and a podium near a projector screen at the head. However, unlike other conference rooms I have seen this one has a set of computer monitors covering half a wall at the far side of the room. To my right are three bookcases filled with both ancient looking and modern books, genre of which I cannot determine from the doorway.

Hanging on the walls are various weapons and pictures. I step closer to one image on my left and see it is a humanoid figure with pointed ears and ethereal features. It reminds me of the elves from Lord of the Rings but with larger eyes. I walk down the side of the room, taking in the other images on the walls. It isn't until I reach the computer monitors that I realize they are all pictures of mythical creatures. Interesting décor. Odd for an order of assassins though.

"Take a seat," Dorian orders, moving to the podium. "The others will be here soon."

I spin around. "Others?" My nerves take a turn for the worse and I wring my hands imagining what these other elites will be like. Will they like me? Hate me? Try to kill me?

I take a seat at the front of the table near Dorian and face my seat to the rest of the chairs so I will not have my back to the others when they come in.

We don't have to wait long. The door opens and five individuals who can only be the elite assassins stroll in.

The three men of the group sit across the table from me, each giving me varying degrees of curious and wary glances. The one directly across from me is older than the rest, with lines on his forehead and white through his dark hair, however I bet his age does not make him any less lethal. The fact that he is in this room proves that. He gives off a sort of James Bond aura. He nods at me before turning his attention to Dorian.

The other two are a bit older than me but much younger than the first man. One has dark eyes, a small nose, Asian features, and short blond hair with black growing at the roots. He smiles and gives me a small wave though I can see a glint in his eye that tells me his friendliness is as false as his hair color.

The last man has dull brown hair, dead looking brown eyes, average facial features. He is someone I would not be able to pick out of a line up as he looks like an average looking fellow that could easily be lost in a crowd. Perfect for an assassin, I guess. He completely ignores me and stares down at the table with crossed arms.

The last two members of the elites are women. A redhead with a small dotting of freckles gives me a scowl as she sits beside me and takes out a knife, casually placing it on the table between us. The other one, a petite, dark skinned brunette, who looks so innocent she should be anywhere but here sits on the other side of her. Before she sits down, I see the outline of a gun through her shirt at her waistband. I think about the dagger in my boot and the shuriken on my belt. I guess everyone is packing.

"Now that everyone is here, let's get to business." Dorian nods at the woman next to me. "Great work on the senator job, very impressive."

She sits up straighter and smirks at the others, preening under Dorian's attention. I roll my eyes, already disliking her.

Dorian hands a folder to the fake blond guy across the table, a manila envelope to the older man in front of me and has us pass down a thicker folder to the petite brunette woman. He holds up another file but doesn't hand it to anyone.

"I have a high priority case here that I want…" The others lean forward a bit waiting to hear who it will be assigned to, "…our new recruit to take." He reaches over the podium and hands me the file.

The red-head next to me grits her teeth but doesn't argue with his choice. Dorian quickly hands out a manila envelope to the annoyed woman and a file to the last guy before bringing his attention back to me and the file I am holding. He gives me a nod, silently telling me to open it.

It seems as if I will just be thrown in the water for them all to see if I can stay afloat. No introduction. No explanations. Okay. Fine. I can do this. I am Jessie-no-last-name. I can complete whatever mission he gives me. I have been chosen to be an elite for a reason.

I open the folder and skim the contents. A couple of words snag my attention. *Alpha. Silver bullets.*

Okay.

This is one of those hazing-initiation moments. They are giving me a fake assignment to see how I will react.

It seems as if even elite assassins are not above juvenile pranks. I snort and close the folder, pushing the file away from me. I sit back and cross my arms.

"Haha, funny," I say sarcastically. "Now where is the real assignment?"

The assassin next to me bristles. "Dorian, you can't be serious with this," she says gesturing to me and curling her lip in disgust.

Great, I have been reduced to a 'this.'

Two can play that game.

"Don't worry Little Red, you can have the big bad wolf all to yourself," I say waving my hand at the fake assignment in front of us.

Her brows rise to her hairline and her eyes shift from me to Dorian with a *you-see-what-I-mean* look.

Dorian holds up his hand to fend off any more remarks and turns to me with a patient smile. "Jessie, there is a reason the elites are the most secretive team of this Order."

I glance at the others. Two of the guys give me sympathetic looks while the third guy at the end of the table continues to ignore me. Little Red next to me rolls her eyes when I look to her and the other female assassin clasps her hands together on the table and gives me a serious look. It isn't quite threatening but more a look that conveys I'm in for it. Whatever *it* is.

"For a long time, the Infinite Order has eliminated threats and retrieved artifacts from around the world but not many know there are far more serious threats than humans."

At the word 'humans' I turn back to Dorian. Is this related to the case he handed me? Are they really going to play this out?

"Like global warming?" I ask sweetly, knowing he does not actually mean that. I gasp in mock realization. "Are you saying the elites are eco-warriors?"

Something lands on the table with a loud *thunk*. My eyes widen and my heart pounds faster when I see a knife embedded in the wood two inches from my hand. I cautiously pull my hand away and put it in my lap. Little Red gives me a fierce glare, her hand still wrapped around the handle of the knife.

*Ok*ay, she is not playing around. I guess I can hear them out and decide afterwards whether to go along with this or not. I think she will lash out again if I don't shut up and listen and this time she won't miss.

I clear my throat and look to Dorian waiting for him to continue. Dorian eyes us both but does not remark on her outburst or my comment. After a moment, he places his hands on the podium and leans forward, staring into my eyes with a serious, unwavering expression.

"Jessie, supernaturals are real."

If he wasn't my boss and if a knife hadn't almost impaled my hand I would have laughed. He said it with such a straight face! He must have practiced that in the mirror. Is this the initiation joke used for every recruit or do they change it each time?

My first instinct is to give a snarky reply but a side glance at the assassin next to me gives me pause. Not able to completely subdue myself I raise an unbelieving eyebrow at my boss.

He nods as if he expected my disbelief. Dorian sweeps his hand toward the pictures on the wall and another toward the bookcases on the other side of the room.

"Elves, vampires, dwarves, witches, and werewolves. All real." He points to the folder still laying in front of me. "And I need you to hunt one of the Alphas of the werewolves."

Dorian walks around the podium to one of the gleaming silver swords on the wall. He doesn't take it down but runs a finger lightly over the blade.

"You will be equipped with everything you need to complete your mission," he turns back to me with his hands behind his back, "most importantly, silver bullets."

I clear my throat. "Sir…" I trail off not knowing what to say.

I cannot outright refuse a job given to me by my boss as soon as I join the elites, especially in front of the others. I cannot just walk away either. I will have a knife in my back before I reach the door. I have no choice but to go along with this ridiculous prank. If they want me to pretend werewolves are real as I kill my target, then so be it. I will prove I am a good assassin then they will take me seriously.

I snatch the folder from the middle of the table and glare at it. "It shall be done."

Chapter 4

Norden

"Just leave him be, Honey, he is still healing."

"Healing? It's been hours. No son of mine is going to let a couple bullets keep him down."

Someone pats my cheek with enough force it is just shy of a slap. "Norden, get up now. It's time you tell us what happened. Sutton is being unhelpful, and we need to get the Chalice back." A moment of silence before the tapping/slapping starts up again. "Norden, wake up."

Bullets. Chalice.

My eyes fly open and I sit up quickly. Bad mistake because the room immediately starts spinning. I blink a few times until the room stops moving and look around to see I am back in the yellow monstrosity of a room. Mother and Father peer down at me, one with concern and the other with an unreadable expression. Mother's brows are furrowed, and her eyes are watery. Has she been crying?

"Tell us what happened," Father says, straight to the point as always.

A blonde beauty flashes through my mind. "Mate," I whisper.

"What was that?" Father demands.

I decide not to tell them I met my mate. I am starting to wonder if I may have gotten it wrong. Surely if she was truly my mate, she wouldn't have shot me.

"We ran into someone at the cave. She surprised me and shot me before I could move." Not quite true. I moved but it wasn't to get away. "She must have taken the Chalice if South does not have it."

Father scowls, either at my news of the Chalice or from the nickname and turns away to pace the length of the room.

"Did East and West get the Moonstone?" I ask, looking to Father then Mother.

Father ignores me and continues pacing. Mother leans in and answers softly, "They arrived an hour ago with it."

I nod. At least we can still find and make werewolves with the moonstone, but we can't tie them to our pack civilly and give them long life without the Chalice. Let's just hope we don't have to induct any new members until we get it back. I push the blanket back enough to get out of bed. Despite being shot three times, I feel great. I lift my shirt to check for holes or scars but find nothing. Gotta love that fast healing.

"Do you know where the Infinite Order could have taken it?" I ask.

Father stops pacing and spins to face me with a frown. "If we knew where they could have taken it, don't you think we would already be on our way?"

My hands ball into fists at his condescending tone but Mother lays a hand on my arm.

"Honey, let's go send out some forces to search for the Chalice." Mother takes Father's arm and guides him from the room.

I scowl at the door, imagining going after them and punching Father in the face. My shoulders slump and I let the idea go. It is my fault the Chalice is gone. He has every right to be angry. I need to get home and start my own search. I have some of the best trackers in the world in my pack.

The door flies open, and three men rush in.

"North! You're ok!" Sutton exclaims before moving forward to pick me up in a crushing hug.

Any normal man would not be able to pick me up that easily, not even most shifters, but Sutton is bigger and stronger than most.

I swat his head to make him put me down then nod at my other brothers when I am back on my feet.

"Dude, what happened?" Sutton asks. "I was keeping guard, and suddenly I hear gunshots. Who shot you? How did they get in and out without me seeing?"

"I think I met my mate." I grin at them feeling proud. To find one's mate was a miracle.

"What!" All three of them shout.

"She was there, looking like an adventurer from one of those movies you like," I tell Sutton. "She wanted the Chalice and…she shot me." My face falls as I remember the gunshots and pain in my chest both from the bullets and instant betrayal.

Easton whistles. "You got shot by your mate and lost the Chalice? Yikes, no wonder Father came storming out of here."

I wince. "Yeah, not my best moment. Although, Father doesn't know that it was my mate…if it even *was* my mate." I shake my head still puzzling it out. That feeling I had when I met her eyes, the instant pull, had to be the mate bond, but if she is my mate and she felt the same draw then why did she attack?

"So, what are we going to do now?" Wesley asks.

"I am going home first to check on the pack then I will try to pick up its trail. The Chalice must be wherever she is and we need to get it back."

"Are you sure the Chalice is all you want?" Easton smirks.

I rub the spot where I was shot. "I don't know."

Canada is nice but it is no castle-in-Germany nice. I breathe in the fresh air and push open the doors to my castle. The whole structure looks like someone grabbed a bunch of spires and bartizans and meshed them onto a four-story manor then took two extra wings and slapped those on the end facing the back of the property. It shouldn't work but it does, and it is mine.

Home sweet home.

My brothers should be back in their own palaces or manors by now. Easton in Northern China, Wesley in Algeria, and Sutton in India. Hence the nicknames we gave each other—East, West, South, and North. The areas in which we were placed like pawns to exert the King's control to all of the packs.

My brothers didn't want to stay in Canada while our Father was on a rampage any more than I did and had hopped on the first flight out of there. They each promised to do what they could to find the Chalice, but we all know my pack has some of the best trackers.

I wish I could just go straight to the forest behind the castle and run, to forget my worries for a while, but I have work to do.

"Elias!" I shout in the Main Hall as I powerwalk through. My Beta should be around here somewhere. "Elias!"

A woman slips from the shadows and attaches herself to my arm. "My Lord, I am so glad you are back," she gushes in a sugary-sweet, German accented tone.

I extricate my arm and try not to growl. "Not now, Danika."

The petite raven-haired beauty pouts but continues to follow me. I ignore her as I turn down one of the halls that will lead to my security room and pick up my pace. That doesn't discourage her though and despite her shorter legs she manages to keep up.

"The King told me you might need some…comfort."

I scowl at her words. My father has been trying to get me to settle down for years now, saying it is not likely I will find my mate and that I will someday become King of the wolf shifters, so it is time I think about the future. How encouraging, I know. And out of all the female shifters in our world, he believes Danika would be the perfect fit. She is a dominant wolf which is ideal for an Alpha, but she is also manipulating, greedy, and thinks the world revolves around her and has more loyalty to my father than to me. I wouldn't put it past my father if he chose her to be my partner so he can use her to keep an eye on me and my pack. His way of keeping control, I am sure.

"No, I am fine, you can run along now."

"I have planned a party for your return, the whole pack will be there."

I stop and she doesn't try to stop her momentum. She stumbles into me far more dramatically than necessary and grips my upper arm to steady herself, then runs her hand down my arm before letting go.

I roll my eyes and take a step back. "A party is unnecessary. A simple run behind the castle will do."

She waves a perfectly manicured hand at me. "Nonsense. Everyone will enjoy a fun night and then you can tell us of your adventures. I hired some caterers and musicians, part of the pack obviously, no outsiders. Everyone is already expecting your presence."

I hold back a wince. My adventures will not be told at the party or any night. I sigh since I know nothing I say will dissuade her from throwing this party. If everyone is already planning to go and hoping I will be there, I guess it wouldn't hurt to show up for a short time.

"Alright, Danika, I will attend, but I will not be sharing any stories."

She squeals and leaps forward to hug me, but I sidestep her and continue walking. I hear her heels click behind me as she follows.

"It will be tomorrow night, so that you have time to rest and deal with pack business until then," she says from behind me.

I wave my hand over my shoulder in acknowledgment. I don't understand how she puts together a party so fast. She only heard this morning that

I was coming back today. But I should know better than to be surprised. Danika can do anything if she wants it bad enough. Except mate me.

We stop in front of the entrance to the security room and I reach out to open the door but before I touch the handle, it suddenly swings open and my Beta steps out. I cross my arms and narrow my eyes at him. Took him long enough to show himself.

Elias glances to my side then looks back at me with a sheepish smile when he sees who is tagging along.

"Sorry, Danika, you will have to catch our esteemed Alpha later," Elias says with mock sympathy and grabs my arm, pulling me into the security room and closing the door before Danika can try to weasel her way in.

We both freeze on the other side and wait for the telltale signs of heels clicking against the floor. It takes a moment but finally we hear them getting farther away and we both sigh when we know she is gone.

I punch his shoulder. "What took you so long?"

Elias only chuckles and moves further into the room.

I sit at the table in the center of the room and drop my head into my hands.

"That bad?" Elias asks, suddenly serious.

He is the only one who knows about my mission in Peru and Canada. Though, I haven't told him yet the outcome of said mission. I look up at him with a grim expression.

"The Chalice has been stolen."

Elias curses and frowns at the wall behind me. I know the monitors are on the wall behind me displaying all 200 cameras set around the castle. With our cameras, limited entrances, patrols, and exceptional hearing, our castle is one of the safest in our entire pack. But I know Elias is not focusing on the screens, he is thinking about our new situation.

"And the Moonstone?" he asks, sounding hopeful.

"Safe."

He sighs but we both know it is only a small relief.

"So, what is the plan?"

I scrub at the scruff on my face then slap my hands on the table. "Ok, I need three of our best trackers to trace the Chalice's steps. An Infinite Order member snatched it in Peru and presumably took it back to HQ. We need to find out the Order's whereabouts and where they keep artifacts. I assume they will want to keep this one close."

"Only three?"

I understand his confusion. We have a group of one hundred in our small area in Germany, and many more beyond the town and country, plenty of shifters who could be looking for this but the less people who know about the missing Chalice the better.

I nod and stand then pace the length of the room. "There's one more thing." I hesitate, wondering if I should tell him this next part.

Elias doesn't push. He leans against the table in the middle and waits for me to give my order.

"I need you to find someone."

He quirks a brow at my vague order.

"I need you to find the one who stole the Chalice and keep it quiet. Use the team looking for the artifact for help but don't tell them who you're looking for or why. Only you should be looking for this person, then I want you to bring her to me."

"Her?" Elias asks, picking up on the fact that this is a secret mission within the secret mission and that there is probably some juicy tale behind it if I am wanting this person to be brought to me instead of my Father.

I don't tell him about my mate suspicion so I tell him the only other thing that would make sense for this to be personal. "She shot me."

Elias' eyes widen and he tenses as he looks me over for injuries.

I know what he is thinking, and I shake my head. "Not with silver, thank the Moon."

He sighs and seems to deflate as he places a hand over his heart then nods and frowns determinedly. "I will find her."

Elias then spends the next fifteen minutes catching me up on pack business and working out details for patrols and issues that need to be solved among the pack down in the village. It is a welcome distraction from the bigger issues.

When he is done, he smirks and tilts his head to the door. "Want to run?"

I grin. "I thought you'd never ask."

Chapter 5

I don't have to like the assignment given to me or the fact that I have to go through this ridiculous ruse to prove myself as an elite, but I do have to enjoy the destination. It is not every day I am sent to Germany. To a castle of all places! This target must be very important to be living in a place like this. Which means their security will be top notch.

I look through the file one last time, but it is the same. A picture of the castle and one grainy photo of my target next to a name—Norden Kane—and that's it. As a regular assassin I had more info in my files than this, but I guess that is where the elite part comes in. An elite assassin should be able to find their target with limited info and eliminate them and disappear before anyone notices. Dorian advised me to read up on werewolves using the books in the meeting room before leaving, but c'mon, I wasn't about to sit around researching legends and be the butt of the joke more than I had to. Plus, I have seen Twilight and Teen Wolf—both the old one from 1985 with Michael J. Fox and the newer TV version.

I brought silver bullets and a silver dagger as Dorian ordered, and the rest of my usual weapons, so that will just have to be enough to appease the jokesters.

I decide the best start would be in the small village just a mile from the castle. I peer down at it from the hill I am on then at the castle beyond. It took some time to find this particular castle because it is not truly a castle. It is more of a giant manor that looks like someone just meshed a bunch of architectural styles from both medieval and modern times onto it and called it a castle. Also, it is not on any map I could find on Google.

I tuck the folder into my backpack, tighten my ponytail, and don my sable fedora before making my way down into the village. I would play the tourist card until I could gather enough intel to break into the manor/castle. I spend the day trying the native food, taking selfies in front of locations I need to take note of, and talking to the villagers about their town and the uniqueness of the castle up the road, making sure to gush and snap pictures like a tourist would. Not that it is a hard task, because I do find this little town in Germany and the weirdly formed manor house interesting. It is not as difficult to talk to the villagers as I previously expected it would be since most of them speak both German and English.

I even take a moment to imagine I live here. I close my eyes and breathe in the fresh air. There are cars but not nearly as many as in a big city which reduces the pollution and noise. There are no big brand chain stores or restaurants around, only local shops. A sense of content and warmth settles inside me as I listen to the chatter and laughter around the village. If things were different, maybe I could stay and live a simple life like the people here. They look so happy and my heart clenches at the thought I might never have that kind of life.

I have to physically shake the thoughts away. Enough of that. I need to focus.

The sun is starting to set so I make my way to the only bakery in the village for a last meal before I attempt to get close to the castle to learn of its defenses. When I walk in, the bell jingles and a young woman with round cheeks and dark brown hair in a messy bun greets me warmly in German as she wipes down the outside of a display case.

"Guten tag!"

"Hello," I answer. I do not speak much German but I know guten tag means something like 'good day.'

She stops cleaning and smiles at me. "Ah, American. Nice to see someone new. What brings you here?"

It is a small shop from the outside but it is bigger on the inside. The colors are cute yellow and green pastels and potted plants hang in the windows. But it is the smell that is truly the best part of the place. My mouth waters at the aroma of the baked goods.

"The pastries," I say eyeing a couple of cherry Danishes behind her.

The woman laughs and stands up, wiping one last time at the glass case before turning to me fully. "I appreciate it, but I meant to our little village."

I smile and hold my camera up, the strap still around my neck. "I am interested in the castle's architecture. I am a student from NYU in America. This is one of a few places that I thought would be brilliant for my capstone." That sounded better than the tourist card I had been using earlier.

Her eyes widen and she claps loudly. I startle at the sound, but she doesn't seem to notice.

"I have always wanted to go to New York. If I didn't have the bakery or any obligations here, I may have gone to school there." Then her smile fades and the excited energy she expressed a moment ago turns into a slump of her shoulders. "Unfortunately, you cannot go inside without an invitation and tourists rarely get invitations to Lord Kane's castle." Her brows furrow and her mouth twists to the side sympathetically.

My heart beats faster at the mention of Lord Kane. The man I am supposed to kill. Do they know each other? Will this woman be upset tomorrow when she finds out the Lord of the castle is dead?

I feign a look of disappointment and let my camera drop against my stomach. "Oh. Well… I guess that is alright, I got a few good pictures from the top of the hill."

Her features brighten. "I have always thought they should put a bench up on that hill for tourists. Some of the best pictures are taken there."

I shrug. "Might be a good idea."

She beams at me, and I can't help but give her a small smile in return. Her enthusiasm is infectious.

"So, what can I get you. Everything in the case is half off. Anything look good?" She gives me a friendly smile and glances at the case she just cleaned.

I look it over and see pastries, fresh bread, cookies, sandwiches, and even little cakes. It all looks mouthwatering.

"Why are they half off?"

Her smile dims a fraction, and she looks away. She hesitates but only for a moment. "Lord Kane is having a party for his return, and I will have to close early. Plus, I have been hired to cater part of it."

"Let me guess, you need an invitation to the party?"

She inclines her head, acknowledging the truth of my statement.

I smile so she doesn't feel upset about my lack of an invitation. "Well, that sounds great that you get to cater, the guests are lucky."

She laughs. "How would you know? You have not ordered anything yet."

I nod and point my finger at her. "True." I inhale deeply and close my eyes taking in the bakery's fragrance. When I open them again, I grin at the lady. "But I have a certain intuition for these kinds of things."

She giggles which makes my smile widen.

She holds out a hand. "I am Janie."

I grasp her hand automatically. "Jessie."

I freeze, my hand stiffening and body tensing. I don't know why I just told her my real name. Something about her energy sets me at ease. Is it her positivity? Her affability? Her innocence? It is like being around an old friend. When was the last time I had a friend?

"Jessie? Are you ok?"

Concern lines her features and she hasn't let go of my hand.

A jolt of shock and terror spears me at hearing my real name from a stranger's lips. I pull back and shoot her a tight smile, hopefully one that passes as real.

"I don't know how to choose." I tap my chin thoughtfully, bringing us back to the food order, then point to a sandwich and a Danish. "I will take those."

She studies me a moment but seems to pick up on my mood and follows along with the change in subject. "Great choice."

She moves around to the other side of the counter and opens the case from her side. She pulls out the two items I chose and rings them up. She adds a second Danish and winks. "On the house."

I give her a grateful smile.

The bell jingles behind me signaling the arrival of somebody but I don't bother turning around to see who it is. My eyes are fixed on those pastries.

"Janie, kommst du?" A young boy asks, sounding winded as if he ran all the way here.

Janie rolls her eyes at the boy but gives him a warm smile that seems to be a permanent fixture on her face. "Well, I am one of the caterers, so yes, I am coming," she answers in English for my benefit.

"C'mon, hurry, the castle doors are opening!" He takes the hint and answers in English as well. He takes off without waiting for a response, making the bell jingle over the door again.

Janie chuckles and takes off her apron. "I guess you are my last customer for today," she says as she hangs the apron on a hook behind her.

I open the bag in front of me and immediately take out one of the Danishes while she starts to box up the items in the case for the party.

I bite into it and close my eyes as blissful buttery flakes of bread mixed with cherry filling send my taste buds soaring. I moan and take another bite. "I think I need to live off these."

She chuckles and grins at my obvious delight. "If you are still here tomorrow, I will make you your own batch to take back with you."

Ooo, tempting. But I will be gone tonight. No sane assassin sticks around after their hit is complete. Not even if delicious cherry Danishes are offered.

I smile as I start for the door and call over my shoulder, "We'll see."

I open the door, sending the little bell off, and take a step out of the bakery.

"Wait! Jessie."

I pause and turn back, using my left foot to keep the door open while most of my body turns back to her.

"Yeah?"

Janie bites her bottom lip and fidgets with her thumbs. I frown at her nervousness and step fully back into the bakery.

"Everything ok?" I look at the boxes and my brows shoot up in realization. "Oh, do you need help packing up?" I walk to the counter and place my bag down.

Janie waves away my offer. "No, I technically do not need it, but…"

I wait patiently for her to continue. Whatever she is trying to say is obviously hard for her to get out.

Janie straightens and her lips set in a determined line. She mumbles something to herself about this being her bakery and her rules then she turns a bright smile on me. "I think I can get you inside the castle if you still want to see it."

My eyes widen and my mouth drops open a fraction at her offer. This is it. This is my in. But if she is the one to get me in then won't she be accused as an accomplice when Lord Kane ends up dead and I disappear? I mentally put up walls around my heart and get rid of all the thoughts about friendship and caring about innocents. I am an elite assassin and must do whatever I can, however I can, to get my job done. If sweet, innocent Janie is offering to get me in, there is no way I can refuse, even if it does cause a twinge in my chest at the idea of using her.

"How?" I ask, gripping my camera and making sure to sound like an excited student.

Janie claps and starts pacing as the idea forms in her mind. "I can say you are my assistant for the night, and you can help me bring in the food and set it up then get a few pictures. I can tell you now, you will not be able to see everything, but the kitchens and the ballroom are splendid. Also, the event coordinator will probably notice you are not part of the guest list and may kick you out but hopefully by then you will have what you need." She finally stops pacing and turns back to me with a wide grin and twinkling eyes. "How about it?"

"Where's the apron?"

***

Turns out there is no apron when catering because it makes you look "tacky" so instead I am wearing a blue sundress and wedge sandals that I brought along with a jean jacket and my trusty fedora. I have to leave behind my backpack when we go inside so I made sure to strap a silver dagger to my thigh, some shuriken on the inside of the band around my hat, added a few distraction trinkets and my gun to my purse, and hung my camera around my neck. I wish I could have brought more weapons along but any more and someone would notice.

Janie drives us around to the side of the castle/manor where other businesspeople are bringing things in. On the way past I notice three guards at the entrance. One walking back and forth along the entire wall and checking around the corners, one checking guests in, and another standing a few feet from the entrance with his hands crossed in front of him keeping an eye on the surroundings. Along the side of the place, I spot a few black orbs hidden among fixtures in the walls and near lights.

Cameras.

There is one security check at the business entrance, but Janie takes care of it and gives me the thumbs up on our way through.

I keep this all in mind as Janie leads me into the castle, each of us with three boxes of food in our arms. I play the part of excited architect student by marveling over the bartizans on the outside and the layout inside. Though I find I don't have to fake it completely. The interior of the place is amazing just as Janie said it would be.

The kitchen is enormous with stone accents around the stoves and entryways. The theme is blue and gray and there are at least three islands in the middle. An actual fireplace or hearth or whatever it is called in olden times sits against the far wall with dried herbs hanging from it.

We put our boxes down on an open space in the kitchen and make two other trips before we have everything out of the van. I help her set up trays and put them on a little cart she brought along. At one point I walk around the room and take a few pictures of the kitchen for show, and even include a few of her with her treats. Maybe some day I can anonymously send her the photos.

When everything is laid out and set up to take out, she smiles and winks at me. "Show time."

Ok, getting into the castle was step one. Step two: find Norden Kane.

I grab a couple of the trays that couldn't fit on the cart and follow her into the next room. She said the event coordinator would probably kick me out when she sees me, so part of step two includes avoiding whoever that is. I straighten my shoulders and walk with purpose. I have found that if I look like I belong then I will draw less attention.

The ballroom I come to find out is also a dining room. Tables are set up in long rows around the room and the middle is open for dancers though everyone is just mingling right now. A DJ in the corner is dancing to his music enough to make up for the lack of it on the dance floor. The ceiling is high and three pointed-arch windows at the top of the room let in the dying light while a giant chandelier brightens the darkening room. I take note of the pillars and dark corners that will make hiding easier.

I didn't realize I had stopped to look around until Janie's voice calls me over.

"Jessie, place them over here." Janie starts unloading her cart and I rush to help her.

When everything is laid out, Janie stands back with her hands on her hips and smiles at the spread. Then she turns and gives me a hug. I tense at the contact and leave my arms hanging limp by my side. If she notices, she doesn't comment on it.

"Thank you, Jessie." She pulls back and looks around before leaning closer and whispering, "Now I suggest getting your pictures of the architecture before this table is overrun with hungry wolves."

I chuckle at her metaphor and pat my camera. "Will do. Thank you, Janie, for giving me this opportunity." Even though you will regret it soon.

A couple of people approach her table, and she waves me off.

I skirt around the edge of the room, hiding in dark corners and ducking behind pillars when people start to look my way. This is a party for the Lord of the castle, so where is he? There are too many people in my way and the entrance to the room shows more people entering. It is like the whole village is here. I look up to the second-floor landing and decide my view would be less hindered up there. I search the room for cameras and notice one on each end of the room. Unfortunately, one is near the stairs. I pull my hat down over my face before heading up to the second floor. Enough people are going between the first and second floor that my presence upstairs will not be suspicious.

The second floor is quieter since there are less people, but I can still feel the music all the way to my bones. The DJ has some great beats, which I shouldn't be surprised by since he was hired for a castle event. If it were any other time, I might have been tempted to dance.

Instead, I find a spot near a pillar that has good cover but enough of a view of the people below me and watch the partygoers. I expected high class, fancy type people to be here. It is a castle after all, one with a 'Lord'.

However, there are men and women of all ages, even children, and some I could swear I saw running shops or stalls down in the village earlier. Some of the younger women are dressed a little more like clubbers in America, probably hoping to catch the eye of Lord Kane. I wonder what it took to get an invite if anyone, it seemed, could be invited.

"I change my mind."

A deep male voice, one that sends shivers down my arms and heat pooling in my belly, speaks from down the hall. I press my body against the closest pillar to stay out of his way. Instead of moving past me he stops near enough for me to hear but not enough for him to see me quite yet.

"Why? You said you would be there," another male voice says, this one German accented and a laughing note in his voice. "The whole village is here to see you."

Whole village? I knew it.

Wait.

The village is here to see him? Does that mean…?

I peek around the pillar at the men and have to hold in a gasp. My eyes widen, and my heart nearly bursts from its place in my chest. Dread slithers down my back and I grip the banister to keep from falling in shock.

No. No, no, no.

There is no way he is still alive.

Next to a platinum-blond man with a teasing smirk that I have never seen before is the man I shot in Peru. Every tall, muscled, dangerous, sexy inch of him.

Sexy?

I meant, surprising.

No, I didn't.

However, his presence *is* surprising. He is supposed to be dead. I shot him, like, three times and watched him fall, unmoving, unbreathing.

The man, Norden Kane I guess I should call him, no, *my target*, shoves his hands into his pockets and frowns down at the ballroom below. He has stubble around his jaw and upper lip which is different from the last time I saw him but makes my heart rate kick up a notch. He is wearing a suit tonight but looks uncomfortable in it. Uncomfortable but totally rocking it. That weird sensation I had when I saw him in Peru comes back and all I want to do is step out of my hidey hole and crawl into his arms. I bet he is warm. Not just his body but his lips too. My eyes flit to his lips and I bite my own when I have the sudden desire to go kiss him and find out how they feel. Home. That's what he will feel like my instincts tell me.

I shake my head. What is wrong with me? My chest clenches and I realize I had stopped breathing. I step back and take a deep breath then let it out slowly.

Home is in New Jersey. Where I have lived my entire life. Where my job is. Where the Infinite Order gave me a mission to assassinate that man that I was just imagining kissing. I have to kill him. For good this time.

Why does my chest hurt at the thought of him being dead? Stop it, Jessie. You're more professional than this.

His voice makes my ears metaphorically perk up and my body leans toward it on its own accord.

"Yeah, but we should be finding the Chalice."

"It's just for one night, the team has been working hard. We'll find it," his friend says.

Norden Kane grunts his acquiescence. "Fine, but…a throne? Really? What is she thinking?"

Throne? I look down into the room below and what do ya know? An actual throne, well a little smaller than I expected a throne to be but a throne nonetheless, sits at the back of the room almost near the food tables.

The man next to him sucks his teeth. I hear a muffled smack and imagine the man slapped Norden Kane's shoulder or back. "That's Danika for you."

Who is Danika and why does that statement make me want to hunt her down and make sure no one can find her again?

"So, are you coming or should I give you a head start before telling her you aren't attending?" The man has a note of humor in his voice as if he is trying to keep from laughing.

Norden Kane sighs and I can't help but peek out at him again. He is leaning against the banister with his head bowed. His face looks troubled. "Just give me a moment. I will be down shortly."

"Ok, but do not wait too long. She will come after me for answers otherwise and I plan on keeping my distance from her throughout the night."

Norden shakes his head with a small smile and his companion starts my way with a grin on his face. I duck back behind the pillar and look down at the ballroom with my hat lowered over my face. My heart beats fast but the man walks by without pausing.

I watch him descend the stairs and a smattering of those club-looking women swarm him.

This is my best chance. My target is alone and it looks like the other guests are nowhere near us. I pull my silver dagger out, knowing it will make the least noise.

This is where Norden Kane will die.

For good this time.

Chapter 6

It's only been a day since I asked Elias to find the thief and for the team to find the Chalice, but it feels like forever. How can something and someone disappear without a trace. We can access all security feeds from airports, train stations, boat docks, and streets and even run a facial recognition search in our databases, hence why my pack has some of the best trackers. Not only do they have exceptional smelling and memory in their wolf forms but also great tech skills. Yet, they have not found anything yet.

It's only been a day. I have to remember that and give them time.

Now I have to sit through this party and act like everything is okay. I stare at the throne that Danika set up at the back of the room and growl low enough for only me to hear. It is a seat my father had commissioned for me.

You are not just an Alpha, son, you are the next King of Wolves.

I scowl at the throne, imagining it is him. My father declared himself King of all Wolves after our last great war, what the humans call WWII, but what we know as the War of the Four Quadrants. My family had always been the Alphas of the North American packs but after the War of the Four Quadrants, we came out on top when all the other alphas died. When we were born, he set me and my brothers up to take over those quadrants, leaving proxies in place until we were old enough.

It took some time to get the Northern packs to warm up to me after my family took over. They finally accept me as their leader and friend, but I see the look in some of the older ones' eyes when my title is brought up. The hesitation. The wariness. The distant greetings, polite but not warm. The only ones who never treat me differently are my brothers and Elias.

And that woman from the cave.

I scrub my face with my hands. Don't go there, Norden. It will only cause impatience and heartache.

With a heavy sigh, I turn to head down to the party. Elias wasn't kidding about Danika hunting me if I don't make an appearance. Suddenly a sharp, burning pain radiates from my shoulder down my arm. I growl and clutch at the spot where the pain is most intense, stumbling back a step from the shock of it.

My fingers brush metal and the pain spikes, nearly making me fall to my knees.

I look down at the offending object and frown.

A silver dagger?

I look up to search for the source, but I don't have to look far. My eyes land on a fierce woman in a fedora and blue sundress. My heart stutters and the breath leaves my chest.

It's her.

And she is trying to kill me.

Again.

The woman flings something at me and I roll to the side. I hear a *thunk* in the pillar next to me. When I look back, I see it is a ninja star. The woman reaches up to her hat and produces two more from the band surrounding it and throws them with lightning speed. I am just barely able to dodge them but when I straighten, the blade still in my shoulder nearly makes me fall. The ninja stars are not silver, more of a black metal, but it doesn't matter because the dagger in my shoulder causes enough agony to impede my movements.

Thank the Moon I am not a normal shifter.

I yank the dagger out and bite my lip to keep from crying out. My vision turns dark at the edges and my stomach churns. If she had hit me a bit to the right, she would have gotten my heart or a lung. I study her wondering if she meant to miss or if she is not that good at throwing weapons. Another ninja star appears and buries itself in my leg before I can move.

I hiss at the sting, not nearly as painful as silver but still annoying, and decide she must have missed on purpose. She is unnervingly good at throwing those things. I pull out the star and toss it with the dagger down the hall behind me. Her eyes flit to the dagger then to me. Realizing she cannot get to it without passing me, she narrows her eyes and reaches into her purse.

I know whatever is in there will probably be the end of me.

I dive and tackle her to the ground. Her breath leaves in a pained *whoosh* and her wide brown eyes let me know I caught her by surprise. I use my body to pin her, and my right hand grips her left wrist where it is buried in her purse, halting her movement there. For a moment we just lay there, both panting heavily from the fight, our chests brushing with every exhale.

Who did the Moon Goddess send to me? This fierce, brave woman, *my mate*, keeps trying to kill me. Is the Goddess angry with me? This assassin is like fire, if I get too close, I get burned but I can't help being drawn to her like a moth to a flame. I need that warmth. That connection. I look over her face, wanting to memorize every feature. Why is this connection only one sided? It seems cruel. Maybe this is punishment. For what, I am not sure yet.

I feel her heart start to beat faster and her gaze flits to my lips. A slow smile spreads across my face at her look. So, maybe it is not one sided after all.

"I don't think we have been properly introduced," I whisper.

She blinks up at me. Surprised? Wary? I am not sure, but I can't help the excited patter of my heart that wants to figure out all her expressions and emotions. To memorize them and be the only one who can read her.

But first, I have to survive this encounter.

"I'm Norden. But you can call me North."

Her head tilts to the side in the most adorable way. Almost like a wolf pup when it is curious.

"North?"

I grin. "A little family joke." When she stays quiet, I raise a brow at her. "And how about you? What do I call you?"

Her eyes darken and her brows pull down into a frown.

Uh oh. That expression is one I already know. It's the same one she gave me in the cave in Peru right before she shot me.

The next thing I know, she is freeing a leg from under mine and kneeing me in the groin. I can't help but loosen my grip on her arm as I practically curl into a ball. She frees her left hand and punches me in the face with strength I was not expecting. I roll off her, one hand clutching my nose and the other my groin. She jumps up, her hand pulling out the item from her purse that I tried preventing and points it at me.

Well, drat.

I shift into my wolf form on instinct. It's not the bone cracking painful transformation most movies and books describe it as and it is not a monster half wolf/half man that can walk on two legs transformation either. It is a seamless shift that only lasts a second. Unfortunately, my clothes don't shift with me and the tearing fabric makes me sigh internally. Another suit lost to the shift.

The first thing I notice as a wolf is that my shoulder is still bleeding which makes my leg limp. Each step puts pressure on that shoulder making me want to whimper, but I refrain. In no way will that stop me from fighting.

My mate's eyes widen so far, I think her eyes will roll out. She squeaks, surprising me that she is not screaming like a normal human would after seeing that, then scrambles away until her back hits the wall farthest away from me and the banister.

"It's true? They weren't lying?" She says, mostly to herself. "How were they not lying? Werewolves don't exist!"

As you can see, we do exist. Not that I can say that out loud so all I do is huff and take a step forward.

She raises her gun and aims it at me. "D-don't come closer. This has silver bullets."

I pause and eye her gun warily. Why hasn't she shot me yet? Her hesitation gives me hope.

"North, you were supposed to be down two minutes ago, man. Where are—?" Elias stops short when he sees the woman and my wolf facing off.

With an inhuman growl, Elias leaps at her and shifts midair, his own clothes ripping and falling to the floor in tatters.

His wolf has a snow-white coat, unusual among shifters. He is smaller than my wolf but still larger than most and gives off powerful dominant vibes. My mate swings her gun around to aim at the attacking wolf either not picking up on those scary vibes or not caring. Everything seems to go in slow motion. My mate is about to be ripped apart by my best friend. My best friend is about to be shot with silver by my mate.

I react on instinct and jump between them. My body manages to knock the gun away so when the shot goes off, it ricochets off the wall and hits the floor. Screams erupt from the party and the DJ's music cuts off. People start rushing about and I hear more than a few heading this way to see what caused the shot.

I tumble into the woman from the impact of Elias crashing into me and all three of us fall to the floor in a heap. Elias and I recover quickly and face each other, both with snarls and lips pulled back to reveal our teeth. I step to the side so I can have them both in sight.

The woman reaches for the gun she dropped, and I snap at it, not trying to bite her hand off but trying to keep her away from the weapon. She yanks her hand back and cradles it against her chest as she stares at us fearfully.

Elias growls, bringing my attention back to him. *"Why don't you attack her?"* Elias says into my mind.

Shifters can communicate with others in the pack when they are in their wolf forms as long as they are connected to the Alpha of the same pack. Which is another reason we need the Chalice back. Without it, we cannot connect any new wolves to the Alpha without resorting to the archaic ways of pack claim.

"We can't kill her."

"Why?!"

I huff and shake out my fur then send out a tiny warning burst of Alpha power, signaling the end of the discussion. Elias lets out a frustrated whine and steps back. About ten wolves race onto the second-floor landing, coming to a stop near Elias with hackles raised.

The woman reaches into her purse again and grabs something. Before I can prevent whatever it is, she throws it at the ground between her and the other wolves. Three *pop, pop, pop* sounds followed by flashes explode from it and smoke starts to fill the area. Not enough to completely hide everything amongst the cloud but enough to stun us long enough for her to escape. Since I was set apart from the others, the smoke and flashes do not affect me as much as the others and I am able to see her race down the hall, picking up the dagger and ninja star I tossed as she goes.

I don't wait for the others. I race after her, my wolf's speed no match for her human legs. We leave the landing and make it deeper into the castle before I catch up. I nip at her heels which only makes her swing at me with her dagger. I dodge the attack then pounce at her. My body hits her back, sending her tumbling forward. She screeches as she falls, and I make sure to jump out of the way, so I do not crash on top of her.

She rolls over so she can see me and holds up her dagger threateningly. She glares and sits up slowly.

I hunch a little lower and let out a warning growl.

She freezes.

"So, what now?" She asks, sounding calm despite the fear I smell.

I shift back to my human form and have to clench my teeth at the sharp pain in my shoulder. I really need to see a doctor soon. I push through the pain and crouch down so I can speak to her at eye level.

"Jeez!" Her eyes widen and her cheeks turn an adorable shade of red. Her eyes flit around the room trying to look anywhere but my naked body.

I chuckle. "Sorry, clothes don't shift with us." Then my voice drops, and I frown at her. "There are only two choices for you right now and you have to choose quickly before the others catch up to us."

She eyes me warily, her gaze pointedly fixed on my face. "Ok…?"

I hold up a finger. "One, you can surrender which includes giving up all weapons in your possession and letting me escort you to a holding room."

Her eyes narrow. "And the second option?"

I shrug and gesture behind me. "I can feed you to the wolves." My heart clenches at the thought of letting my pack tear her to pieces. There is no way I would let that happen, but she doesn't need to know that.

Her lips twist in thought and she points at me with her blade. "Or third option. I kill you right now then make my escape."

I smirk and rest my arm over my knee. "You could try."

"Try what? The killing you part or the escaping part?"

I quirk a brow. "You've already tried to kill me twice now. How'd that work out for you?"

Her eyes turn to slits as she bites the inside of her cheek. Holding back a retort, I am sure. I find I kind of like pushing her buttons.

Wolves howl and pound down the hall after us. I tilt my head at my nonexistent watch. "Tik tok, Moonfire."

I don't know where the nickname came from, but it suits her. She is a fiery soul sent from the Moon Goddess. My Moonfire.

Her head tilts and her brows furrow at the name.

My pack, lead by Elias, comes thundering down the hall. Her eyes widen when she sees them and she stands. I stand with her and turn so my body is facing the wall where I can see my pack and her at the same time. She glances over her shoulder and her hand tightens around her weapons. A ninja star in one hand and her dagger in the other. For a second, I think she is about to make a run for it and I tense, ready to chase after her again.

Instead, her shoulders droop, the fight leaving her, and she drops her weapons at her feet.

"The purse too," I order, as I hold my hand up to stop the wolves.

Elias comes to a halt near me and growls at the woman. The others stop behind him, all waiting for their orders. Some of them snarl, others pace anxiously.

She sighs and, with a roll of her eyes, drops her purse next to the weapons.

I smirk. "Good choice." I look down at Elias. "Take her to a windowless room, place guards around it, report to me when it is done. And Elias..." I wait for him to look at me, "Don't. Hurt. Her."

Elias stares at me a moment then nods once. He barks at the other wolves and three follow him. Elias walks over to the girl and nudges her. The woman draws away from the wolf and looks up at me with a worried frown. I nod at her to go on and her frown deepens. Elias nudges her a bit more forcefully and finally she moves in the direction he wants her to go. With one last look at me she turns and walks away.

I turn to my wolves and send a little Alpha power out through the link. "No one harms her." I wait for them all to give me a nod of acknowledgement before letting go of the power. "You are dismissed and thank you for your support today."

They start to leave but I call out one last thing.

"And someone please get me some clothes."

Chapter 7

Jessie

I screwed up.

I don't know what happened when I threw that dagger but for some reason panic flooded me at the idea of killing him and my hand shifted a little to the right on its own accord. I ended up hitting him in the shoulder instead of his heart. I also had an opportunity to shoot him but again I hesitated. Lastly, I could have stabbed him and escaped in the hall before those other…werewolves appeared, but that smirk and his naked form distracted me.

Some elite that makes me. Now, I am in the wolf's lair.

Do wolves have lairs?

I groan and cover my face with my hands. What am I going to do? What are *they* going to do?

I don't know why Norden Kane kept me alive. He has every right to want me dead. Instead, he saved me…sort of.

I've got to get out of here.

For the third time since being put in this room two hours ago I search for an escape. The room is as Norden ordered, a windowless one with a guarded exit. There is a bathroom and a closet attached to the spacious bedroom. A large canopy bed and dresser make up the only furnishings. Searching the drawers, closet, and bathroom reveal nothing useful unless I want to fight off a pack of wolves with a toilet brush.

I place my ear against the door and immediately hear a low growl.

Ok, so guards are still there.

It is uncanny how they know when I am close. When I first got put in here, I kept tapping on the door just to annoy the wolves but that got boring fast when all they did was growl. I also banged on the door, tried opening it from my side (it's locked from the outside), and promised that if they let me go I will let them live. Nothing I did made them open the door for me to try and escape.

I flop on the bed with a sigh. At least they didn't take my camera. I take it off from around my neck and go through the pictures. Images of Janie are the first I see and I can't help a twinge of guilt. Have they realized she was the one to let me in? Have they asked her about me? Just in case they haven't figured it out yet, I should probably delete the pictures so she is not connected to me. I hover over the delete button, hesitating a moment but with a grunt I press down and delete all pictures from the camera including my recon pics then toss the camera onto the bed beside me.

Voices outside catch my attention and I spring from the bed. I stand in the middle of the room with my feet slightly apart and hands fisted, ready to attack or flee, whichever comes first.

A second later the door opens and two men walk in. One has platinum-blond hair and icy blue eyes. In the hall before my attack, he had been smirking and seemed to enjoy joking around. Now he stands behind his Alpha with arms crossed over his chest and a glare sure to freeze anyone it lands on. He is no longer wearing a suit but a plaid white and blue shirt and jeans. I ignore him, not intimidated by his look, and focus on the other man in the room.

Norden Kane finally put some clothes on, a red T-shirt over dark jeans. A little sweat mars his brow and his left arm hangs limp making me wonder how his shoulder is doing. If Dorian is correct, and he probably is, silver hurts worse than a third-degree burn for these guys. Yet here he is, looking tough and steady. If it wasn't for those two little signs, I would think he is totally fine. His dark blond, almost brown, hair is combed back as usual, but pieces fall forward across his forehead. His golden-green eyes glitter with amusement though I don't know what he could possibly find amusing right now.

Norden gestures to the man behind him. "This is my Beta, Elias."

Elias doesn't make any move to greet me. If anything, his eyes narrow further.

I stay silent and study them. What is their aim here?

"We'd like to ask you a few questions," Norden says.

When no one says anything Norden clears his throat and continues. "Let's start with who you are. Now I know from experience you will probably attack me if I ask your name so we will skip over that for now." He smirks and shoots me a look like we have our own inside joke.

I mean, he isn't wrong.

The last two times he asked me who I am helped snap me out of my fog and focus on my main task. It just so happened that my main task involved hurting him. I feel my lips pull up and I fight to keep my own smirk down. I cross my arms and raise my brow instead.

"We know you work for the Infinite Order and that you are an elite assassin thanks to the silver weapons." He shrugs and nods his head side to side in thought. "Most likely new to the elite part due to your reaction when we shifted." Norden studies me, looking for a response to anything he said.

I am surprised by how accurate he is, but I keep my face stoic. After this failed mission, I will be lucky if I can still be an elite let alone work for the Infinite Order.

"You were the one to steal our Chalice, so that leads me to my first question. Where is it?"

I blink at him. Of course. The Chalice. It must be a supernatural artifact seeing as how an Alpha of werewolves was there retrieving it and I got promoted to elite who kills supernaturals after delivering it. Oh my goodness. I escaped two werewolves with an ancient supernatural artifact in Peru before I even knew their kind existed. They could have ripped me to shreds. If I stayed longer, would more creatures have shown up wanting the cup?

Laughter bubbles up and I cover my mouth to hide the snickers that escape.

Elias and Norden share a confused look which only makes me laugh harder. I clutch at my stomach and squeeze my eyes shut hoping to contain the laughter. This is all so crazy. How is all this real?

I stand up straighter and wipe away a few tears when my laughter dies down. The two men—werewolves—study me with small, curious frowns.

I hold up a hand. "Sorry. It wasn't you I was laughing at, really. This is all..." I wave my hands at the two men, "...so crazy. Why do you even want the old cup? Is it magical?"

Elias scoffs and turns away shaking his head. "'Old cup,'" he mutters.

"Your boss didn't tell you?" Norden asks surprised.

"Tell me what?" My humor is completely gone now. There is obviously something dear old Dorian kept from me about that chalice. How did Dorian know about it anyway?

"It is a very important shifter relic. Necessary for the survival and connection of our species." His eyes are fixed on mine, locking me in place. "Moonfire, please. We need it back."

That name. Why is he calling me Moonfire? It sounds so personal. The sound of his voice calling me that name sends warm tingles through my belly and heat to my cheeks. I cross my arms and squeeze, hoping to rid myself of the feeling.

I press my lips together into a firm line. Why does Dorian want their shifter relic? Why does he want Norden dead? I think about the other assassinations I have committed. All human but dangers to society, or so I was told. Maybe shifters are a danger to humanity and the Infinite Order is trying to eliminate them before they kill us all. Something about that doesn't seem right, but I am not about to betray the Order.

I shake my head and avert my eyes. No way am I going to let gorgeous werewolf eyes hypnotize me into telling them anything.

"Ok then, we can circle back to that. How about, where is the Infinite Order located?"

I snort and shake my head.

"Are you here alone? Did anyone help you with this assassination attempt?"

I bite the inside of my cheek and continue staring at the wall.

Norden sighs.

"There are other ways we can get the information from her," Elias not-so-ambiguously suggests.

Norden turns on him and since his back is to me now, I cannot see the look he shoots Elias, but it must be in my favor because Elias huffs and mutters, "Whatever you say, boss."

Norden turns back to me and inclines his head. "This is not over. Until next time, Moonfire."

Before I can respond, the two shifters are gone and the lock engages once again.

The door handle jiggling interrupts my fitful half-sleep and I bolt upright on the bed, reaching for the dagger on my pillow beside me only to feel my hat instead. I have no idea what time it is since there are no windows or clocks in here, but it feels like hours since the last time I saw anyone. The door opens and I leap out of the bed, so I have more mobility to fight if need be.

The platinum haired man from yesterday, Elias, steps inside but keeps the door open behind him. I eye the doorway, wondering if I could make it past him. He crosses his arms and arches his brow at me, silently daring me to try.

I mimic his stance. "So…what brings you here to my lovely abode?" I say sweetly, as if greeting a friend to my home.

The corner of his lips turn up on one side just the slightest to let me know he found my statement amusing but so faint that I could have missed it if I wasn't watching him so closely.

"You are to dine with the Alpha for breakfast."

He steps into the hall and reaches down to something beside the door. For a second, I think he is talking to the guard wolves but realize my mistake when he comes back with a black backpack. He holds it out to me.

"I believe this is yours. You can change first."

My brows rise a bit at the sight of my bag. Does that mean they found out Janie helped me get inside? My stuff was in her van. I want to ask about what they did to Janie, but I don't want to make it seem like I care about anyone. Caring about people leads to friends and friends lead to weaknesses and targets for my enemies. I am sure they already went through the bag and must have found my other weapons and the file with my target info in it. Thankfully, there is nothing that can lead them back to the Order.

Instead of taking it, I shrug and turn back to the bed. "No thanks," I say nonchalantly though a thousand butterflies flutter in my belly at the thought of seeing Norden again.

This time he doesn't try to hide his smirk. "It was not a request."

He tosses the bag onto the bed and backs away toward the door, making sure not to give me his back. Smart man.

"Get changed. I will be right outside."

"And if I don't?"

He arches a brow again. "Then I guess you will have to go to breakfast in that." He nods to the dress I am wearing.

I roll my eyes knowing he misunderstood my statement on purpose. "What if I don't go to breakfast?"

He pauses a moment and looks at the doorframe to his right. "Then I am sure he will come get you and carry you over his shoulder if he has to."

I narrow my eyes but not quite in a menacing way, more out of curiosity. Elias said *he* will come get me, as in Norden Kane. Why would Norden come get me when

Elias is just as capable of throwing me over his shoulder?

Elias taps on the wooden frame once and says, "Five minutes." Then he leaves, closing the door behind him.

I wait for the telltale click of the lock, but it doesn't happen. I am tempted to try to escape now that the door is unlocked but his warning replays in my mind. *I will be right outside.* I grumble and unzip my bag. The first thing I do is take inventory.

As predicted, all my weapons and distraction trinkets are gone as is the file. Even my passport was taken. Luckily, it had a fake name and address on it so they won't get far with it. All that is left are my clothes and a few toiletries. I grab the first things in sight and quickly change out of my dress. I have a feeling Elias won't hesitate to waltz in once the five minutes are up whether I am done changing or not.

Five minutes later, I am surprised by the warning knock before he comes in but not surprised that he opens the door without waiting for my permission. Thankfully, I am already clothed and only need to brush and braid my hair which I do quickly then throw the brush and other items back into the backpack.

"Let us go. Breakfast is about to be served." Elias steps to the side and waits for me to go past him so that he can walk behind me.

I watch him warily as I draw closer to the door and quickly run an attack/escape scenario through my mind.

I could take him. When I reach the doorway, the doorframe at my back and Elias mere inches away, I ball my hands into fists but a low growl from the hall stops me from going further than that with my plan. I may be able to take one of these guys in their human form, but a human and two wolves is a no-go. Relaxing my hands again, I follow wolf number one while wolf number two and Elias follow behind us. I expect to be led to the right to go back to the ballroom/dining hall, but we go left from my room deeper into the castle.

I make a mental map as we go along making sure to remember the turns we make and lay it out in comparison to my room and the ballroom. We take a different set of stairs down to the first floor then turn down a couple of hallways until wolf number one comes to a stop in front of a nondescript door. Elias steps forward and opens the door before leading me inside, still keeping his body turned toward me so as not to give me his back.

The first thing I notice are the three pointed-arch windows that let in the bright daylight. I squint until my eyes adjust to the light then look around. It is bigger than my room but much smaller than the formal dining/ball room. A white settee is laid against the back wall and a side table sits next to it. There is a sliding door on the left wall but it is closed so I do not know what it leads to. A dining table sits in the middle with six chairs set around it and in one of those chairs is

Norden Kane whose elbows are resting on the table and hands are folded into a steeple.

The sight of him sends a rush of excitement through me. He is dressed in a simple blue t-shirt and jeans and his hair is brushed back but pieces fall forward across his forehead. He runs his eyes over me slowly, causing heat to pool in my belly. Finally, his eyes come up to rest on mine and my breath nearly falters. Man, his eyes are gorgeous.

"Morning, Moonfire. Glad you chose to join me."

Chapter 8

Norden

"I wasn't aware I had a choice," Moonfire says dryly and goes to sit at the opposite end of the table as far from me as she can get.

My wolf whines in my head at her distance, but I shush it. I am glad she showed up. Knowing Elias, he probably told her I would throw her over my shoulder and force her to have breakfast with me if she didn't come along on her own. While throwing her over my shoulder seems enticing, I would not have forced her to be here if she truly did not want to be. If a bit of distance means having her in the same room, then I can handle it. For now.

Since she is no longer in her sundress, I assume Elias gave her the bag that we retrieved from the baker in town, Janie, after watching all the security footage from last night. After hours of interrogation and analyzing footage, we concluded that Janie had been an unknowing accomplice and was therefore innocent. The baker seemed quite upset and a bit hurt to find out the NYU student she had helped was the assassin.

Today the woman, or Marion Ravenwood if her passport is to be believed, is in a white tank top and tan shorts that only reach mid-thigh showing off her long legs. Her light blonde hair is braided, and her brown eyes seem to scan me just as I was doing to her even though she is trying to feign disinterest. I smile to myself, my wolf and I feeling pleased at her perusal.

"Everyone has a choice."

She only glares.

I hear someone approach and know our food is about to be served. I sit back and look to the door that leads to the next room just as one of the kitchen staff comes in rolling a cart. He silently places two plates in front of her, then two in front of me. I gesture for Elias to take a seat, feeling awkward that he has been standing broodingly at the door the whole time. The server places the last two dishes in front of him when he sits in a seat in the middle of the table between the woman and me.

"Have you ever had speckpfannkuchen and senfei?" I ask as I pick up my fork and take my first bite.

"Speck-a-what-now?" she asks, frowning with confusion at the German word.

I curl my lips inward to stop myself from smiling then answer by gesturing to the food in front of me.

Her eyes widen with realization, and she looks down at her plates. "Oh, I have had bacon pancakes before," she says referring to the speckpfannkuchen, "but not this mustardy-stuff." She pokes the senfei with her fork.

"It is good, I promise. It is only potatoes and eggs in a mustard sauce. Try it."

I watch as she tries a bite of the senfei and her eyes widen. "This is delicious."

This time I don't try to hide my smile. "The cooks here are great."

She digs in with a bit more enthusiasm.

I hold my questions until we are done eating but as soon as our plates are cleared, I fire off the first of many.

"So, Marion is it?"

`She doesn't even bat an eye. She quirks an eyebrow and sits back, lacing her fingers in front of her as she settles in for her interrogation.

"Or is it Jessie?"

Janie, the baker, had revealed that was the name this woman introduced herself as when they met, but since it contradicts her passport, it could just be another alias.

Again, the woman doesn't react.

I shrug. "I guess the name is not important right now." It is important but I don't want her to think so. She will be less likely to watch herself when speaking about names if I don't push for hers. I lean my elbows on the table and steeple my fingers. "Where is the Chalice?" I throw a little bit of Alpha power behind the words.

Elias' head snaps up and he looks from me to her, having sensed the power. Humans cannot be compelled by the Alpha power like shifters can, but they do sense something. Whether it is danger, or authority, or just that something is not quite right.

Her eyes grow bigger as the Alpha power grows stronger and her fingers go white with how hard she clenches them. I release the power and watch as she relaxes her fingers though her posture stays stiffened.

Her eyes narrow. "What was that?" she asks.

I expected her to sound scared, so the anger surprises me.

I ignore her and get back to my questions. "The Chalice. Where is it?"

She bites the inside of her cheek and looks toward one of the windows, clearly dismissing me.

A low growl rumbles in my chest. As an Alpha, I am not used to this kind of behavior. My questions are usually met with immediate responses and my orders followed without delay. While it is amusing to watch my mate do something no one else would dare I remind myself that this woman is an assassin and thief and I need to do something to get our relic back.

My tone gets lower after each question, and I push more Alpha power at her until even Elias looks uncomfortable. "Where did you go after Peru? Who did you give the Chalice to? What does the Infinite Order want with it?" I let out another low growl, reminding her that she is in a room with shifters.

She continues to look out the window, ignoring me, but I can tell she is sensing the power. It is odd that she is so effected by it. Her fingers have gone white again and a bead of sweat breaks out on her brow. I can hear her heart race even in my human form. This time, she is scared.

A part of me hates that I am scaring her, but another larger part is more worried about the Chalice. I slam my hands on the table and shout, "Tell me!"

Suddenly, a fork is flying toward my face, the prongs aiming straight for my eye. I duck to the side to avoid the projectile and hear the cutlery *thunk* against the wall behind me.

I look to where it came from with wide eyes and see the woman glaring at me. "Do not threaten me with your voodoo," she says.

I choke on a laugh. Voodoo?

Elias jumps out of his seat and nearly leaps over the table to get to the woman. He snarls and his fangs descend as fur sprouts over his arms. The woman stands up, knocking over her chair and backs away. She looks around for a weapon but other than the fork there is nothing she can use against a werewolf. Elias makes it around the table and advances on her. By the time he reaches her he has fully shifted into a white wolf. His hackles are raised, and teeth bared as he snarls at my mate. I stand from my seat and reach out though it is a useless gesture.

"Elias!" I call out to my Beta, but the wolf is not backing down.

Suddenly, Elias jumps forward, aiming for her legs, attempting to hobble her so she cannot run away.

"No!" I shout.

Despite not having a weapon, my mate doesn't back down or shrink away in fear. I can definitely smell the fear coming off of her, but she doesn't let it hinder her. She swings out and punches Elias in his snout before he can bite her. The wolf yelps and misses his mark. He snarls again but that punch gave me enough time to gather myself.

"Enough!" I shout as I push out enough Alpha power to force Elias to his belly.

My Beta whimpers and lowers his head though in between each whimper is a growl aimed at the woman.

The woman has her back pressed against the wall and her chest rises with heavy breaths. She grits her teeth against the power and scratches at the wall trying to find something to grip. Once both of them are not trying to kill each other, I release the power and Elias shifts back to his human form.

He stands up and glares at me then shoots a glare at the woman before stalking out of the room to find some clothes.

The woman and I stand there for a moment trying to process what just happened. After replaying the whole scene in my mind, I start chuckling then full on laughing. She tilts her head and eyes me like I have just jumped off the deep end.

In between bits of laughter, I say, "You just punched a wolf. A Beta of wolf shifters to be exact."

The woman stares at me then lets out an amused snort which turns into a chuckle. Then she starts laughing fully and soon we are filling the room with our mirth.

"I just punched a freaking wolf!" She says, tears pooling at the corners of her eyes from how much she is laughing.

When our outbursts fade and we catch our breath I tilt my head to the fork in the wall across the room. "How about we make a deal?"

She eyes me warily. "Ok…?"

"I promise not to use my Alpha power on you or threaten you with my…" I smile as I remember her words, "…voodoo, if you promise to not try to kill me." I know that is asking a lot. It is her job after all to kill me, but I have to have hope that with this truce, we can form some sort of trust and maybe that will be a step closer to finding out more about her and where the Chalice is. Force and threats obviously will not work.

She searches my face for deception and narrows her eyes in suspicion. I keep my face open and honest, wanting her to sense that I mean what I say. She presses her lips into a thin line and looks to the window.

A minute passes and I think she is going to refuse then try to attack me again, this time with Kung Fu skills or something.

"Do we have a deal?" I ask again. I tense, ready to fight if she attacks.

She turns back to me and nods once then says through gritted teeth, "We have a deal." She closes her eyes and frowns.

I grin. "Now that this is settled, why don't I escort you back to your room?"

Trees whip past me and my heart thuds loudly in my chest as I race through the forest. I sniff the air and immediately change direction, veering to the right to follow the trail I had been tracking for the past few minutes.

My paws fly over the ground and for a minute I think about forgetting the scent and just racing off to be alone for a while, but I have responsibilities, and one of them is my Beta.

The scent gets stronger and I know I am close so I put in a little extra burst of speed to catch up to the owner of that scent. When I spot white fur I sprint at it until I am right up on his tail then nip at his heels. The wolf in front of me lets out a warning growl but I nip at him again then speak into his mind using our pack link.

"Stop for a second, would ya?"

The white wolf ignores me and keeps running. I grumble but it comes out as a whine-growl, then I leap and tackle the wolf to the ground. Since we were running fast, the impact sends us rolling. Elias manages to twist around so we are facing each other then tries to bite me. As we roll around the forest floor, Elias and I nip and swipe and go for each other's ears as we play. But with shifters, playing is never just that.

I get the upper hand, well...paw, then pin him beneath me and snap at him, stopping just a breath away from his snout. I need to show that even in a play fight, as Alpha, I will always come out on top.

Elias stills and I wait a moment to make sure he is not going to surprise attack then back off. He rolls over and stands until he is on all fours again then faces me with a low stance. I wait to see what he is going to do. Run? Fight?

Elias stares at me with ice, blue eyes, the color eerily similar to his human ones, then opens his mouth. His tongue lolls out and he plops onto the ground for a rest.

Smirking in my mind, I sit in front of him, our paws almost touching.

"I think we should talk," I say with mindspeak.

Elias makes a huffing noise before answering. *"I just do not understand. Why are you giving her a room? Inviting her to breakfast? Defending her? All she has done is try to kill you. We should be torturing her and finding the Chalice."*

I shake my head. *"It's not that simple."*

He stares at me, waiting for me to explain. I turn my head to look at the forest around us, hesitant to tell him what I have been suspecting. After a minute, Elias huffs again, bringing my attention back to him.

I sigh. *"I think she is my mate."*

Elias stands abruptly. *"What?"* His wolf face doesn't show as many expressions as a human face does but his voice in my head holds a tone of surprise and disbelief.

I nod. *"I knew from the moment in the Peruvian cave."*

Picking up on my uncertainty despite my words, he lays down again slowly. *"But...?"*

It was my turn to huff. *"But I am not totally sure she is my mate because if she is then she should not be able to kill me, right?"*

Elias puts a paw forward, almost touching mine. *"Tell me everything."*

I explain the feelings I had when I first saw her and again when she appeared at the party. How everything disappeared and the only important thing was her. How my heart fluttered, and I wanted to protect her even when it didn't make sense to do so. How everything felt right and clicked when I was with her. All the things older shifters say happens when we meet our mates. I do not need to explain why I think I might be wrong because he has been there or heard of all the times she has tried to kill me.

"And I don't even know her name," I finish.

Elias is silent for a moment, and I shift restlessly waiting for his reply. Maybe he will know what is wrong with me. With this dynamic between me and the assassin.

Finally, he shakes his head. *"A name will come later, right now you need to know if she is the one. Technically she didn't kill you. She probably could have last night but she didn't. It is possible she feels the same. That fact, and if what you say you are feeling is true, makes it seem like she may be your mate."* He looks around the woods as if someone could overhear us even though we are using mindspeak then asks, *"Has the mark appeared yet?"*

If I was a human, my cheeks would have turned red. Blessings of a wolf body.

"No, of course not. Remember, they say it appears after the first kiss." A picture of her in my arms, her lips on mine, my hand in her hair, pops into my head. What would it feel like? Soft and gentle? Hot and intense? Would the mark hurt when, *if,* it appeared?

Elias chuckles in our minds. *"You are picturing kissing her, right?"*

I snort my denial but we both know I am lying.

"I am going to regret suggesting this, I am sure of it, but maybe you should kiss her. At least then you will know. And if it turns out she is not your mate, then we can torture her for information."

I growl at his suggestion. *"One, we are not torturing her, and two, I am not going to force her into a kiss when she doesn't even like me. She probably thinks I am a monster and she is an assassin. No. No kissing."*

I have never seen a wolf shrug but somehow Elias manages it. *"Well, either way, we need to know where the Chalice is and I am sorry but that needs to take precedence over this whole mate-or-no-mate thing."*

I nod. *"Agreed. We still have our team searching for it so hopefully they find something soon. Are we good?"*

Elias nods and stands. *"Yeah, you and I are good. I understand your weird behavior now."*

We snort our amusement then I nod in the direction we came from. *"Ready to head back?"*

As his answer, he darts forward and races through the forest back to the castle issuing a challenge I cannot refuse. Immediately, instinct takes over and I chase after him.

Chapter 9

Jessie

I am the worst assassin ever.

What kind of assassin makes a deal that she will not kill her target?

A stupid, unprofessional one, that's what kind.

I have barely been an elite for less than a week and I am already a failure. Maybe I should have stuck to artifact retrieval and small-time assassin jobs.

Then again, I could always break our deal and kill him anyway. The thought sends disgust pooling in my belly.

Killing someone has never been this hard for me. I don't usually have qualms about assassinating a target but for some reason I cannot stomach the thought of Norden Kane being dead. Yet, look where that got me.

Locked in a room in a castle full of werewolves. Freaking werewolves!

I groan and slump onto the bed.

I have to get out of here.

My thoughts go to breakfast before the attack. I had been let out of my room for it even though I am sure someone could have just brought me a tray. Or not fed me at all. I know now it was to get me to relax and maybe trust them so that I would answer their questions which I caught on to quickly. But maybe I could do the same to them. Act like I am playing along so they will give me more freedom, then when they are not paying attention, I can escape.

The fangs and distrust on that Beta though means my plan will take a while to accomplish but I do not have any other options. For some reason they have not turned to torture yet and after that ridiculous deal I just made I am sure I can get Norden to trust me enough to let me out more often. As long as I do not try to kill him and he does not use his weird werewolf power on me again.

I shudder, remembering the strange sensation of pressure on my chest; of fear wanting me to flee from the predator. I felt powerless, hence the flying fork.

I nod. Yes, that is what I will do, but there is no way they will believe me if I say I am ready to talk now after the breakfast and party incidents. No, I will have to see what their next move is then go from there.

Their next move does not come until the following day. After spending hours staring at the four walls, pacing the length of the room, trying to sleep, and unpacking and repacking my backpack, the lock at the door clicks. I almost smile and shout with joy, feeling relieved that my boredom will end even if only briefly, but I school my expression to one of indifference and cross my arms.

The door opens, once again without my permission, and Elias and Norden step in. Elias' eyes flick over my room, looking for danger I am sure though what I possibly could have done with the minimal items in the room to cause danger is a mystery. Norden's eyes immediately find mine and stay there. I feel a rush of…something the longer he stares and I force myself to look away before I get lost in it.

"What will it be today boys? Take me down to the kitchens to make kibble out of me? Set me loose in the woods for the pack to chase? Oh! Lock me up in the stocks and let the villagers throw tomatoes at me?"

Norden chuckles and shakes his head. "Nothing so medieval. No, today I thought we could get some exercise by walking around the castle."

They have to know that it is a terrible plan to let an assassin see the layout and inner workings of their home. They are either overconfident that I won't use that knowledge to escape and kill Lord Kane, or it is another ploy to get me to trust them and let down my guard. Probably both.

I hook a thumb at the Beta. "Is he coming?"

Elias scowls. "Of course, I am."

I tap my lips and look up toward the ceiling as if thinking about it. "Hmm, his presence will make the walk less enjoyable but my desire to get out of this room is stronger than my dislike for him so let's go."

I don't miss the Beta's eye roll, but I ignore it and move to the door where Norden is waiting for me. We head down the same path that Elias took me on yesterday. I imprinted the path in my mind and am able to identify the door that leads to the private dining area. However, Norden doesn't stop or acknowledge the door. We continue through the castle, making turns down halls and looping around to cover the same ground before going around what appears to be the back of the castle all the while Norden talks, attempting to make conversation without actually giving me a detailed tour. I know what they are doing. They are trying to confuse me by going in circles to make the place seem like a labyrinth and talking to distract me from that fact, but when it comes to memorizing paths and layouts, I am a master. I have to give it to him though, it is a solid plan that would have worked on any normal person.

Norden doesn't try to ask me any questions about who I am or where the Chalice is. He sticks to mundane topics of which I am able to partially tune him out to focus on my surroundings. However, my mind and body are too aware of him to tune him out completely and when he brings up shifters and his pack, I can't help but participate, my curiosity too much to contain.

"…Elias and I have been friends ever since we were pups and he joined me here when I came to take over as Alpha of the world's northern packs. We had our choice of homes to choose from but something about this strange architecture intrigued me and next thing I knew I was choosing this little village of Germany to set up HQ."

"World's northern packs? How many packs are there?"

Norden tilts his head as he thinks about it. "Hmm, hard to say but the last time a census was done there were approximately sixty thousand."

Sixty thousand? How many times have I passed a shifter on the street or on my travels and never known? Does the Order know about all the packs?

"And you're in charge of the northern ones? How many is that? It seems like it would be a lot of shifters to look after for one person."

A dark look passes over his face, and he turns away. He doesn't answer me for a moment, and we continue down a long stone hallway. Are they taking me to a dungeon?

Finally, he speaks but avoids looking at me. "It can be hard. Especially when some of them do not believe I should be here."

There is much in that statement that I do not understand but can see weighs heavily on him. My fingers twitch, almost reaching out to comfort him but I clench them into a fist instead to hold myself back. If I reached for him, Elias would probably take it as a threat and rip me apart.

Norden shakes his head to rid himself of the thoughts plaguing him and answers the rest of the question. "Our world is divided into four quadrants, well technically five. My father is King of all the wolf-shifters and runs things from his place in Canada while his four sons are in charge of the northern, eastern, western, and southern packs in the rest of the world with approximately 12,000 packs in each give or take."

He is Alpha of over 12,000 packs? How many wolves is that? Wait, did he just say his father is the King of all wolf shifters?

"You're a Prince?"

He doesn't answer the question, but he doesn't need to. The throne from the party and the target on his life makes more sense now. I am still reeling from the information when we stop at a wooden door. He shoots me a small, hesitant smile before opening it and gesturing for me to go inside ahead of him.

Alright, if this is a dungeon then we are going to have problems. I step through the door and can't help but gasp at the sight. It is definitely *not* a dungeon.

For a second, I think he took me outside but on closer inspection, the stone walls are still there, just hidden among tons of ivy and flowers. Bushes, flowers, and loads of other plants fill the room. There are a few trees which reach up and nearly touch the glass dome above us where sunlight streams down to cover the room in bright, golden light. Little dirt pathways wind through the greenery and stone statues can be seen on the edges of the room.

"Wow," I breathe out. I turn to Norden who is beaming at me. My cheeks flush at his look and I turn back to the indoor garden. "Can…Can I take a look around?"

"Of course, let me give you a tour." Norden shoots a look at Elias who frowns but backs up until he is leaning against one of the walls and leaves us alone, though he gives me a warning look to remind me we are not truly alone. Norden leads me to one of the paths and we slowly make our way through the garden.

We walk in comfortable silence for a bit until we reach a stone bench halfway down the path. He holds out his hand toward it and I take a seat. He sits beside me and our thighs touch sending heat racing to every part of my body.

I try to ignore it and stare at a lily on the other side of the path. He sees my look and stares at the flower too.

"I love to escape to this garden when shifting and running through the woods is not optional."

I nod. "I can see why you love this place. I've always loved plants. I have many at home. One is a small succulent like that one." I point to a plant on my left near the trail. Suddenly, my words register and I suck in a sharp breath as my heart pounds in my chest. I just gave him a personal detail.

Something about him and Janie sets me at ease until I can't help but drop my guard. The thought of Janie sends a spike of guilt through me and I have to ask, "What did you do with Janie?"

He tilts his head at the change of topic but continues looking at the succulent. "The baker? Nothing. We know she is innocent." He casts me a sidelong look. "Why?"

I shake my head. "Just that it would be a shame if she couldn't bake those Danishes anymore."

He turns his head until he is looking at me directly now and studies me.

"What?" I ask, trying not to squirm under his gaze.

A small smile pulls at his lips and he shakes his head. "Nothing." He kicks at a pebble near his foot and sends it skittering over the path.

"Mhm," I make the disbelieving sound before moving on to something that has been on my mind. "So, does it hurt to shift? Can werewolves shift whenever they want?" He has been forthcoming with information today so I want to get as much out of him as I can before he clams up.

He said he came to the garden when shifting was not possible which made me think about the times I have seen him and Elias shift into wolves. Elias was a snowy white wolf with ice blue eyes and sharp teeth. Norden was a big, gray and brown wolf with thick fur, big paws, and yellow eyes. I have seen a werewolf shift a couple times now, yet it is still hard to wrap my head around.

He shakes his head then tilts it and frowns a bit as if thinking about the answer more carefully then bobs his head side to side. "It depends."

I wait for him to elaborate but he stays silent, his small, thinking-frown still in place.

"What does that mean?" I prompt.

He purses his lips. "Do you know how a shifter comes to be?" He looks at me and seems to realize who he is talking to. "I suppose you don't."

I feel affronted but he is right. Two days ago, I never knew shifters existed and other than movies, I don't have the slightest idea how one may 'come to be'.

"A shifter can either be born or made. The ones who are born are able to control their wolf better because they grow up with it and it is a part of them from the beginning, you cannot have one without the other, but a made-shifter is a human who suddenly shares a body and soul with an animal after years of being alone. The urges to shift and the battle for dominance are a constant struggle. So, maybe you can imagine how it is difficult to answer those questions."

"You're a born wolf, right?"

He nods.

He is living proof that these myths exist and yet I still cannot comprehend that this man has an animal inside of him, one that he was born with—his other half. Is it like a spirit animal or something more?

"And…how does one become a wolf?" Images of a wolf's teeth biting into my arm and shaking me like a ragdoll as I scream makes me shudder.

"That is a story for another time." Before I can argue or ask him more questions, he stands abruptly and holds out a hand. "Ready to continue?"

I nod, letting the topic go for now, and stand. I ignore his hand despite my whole being wanting to reach out and have his warmth envelop me even if only through that little contact. He drops his hand but stands close as we continue down the path and I hate to admit my body hums at his nearness.

We are silent for a few minutes. I look out into the garden and admire the beauty of it, wishing I had a place like this back home to escape to.

Norden has since put his hands in his pockets but keeps bumping his arm into mine which sends little jolts of electricity zipping across my skin. We turn the corner, and I can see the end of the trail up ahead. I feel a pang of sadness that our time alone is coming to an end but immediately feel ridiculous for it.

He stops suddenly and bends down. He picks a yellow dahlia from the side of the path and turns to me. Before I can move away or say anything, he is standing in front of me and grabbing my hand with one of his and placing the flower into my palm with his other. Butterflies take off in my belly and I feel my cheeks heat. This is completely unexpected and probably inappropriate behavior between supposed enemies, but I can't help feel giddy at the exchange. What is wrong with me?

"Norden…" I start to protest and hand the flower back, but he holds up a hand refusing it.

"Call me North, please." Norden, or North, clears his throat. "I have something I want to…" he searches for the words, "discuss with you." He shifts his feet and crosses his arms.

I frown at his nervousness. First a garden walk then a flower and now he is acting nervous and needs to discuss something? Is this his way of telling me they are going to kill me after all or that they are giving me twenty-four hours to fess up to the Chalice's location before they start the torture? A tiny voice in my head wonders if he is about to confess feelings for me since these are typical romantic things. A weird feeling unfurls in me at the thought. Then the larger part of my brain laughs at that tiny voice and scolds it for being foolish. I have watched too much TV. He is just trying to make me drop my guard. That's all this is.

"Ok...?" I start but stop almost immediately, unsure what to do or say.

"Ok, here it goes. I think, no, I strongly believe that you...Well, I am...We... This is harder than I thought." He pinches his chin and frowns.

"North, what are you trying to say?"

He opens his mouth but a figure at the end of the path cuts off whatever he was about to say. The figure gets closer, and I see it is Elias. I glare at him, and he reciprocates before focusing on his Alpha.

"North, you have a call waiting for you."

"Can't it wait?" North asks, annoyed, and gives his Beta a meaningful look. I look between the two of them trying to pick up on the unsaid message but am unsuccessful.

Elias shakes his head. "No, you should take this." He glances at me and hesitates but seems to think it is fine for the enemy to hear whatever it is and says, "It's your father."

Chapter 10

Norden

I sit in the security room in front of the many monitors, each showing a different part of the castle. My eyes land on one particular screen. The door to Moonfire's room is closed and two wolves stand guard in front of it. I think back to the moment I was about to tell her about mates. How would she have taken it? Not well I suppose. This is all new to her and dropping that bomb would only confuse and possibly make her feel more trapped than she already is.

But she needs to know. I cannot keep hiding it.

I watch the door on the monitor for another moment. It is unlikely, but I half expect the door to open and for me to see the woman step out only to flip off the camera, knowing I am watching. I smile at my imagination and open my laptop, ready to see what my father wants now. Probably an update on the Chalice.

The call connects and my father's face appears on the screen. "Any news on the Chalice?" He immediately asks. How predictable.

"Hello to you too."

He snorts and rolls his eyes then lifts his eyebrows as if to say *well?*

I resist my own eye roll and sigh instead.

"The team has traced them to The States, but they are still narrowing it down." I got the update of our team's work from Elias on our way to the room in anticipation of my father's question.

"We suspected that much," he says with annoyance.

Suspected. Which means his team was not able to track it even that far and he is upset by it.

"Keep me updated," he orders.

I expect him to end the call, but he hesitates.

"Yes?" I prompt which makes him scowl. He is an Alpha, not to mention King of all wolf shifters. He is not used to sass.

"Danika tells me there has been an assassination attempt?"

I roll my eyes and make a mental note to talk to Danika after this call. "Ah, you care, how sweet."

He frowns, his bushy eyebrows nearly covering his eyes. "You are the heir. Without you I would have no one to take over after I am gone. Everything we have worked for would be for naught."

I resist pointing out that he is the only one of us who wants the world united under one family. I shake my head and give him a wry smile. "You're right, it's not like I have three brothers or anything."

"What of the assassin?" He asks, ignoring my comment.

I pause for a moment and make a conscious effort not to show anything on my face. "It's been dealt with."

He stares at me a moment waiting for me to elaborate, or apologize, or…something. I lean back and cross my arms over my chest. He probably already knows, and if not, then Danika will surely tell him soon enough. Moonfire's days here are limited if that happens. I would like to think everyone here is loyal to me, but Danika proves there are spies who are more loyal to my father and would probably kill the assassin if asked to. I keep my face blank despite my rage and panic simmering underneath. My wolf pushes against me from inside wanting out so it can run to Moonfire's room and protect her.

"I better not hear of another incident." As if I was the one to order the hit on my life. "Keep me updated on the Chalice." He does not wait for a response and ends our call.

I let out a deep breath and spin around in my seat to find Elias. He is standing against the wall near the door, out of sight of the computer screen where my father had been but still near enough to have heard everything.

Elias presses his lips in a firm line and shakes his head.

"Father of the year award everyone," I say wryly.

Elias doesn't say anything. He doesn't need to. He has been with me long enough to know how my father is. He pushes away from the wall and turns to the door. "I assume we are going to pay Danika a little visit?"

I groan. "Must we?"

He arches a brow at me.

I stand and head to the door. "Yeah, yeah, I know.

With a few calls, Elias is able to pinpoint her location. I hate to leave the castle and more importantly, leave my mate alone with possible assassins—ironic, I know—but I must speak with Danika, and she would most likely be in town for most of the day. She loves attention and letting everyone know how important she thinks she is since she has the King's ear, so she likes to spend time in town, specifically the nail salons, local shops, and community center. If she wasn't doing it all for selfish reasons, she would make a great community liaison.

The mood in town is a refreshing change to those in the castle. Everyone is going about their day with calm, happiness, and no worries. Unlike in the castle when people tense whenever I walk past or look frightened half the time even if they try to hide it behind a smile.

As if at any moment their lives or jobs would be disrupted. I hate the fear my father has put in people despite years having passed now since the takeover. I shake it off and continue on my way.

Elias leads us to the main street where most of the shops are set up. He checks his phone then looks around at the shops. I wait for him to find what he is looking for knowing his security team is sending him the info about Danika. When he spots it, he nods his head at it directing my attention to the shop where she is located and letting me take lead on our approach. I glance up at the sign when we get closer and see it is the bakery. Janie's bakery.

I reach out a hand to the door handle but hesitate. Why is it so hard to go in here? Is it because of our brief suspicion of Janie and the guilt over that? Or is it because Janie knows my Moonfire if only briefly or that Moonfire loves the food from here?

"North?" Elias prompts.

I shake my head and open the door. The smells hit me immediately and it is like stepping into a warm, sun filled, happy home full of delicious, sweet treats. I don't remember the last time I actually came into this shop rather than have the food from here ordered to the castle, but I should have come much sooner. I spot Danika at the register talking to none other than Janie.

The two couldn't look more different. Danika is wearing a white dress with gray geometric designs all over it and a white sun hat. On one arm is a small purse and on her feet are shoes with a three-inch heel. How she can walk in them is anyone's guess. Her black hair is perfectly styled even as it rests loosely against her back. Her whole attire looks expensive and out of place in this quaint little village in Germany and yet it is so…Danika. I wouldn't expect her in anything less.

Janie on the other hand has her brown hair up in a messy bun and wears tan pants with a light blue, simple shirt with an apron over it all. She is taller than Danika (most people are) ad thicker in the middle and cheeks. The woman does not wear any makeup and smile lines around her eyes show she is never slow to express her happiness. She looks relaxed, homey, and friendly.

Janie spots me and stiffens but immediately eases and gives me a small wave and welcoming smile. "I will be with you in just a moment, my Lord."

Danika straightens at the title and spins around. When she spots me she gives me a slow grin. Her eyes flit to Elias but immediately dismiss him and rests back on me.

I nod at Janie. "Thank you but I am here for her," I say nodding toward Danika.

"*Ooo,* and to what do I owe this…pleasure?" Danika practically purrs as she glides toward me and runs a hand down my chest.

I clear my throat and take a step back letting her hand drop. "We need to talk."

The smallest of frowns passes over her face before she covers it with a smile that I think she is meaning to be flirty.

I gesture to a table nearby. I sit and Elias is about to take the seat next to me, but Danika beats him to it leaving him to sit across from us. Elias glares at her but does not say anything.

I take a deep breath and let it slowly out, knowing this conversation is going to be a roller coaster. "Danika, have you been speaking to my father again?"

Wide innocent eyes blink up at me. "Of course I have. He is our King and wants to be updated on all the packs. He also loves you and wants to know how you are doing." She gives me a disapproving frown. "You do not talk to him nearly as much as he would like."

A growl slips from me and has her raising her eyebrows in surprise.

"I am the Alpha here. Elias is the Beta. We are the only ones who should be sharing information with anyone. There is no instance where you should be telling him, or anyone else, anything."

We have had this conversation many times before, but the King's protection and his approval of her actions keep her going. Not only that but her assumption that she will one day be my mate and therefore Lady of the Pack makes her think she can do certain things.

She pouts dramatically, complete with a protruding bottom lip and head down as she gazes up at me through her lashes. She places a hand on my arm. "Oh, My Lord, I am sorry if my actions have upset you. However, what have I told him that has prompted this discussion?"

"The assassination attempt," I state simply.

Behind her I see Janie stiffen. She had been cleaning and organizing her displays, but I guess she had been listening as well. Not hard to do with enhanced hearing and our lack of whispering.

My attention is drawn back to the woman sitting next to me when she gasps and squeezes my arm.

"Oh, how could I not tell him? That…that…*Depp* ruined my party and almost killed our beloved Prince."

Interesting how her first concern is the ruined party.

I bristle at the name calling. Anyone who had been there that night might say the same about an assassin even if that word makes me want to punish any who uses it in reference to Moonfire.

"I am honestly surprised you had not already told him. He seemed very surprised to hear it."

To Danika, this was the first attempt on my life, but my father knows that it was the second in less than a week. Elias and I share a look. There is still something we need to know.

"You did not tell him she is still in the castle, did you?" I study her for a reaction. I need to know if Moonfire is in danger.

Danika does not disappoint, however, her response is a surprise. "What?! The assassin is still in the castle?"

She starts fluttering her hands about. "We are in danger. Call the pack. Get them to hunt her down." Her hands suddenly still. "Wait, did you say '*she*'?"

I glance at Elias whose wide eyes, which probably match my own, show we both know I made a mistake. I had assumed she knew since many of the wolves on guard in front of Moonfire's door and those who chased her that night knew about her stay in our castle.

"We are keeping her under guard and trying to…" I look to Elias for help. We cannot exactly tell her we are trying to get information about our sacred Chalice that is stolen or that she is my mate.

"Trying to get information about the Order and…maybe get her to be on our side and infiltrate them as a double agent." Elias shrugs minutely and I incline my head infinitesimally, appreciative for the save and impressed by the lie. It would make sense to the others who are probably wondering why we have not killed her yet.

Danika snorts and sits back, suddenly serious and with anger reflecting in her narrowed eyes. "As if that will work. Those Infinite assassins are loyal dogs and would rather die than double cross their Order. Just kill her."

A growl slips from me before I can stop it.

Elias and Danika raise their eyebrows at me, Elias in warning and Danika with shock.

I swallow and try to cover my reaction. "I need her."

I realize how that can be interpreted but I don't change it.

Elias however, feels the need to elaborate. "For information."

Danika looks between us with a frown, suspicion growing in her eyes. Oops, we need to end this conversation now before she picks up on anything else.

"Danika, we need you to keep quiet about this. Do not go blabbing about it to my father. I have this handled and as your Alpha you need to trust that for once."

Danika starts to protest. "I do not blab—" At my hardened look she deflates and gives me a single nod. "Fine." She mimics zipping her lips shut. "Is that all?"

She looks between me and Elias and when neither of us say anything she stands and grabs her purse. She starts to leave but turns back and places a hand on my shoulder.

With a serious and non-dramatic tone, different than her usual style, she says, "Norden. I do trust you. I always have. I am just worried about you."

With that she walks to the counter and takes a box that Janie had ready for her and leaves the bakery.

It is not often that Danika calls me by my name and that is probably the first time I had ever seen her show loyalty and trust to me alone rather than to me because of my father. Now let's see if she can keep quiet about it long enough for me to figure out what to do with our little assassin.

"Well, that went…well," Elias says, staring after Danika despite her no longer being in sight. "I think she is actually going to listen to you this time." Then he shakes his head as if clearing it of thoughts and turns back to me. "Ready to head back. There is work to be done."

"There always is," I chuckle and stand.

We wave goodbye to Janie who nods back with a strained smile. We are at the entrance, Elias already stepping outside and me with a hand on the open door and one foot out when I pause as a thought strikes me.

"Hey, I will catch up with you, I am going to grab something while I am here."

Elias waves a dismissive hand at me. "Sure, get me a schnecken."

I chuckle and nod then step back inside. Janie shifts on her feet nervously, but her professionalism takes over and she gives me a warm smile as she gestures to the case. "Anything I can get you today, my Lord?"

I smile as I think about Moonfire. "Yes, what kind of Danishes do you have?"

Her eyes narrow suspiciously, and she studies me. "Are these for you or—Never mind. I have custard, strawberry cream, chocolate, cherry, and apricot." Janie leans her hands on the counter in a relaxed pose and glances from me to the Danishes.

"Hmm," I tap my lips with a finger as I study the different flavors and try to guess which one Moonfire would like. "I will take two chocolate Danishes and throw in a schnecken please." I nod, feeling good about my decision then move to the register. Women love chocolate, right?

She starts packaging the order but as she reaches for the second Danish she pauses and stares at the pastries for a long moment.

I clear my throat to get her attention, but she continues staring at them, her mind far away.

"Janie?"

She shakes her head a little then turns to me, the bag in one hand and a pair of tongs held up in another. "Tell me, are these for…her?"

I know she does not mean Danika. She heard the conversation between us all and knows I have the assassin in the castle. If I say yes will Janie not want to give me the treats? And if I say no, would she see through me?

My hesitation seems to be answer enough. She turns back to the case abruptly. "You will want cherry Danishes then." She stuffs a couple in the bag with the one chocolate pastry she had already put in there.

I stare at her, baffled. How does she know what kind Moonfire would want and why is she being kind towards the one who betrayed her? The answer to that first question is obvious. Moonfire stopped here before going to the castle that night. She must have gotten the cherry Danishes and fell in love with them. The thought makes me smile.

"Um…" I try to say something, but my mind gets all jumbled and nothing comes out.

She comes to the register, avoiding my eyes, and rings up the purchases. She places the bags in front of me and nods a goodbye.

I take them and start to leave but turn back to find her watching me curiously. Her eyes widen when she notices she has been caught and her eyes skitter to the side to avoid my own. Whether in nervousness or because she senses the Alpha in me, I am not sure.

"Thank you, Janie."

She nods again and gives me a small smile. She knows I am thanking her for more than just the food. She may not know exactly what my goal is by giving the Danishes to the assassin, but she seems to suspect there is more going on than I am letting on.

Perceptive and kind little wolf.

I leave the bakery feeling excited to see the look on my Moonfire's face when I give the treats to her.

Chapter 11

Jessie

What was he going to say?

I pace the length of my room with hands on hips trying to figure it out. After a while I throw my hands in the air and flop on the bed. There is no use trying to figure out what he was going to say. I would only be assuming and there would be no way to know if I was right until he actually told me.

Instead, I spend the next hour doing workouts. Just because I am stuck in here does not mean I should let my exercise routine go. I need to keep up my strength and stamina.

After my sixtieth sit up, I rest my arms on my bent knees and take deep breaths. Despite having just done a workout, I still feel the need to be doing something.

Feeling bored for the umpteenth time, I cross to the door and sit next to it on the floor. I know the guard wolves are there, but I cannot hear them. I start tapping on the wood with my fingernail and instantly hear one of the wolves give a warning growl. I stifle an amused chuckle and do it again. This has become our routine for a couple days now. I wonder if the same guards are out there each time or if I am annoying the whole pack as each of them changes shifts.

I start tapping out the rhythm to Eye of the Tiger and when it reaches the point where the singers in the song would begin, I do the same. Now, no one has ever heard me sing before, except maybe my mother when I was younger, but I know for a fact that if they did they would run as far as they could to get away and make sure they never heard it again. I was hooked on American Idol when I was fifteen and recorded myself singing for an audition tape once. I replayed that video before sending it then immediately deleted it and rid myself of those dreams forever. Singing is fun but it is not something pleasant to hear coming from me. That might be self-deprecating, but I know when to face the truth. Right now though, I decided my guards should have a taste. When I reach the chorus, I tap and sing louder. Not to be annoying—ok well, kind of—but mostly because it is a good song and it needs to be dramatic.

I am interrupted by the door opening and I scramble back before I am crushed by it.

Oh no, I took it too far. The guards are coming to end me before I can finish torturing them with my song. Unfortunately, since I am still on the floor, arms splayed behind me to hold myself up, I will be easy pickings.

Instead of wolves, a familiar face appears around the open door sending my heart immediately aflutter which is quickly replaced by burning cheeks as embarrassment heats my body knowing that he heard me singing Eye of the Tiger.

North's eyes flit around looking for me then widen when he finds me on the floor a few feet away. My heart skips when he grins down at me and steps the rest of the way into the room. Surprisingly he is alone, no guards or Elias accompanying him.

He tries to fight a smile but his lips tug upward anyway and his golden-green eyes sparkle with mirth. "Outstanding performance. 10 out of 10." He uses his thumb to point over his shoulder at the door without taking his eyes off me. "Ralf and Lenny do love karaoke. I think I even saw Lenny tapping his paw to the beat, maybe even heard a low hum too."

"You sure he wasn't flexing his claws and growling?" I ask, as I stand up to face the Alpha.

He chuckles and moves to the dresser where he places a white paper bag on top.

"What's that?" I ask and nod to the bag.

"A treat." He opens the bag and pulls out a cherry Danish that instantly has my mouth watering.

"Is that…?"

He turns to me and offers me the pastry.

I grab it and enthusiastically take a bite then another, only regretting my fervor a second later when I realize he could have laced it. That's what I would have done.

I rush to the trash can in the bathroom and spit the pieces out. Luckily, I did not swallow any.

North is frowning when I return. "Was it not to your liking? Janie assured me the cherry ones were your favorite."

A pang tightens my chest at her name. Janie told him what I would like? Even after what I did to her? She is truly one of a kind. I mentally shake my head. I can think about that later.

"I will not fall for one of your tricks. What did you do to it? Truth serum? Poison? Sleep meds?" I wave the Danish at him accusingly.

North scoffs. "You are really untrusting, aren't you?"

When I continue to glare, North sighs and steps forward. He snatches the pastry from my hand and takes a large bite out of it. He chews for a few moments while I stare at him with an open mouth and wide eyes. He makes a dramatic swallow then opens his mouth and holds out his tongue to show me he truly swallowed it then raises his eyebrows at me.

"Satisfied?"

He turns to the bag and produces another cherry Danish and holds it out to me while he continues to hold the half-eaten one in his other hand, I guess keeping that one for himself.

"I would *never* trick you like that." He looks me in the eyes and holds my gaze, sincerity shining in them.

I slowly take the full Danish from him and nibble on it, feeling sheepish that I overreacted that way.

"If I really wanted to kill you, I would just throw you to the wolves."

His words catch me by surprise, and I end up choking on a bite which leads to a fit of coughing all the while he munches on his own treat as laughter dances in his eyes.

I shake my head as I fight a smile and turn away from him, my gaze landing on the white paper bag on the dresser. "What else is in there?"

He moves to the bag and opens it so I can see inside.

"A cinnamon roll? Is that yours or mine?"

He closes it and shakes his head. "It's a schnecken, which I guess you could call a German cinnamon roll though there is more to it. It's for Elias." He nods his head to the door and sighs. "Speaking of which I should probably go. I have work to do."

I frown. "Must be nice."

"What is nice?" He asks as he picks up the bag and holds it in front of him with two hands, waiting for my answer.

"Working. Leaving the room." I cross my arms and lean against the bed.

"You miss killing people?" He asks, a thoughtful frown pulling his brows down as he studies me. He takes a couple steps closer.

I start pacing and waving my hands around. "I do not do it for fun. It's a job. Plus, I am also an artifact retrieval expert, not just an assassin. I am used to going out, traveling, doing…something," I say defensively. Then I curse.

I told him about my job. I may not have given details but now he knows a little more than he did before. Gah, maybe there is truth serum in the pastry after all. I sigh internally at that thought. No, I know there is nothing like that. I told him because I instinctively trust him for some reason. I have to be more careful.

He stares at me a moment, his face blank, and suddenly I want to know what he is thinking and feeling. I take a step closer before I can stop myself.

He blinks as if coming out of a deep thought then looks around the room and winces. "Yes, I suppose being locked in here for days does have its…frustrations."

I roll my eyes and grin. "Ya think?"

He chuckles and heads for the door.

That's it? I thought he was going to say…I don't know… something else. Not just leave me alone here again.

"North—"

At the same moment I call out he spins around, raises a finger and says, "I have an idea."

I shut my mouth and gesture for him to go on.

"Do you like reading?"

My nose scrunches up and I tilt my head side to side. "I prefer watching TV, but reading is ok I guess."

"I will send over some books. Look through them and we can discuss them tomorrow."

I frown but it is lessened by my teasing smile. "So, after my whole speech about needing to do something and my insinuation of my boredom, you think 'ah yes, I know, book club'?"

He chuckles, his smile lighting up his whole face. A little butterfly dances around in my belly at the sight and a warmth fills me knowing that I made him laugh.

"Let's see how it turns out then go from there," he says and opens the door. "In the meantime, please, continue serenading my wolves."

The guards outside growl low which makes us both laugh.

An hour later, four books are dropped off and shoved through a tiny opening in the door. I pick them up and take them to the dresser, laying them out on top to take a look at what North expects me to read to fight my boredom in this room. Two look to be informational texts set in old leather-bound covers. I flip through a few pages of each one and see that the thicker one is about all the different types of supernatural creatures, and the other one is more specifically about wolf shifters and packs. The third book is more of a thin black journal with no title or writing on the cover. I open it and see elegant, handwritten filled pages. I skim a couple pages trying to figure out what the journal is about. The words *Infinite Order* stick out multiple times and I shut it quickly. This must be the information they have on the Order, but why would he give it to me to read? I shake my head and look over the last book. It is the only one that is for entertainment rather than information. It is a complete collection of the Adventures of Sherlock Holmes. I grin down at it but place it next to the others.

I can't read all of these before tomorrow. I put my hands on my hips and bite my lip as I look at the four books. Which one would he want me to read first? My first thought is the black book about the Order. That might be the one he wants to discuss but I would rather learn more about the supernatural world. My mother must have known about the supernaturals. That must be why she said I had to become an elite so I would know the truth.

A pang of longing and loss hits me hard, and I rub my chest to try to ease the pain. I usually bury my sorrow down deep when it comes to my mother but right now, knowing this is what she meant by *the truth,* it is hard to ignore. I wish I could talk to her about it all.

I pick up the thicker leather book and go to my bed to read it. I sit cross-legged on top of the covers and lay the book in front of me. I should have listened to Dorian when he said to read up on my target's species when I had the chance. Better late than never, I guess. With this book I will be able to learn about the *others* out there too.

I flip open the first page which is blank then go to the next page which is the table of contents. The book looks old, so I was not expecting there to be a table of contents but am pleased there is. I use my finger to brush over every word as I skim the page's contents.

Vampires. Faeries. Witches. Shifters.

There are subcategories for each of them and my eyes grow larger as I take in how many supernaturals there really are in our world. I flip to each section and briefly look through the information. This book is going to take days to analyze and absorb.

An hour later, I start to feel overwhelmed and shut the book. I sit back against my pillows and breathe slowly as I take in all this new information. I think about Norden and our garden talk and sit forward again then flip to the shifter section, subcategory wolves. After reading it I sigh in disappointment and sit back again. There are not many details about them in the book. Just a broad page about them covering the basics.

I look to the dresser then scramble off my bed. I switch out the thick leather book for the thinner one, even though this one is still a thick tome, and take it to the bed. I find myself getting nervous for this information as if my body is expecting to find something that will change my life forever, but that is absurd. The other book already did that as well as the whole assignment that brought me here. It must be excited nerves. I have been wanting to know more about these werewolves and now I have the book that will tell me everything.

I open it and sit back for the rest of the night, reading each page carefully until I fall asleep with it open on my stomach.

Chapter 12

Norden

I knock on Moonfire's door and wait a moment. No singing today. A little part of me is disappointed and I can't help a soft chuckle at the memory of it from yesterday.

The guards by the door look up at me and I nod to them, still grinning at my thought, but their wolf faces give nothing away. I really am shocked that Danika did not know about the assassin staying here with how much she likes to talk to the guards and people in the castle. The guards switch out every eight hours so most of them, if not all, know of her by now. Maybe they are not as gossipy as others in this place.

I open the door, feeling as if enough time has gone by, and enter. Elias would not like it if he knew I was in the room once again without someone with me for protection. He scolded me for it last night when I delivered his schnecken but he forgave me because…well…I gave him a schnecken. Elias would forgive anyone if they gave him that treat. But he warned me not to do it again, however, I want to be able to talk to her without a bodyguard hovering about scaring her. How can I show her I trust her if I have someone in the room ready to rip her head off if she makes one wrong move? Also, I want to know what she thought of the books I gave her, and I do not think Elias would be happy about me giving those to her either.

I look around the room for Moonfire but do not see her. I take a couple more steps inside and close the door behind me.

"Hello? Moonfire?" I call out.

No answer.

I spot the books on the dresser and walk over to them. I brush my fingers over the covers then put my hands behind my back and analyze the room, trying to locate my mate.

The door on the other side of the room opens and steam billows out. Then out she comes, wrapped in only a towel, and my cheeks heat enough to know I am furiously blushing.

"Oh! Uh, I, uh—" I scramble for something to say as I avert my eyes and turn around to give her some privacy. I squeeze my eyes shut and try to rid myself of the image of her and resist the temptation to go over there and run my hands over her bare shoulders or slip my fingers into her wet hair.

Moonfire yelps then scolds, "Jeez! North!"

I hear the bathroom door slam shut and her muffled voice calls through the wood, "Um, can you please grab my bag?"

I open my eyes and look around for the black backpack. I find it laying on the floor at the foot of the bed and grab it, holding it out at arm's length as I take it to the bathroom. I find my cheeks heating again and embarrassment tightens my chest as well as something that feels a lot like longing.

I knock softly and the door opens a crack. I hold her bag up to the opening and she yanks it through before slamming the door.

I hear the zipper of the bag and clothes rustling. I take a few steps away though my hearing can still pick up the sounds.

"We need to have a serious talk about boundaries," she says a moment later as she throws open the bathroom door and walks out fully clothed.

She is wearing a simple black tank top and skinny jeans. Her blonde hair is braided and hangs over one shoulder to rest against the front of her body.

I clear my throat and nod. "Yes. Boundaries." I look to the side, not quite able to meet her eyes.

Amusement colors her tone. "North…are you…blushing?" She takes a few steps closer and peers up at me with a smirk.

I bite my lip and try to tamp down my feelings. This is not how I expected my visit to go.

Her smile drops and she crosses her arms. "New rule. You, and anyone else, cannot enter without my permission. Deal?"

I tilt my head to the side and finally meet her eyes. Her attention sends warmth through me and I smile.

"What if you are in danger?"

She looks at me askance and gestures to the room. "How would I get into danger in here?"

I shrug then hold up a finger. "Ah, but what if—"

She slaps my finger out of the air. "No, there is no *if*. Just do not come in without my permission."

I cross my arms and stare at her a moment then nod. "Deal."

She relaxes. "Thank you."

"So…" I move to the dresser and pat one of the books. "Did you read any?"

She comes over and stands next to me as she peers down at the books then looks up at me questioningly.

"What?" I ask.

She narrows her eyes and raises a brow. "Which one did you want me to read for our book club meeting today?"

I shrug and gesture to all of them. "Any is fine."

She casts a look of disbelief at me then slowly points at two of them. "I looked through these."

I nod. "Good choices." I pick up one of them. I told her it didn't matter which one she read but I admit I was lying. I gave her a range of books that might interest her but one in particular had me nervous for her opinion and it wasn't the thin black journal about the Infinite Order.

"What did you learn from this one?" I hold up the thick tome about wolf shifters.

She takes it from me and starts flipping through it.

"Shifter history goes back thousands of years and in all that time they grouped up in packs run by an Alpha and made alliances with other packs for protection, yet they were not one single unit. That is what the book said anyway. However, I remember you saying your dad was the King of wolf shifters, like the ultimate Alpha or something, who rules over all the of the packs and you and your brothers rule over a portion of those packs as Alphas. What changed? I didn't find anything about it in here." She taps the book with one of her fingernails.

So, that is what she decides to go with. Well, we have to start somewhere and knowing a bit of our history can be beneficial.

I sigh and lean against the dresser. We really have to get some other furniture in here for when I visit. Sitting on her bed would seem too…intimate.

"Well, about seventy-five years ago the battle of the four quadrants ensued—"

She gasps and interrupts my history lesson to say, "World War II? The shifters started it?"

I chuckle and shake my head. "No, humans started it, but shifters were targeted too, and it caused a lot of issues. Alliances were made, others broken, and war started to decimate our population. The packs in North America did not join this war until the States joined and even then, they barely helped. My father was one of the few Alphas in North America who thought they should help end the war of the four quadrants or become extinct."

I study her face to see if she is keeping up. She tilts her head at me, curious eyes begging me to continue.

"Well, long story short, I guess he thought since no one would listen then he should be the one to take charge and unite the world under one leader so that this would never happen again."

Her brows shoot up. "How…noble?" She sounds like she is trying really hard to be nice and ignore the obvious.

I laugh and shake my head. "You can say it. It sounds like a dictator."

She winces and shrugs a shoulder. "Well…I mean…" She sighs and nods. "Yeah, it kind of does, especially around that time period." She hesitates and picks at the side of the dresser as she asks, "How…how did he do it?"

I take a deep breath and let it out slowly. "Public story is the Alphas killed each other in the war and my father waited until the perfect moment to sweep in and 'save them'" I say, using my fingers as air quotes around the last words. "In reality, though it has never been confirmed, I believe he killed them by sending assassins and set up proxies until he could form a new pack dynamic in our world. Meaning him as King and his sons, who were born later, to take up the four quadrants." I shake my head.

"You don't agree with his plan?" She seems surprised and I look into her brown eyes searching for the disgust or disappointment that is so ready in my father's gaze when I talk about my disagreements with his rule. I do not find either one, only curiosity.

"I guess it is good that the packs no longer fight but… I do not believe all wolf shifters should be under one ruler. There were various Alphas and different packs for a reason. Territory, family, culture, more attention to the packs and the individuals. More people had a say in how they lived."

"Hmm." She taps a finger against her lips as she thinks. "Is there any way there can be life in between those two lifestyles? You said it yourself, no one fights against each other anymore."

I shrug. "I am not sure, and it will be a while before I can do anything about it."

I take a deep breath and let it out before grabbing the book from her and flip through the pages absentmindedly.

"Have you read anything else besides the history?" I hope I do not sound too eager and hopeful. I am being a coward by having her discover the information about mates this way rather than telling her directly, but I hope if she reads about them then she will understand it more then be more willing to accept the bond.

"Not much more, I dozed off before the really good stuff," she smirks to let me know she is joking but I only give her a half-smile back. She is right, history is great and all, but the really good stuff is later in the book, and I am eager for her to find it.

"I am glad you have started to learn more about us." I set the book carefully on the dresser. "I will be back tomorrow, and we can discuss more." I start to head toward the door, but she grabs my arm, halting me.

"Thank you for the books and all, but I am still trapped in here and those will only do so much." She gestures to the room then at the books as she speaks. "Could you take me to the garden again or show me more of the castle? I may have lied about being a college student studying architecture to get in here, but I do truly admire the structure." Her eyes are big and pleading.

I look to the door and bite my lip. I have some work I need to do and I have to check in with the team trying to locate the Chalice but when I look down at her again I already know I am going to say yes.

I nod. "Sure, I will take you to the library."

A flash of a frown passes over her face before she covers it with a forced smile and does a little hop toward the door dragging me along. "Yay, more books. Let's go."

I chuckle at her forced excitement and follow her to the door only realizing when we reach it that she has not let go of me. The spot where her hand lays on my skin warms and I smile down at her fingers, so delicate yet so deadly. What would it be like to hold them between my fingers, her palm against mine?

She opens the door to the growling of the wolves outside and my mind is pulled away from my imagination. She pauses and looks back at me, her eyes wide and nervous. She takes her hand off my arm much to my disappointment and holds it in a fist in front of her chest. I step in front of her and lead the way out and the guards immediately stop their warning. I give them a nod and grab her wrist on my way past and tug her along.

The library is on the third floor, so we only have to go up one level and down a couple of halls until we reach a set of red and brown wooden doors. I pause in front of it and look down at her with a grin.

"Ready?"

She glances from me to the doors and down at my hand still wrapped around her wrist. I quickly let go, assuming she doesn't want me touching her and a flash of hurt passes over her face. Then she twists her mouth and looks at the door again before nodding. I stand there studying her a moment, wondering what I should do. My instinct is to touch her again, so my hand comes up to rest on her back while I reach out and open one of the two doors.

"Welcome to my library."

She stiffens at my touch but soon relaxes and seems to lean back into my hand. My wolf hums inside me, pleased our mate enjoys our touch. She steps forward and takes her first look at the room. I step in beside her and close the door but keep my eyes on her, waiting for her reaction.

She goes farther into the room then turns in a slow circle. She whistles and nods at the room. "This is impressive. If I loved books, I would probably be in heaven right now. As it is, I would say I am in the Beast's impressive library."

I chuckle and come closer until I am standing next to her again, nearly brushing her shoulder with my arm. "Are you calling me a beast?" I joke.

She turns and swats my arm playfully. I do not know where this new...familiarity, I guess I would call it...came from but I like it.

"No, the Beast from *Beauty and the Beast*. He too had a massive library. However now that you mention it, I guess both references fit. I mean, you *are* a werewolf."

"I have never seen *the Beauty and the Beast*, but I do know of it, so if this is similar circumstances, does that mean you are going to fall for me, Beauty?" I am shocked at my boldness, but I refuse to take it back. Instead, I lean closer until my breath feathers over her hair.

She seems just as shocked, and half laughs-half gasps as she turns away, but not before I see the pink in her cheeks.

"In your dreams, Wolfie." She walks away and I chuckle warmly as I follow her.

Chapter 13

Jessie

What was that? Was he flirting? Was I?

I shake it off and continue farther into the room. This room is massive. It has two floors with a rail along the edges of the top level. Every wall is covered in books and there are lines of freestanding bookcases in the middle of the room with even more books. Glass cases are interspersed among them with artifacts that I cannot identify from here. A giant chandelier hangs from the ceiling though it seems like it is more for decoration than lighting.

I wander the stacks and skim my fingers over the spines, not really focusing on what they say, just enjoying the feel of them.

After getting my racing heart back to a normal level I glance at the Alpha over my shoulder. "So, you hoard books? That's your secret huh? I thought hoarding was a dragon thing."

"Nah, if you saw a dragon's hoard you would call this a simple collection, emphasis on the simple."

I spin to face him, my mouth dropping open in surprise. "Dragons are real?"

He smirks at me and walks by without answering.

I really have to read that supernatural species book more.

I catch up to him and he says, "This library is open to everyone in the pack. Not just in this town but anyone in the shifter community who wants to stop by is allowed."

"No humans though." I meant it as a question, but it came out a statement.

He glances at me and shakes his head. "No humans."

"So, I am the first human to see it?" I feel a little warmth bloom in my chest at that.

"On special occasions, a few humans have been here."

I may not be the first, but I am one of a few. I wonder why he would bring me here.

As if reading my mind he says, "As long as you're here, you may come to the library." He looks down and smiles. "With an escort of course."

I roll my eyes but cannot blame him. However, would I actually come here with anyone other than

North? I could not imagine me asking the guards to bring me going over well.

"Do you come here often?" I ask. We reach the end of one row and make our way down another.

"Not as often as I would like. Being Alpha of the entire Northern packs takes a lot of my time. Not to mention having to hunt down a certain missing relic." He glances at me from the corner of his eye, but I look away to the shelves on my other side.

I may be liking this wolf-man a little more and I may be feeling a little less homicidal toward him, but I am not about to betray the Order.

He does not let my silence affect him and continues as if he never mentioned it. "I like reading all sorts of stuff. You learn a lot from books you know."

His tone makes it seem like there is more meaning behind his words. I quickly look at him to find him staring at me with raised brows, as if wanting me to read between the lines. But I do not understand what he is trying to say.

"Reading is okay, but you can never beat a good tv show," I say.

He chuckles and shakes his head then leads me to the second floor of the library. The stairs are metal and spiral up. They are not wide enough for us to walk side by side so he leads and I follow. I try really hard not to stare at his butt...ok not that hard, my gaze may linger just a bit.

On the second floor I go to the railing that keeps people from falling to the first floor and look down. The drop would probably hurt a normal person, but I have fallen from this height before as part of my training, so I am not worried. The library has a different view from up here. While on the bottom it all seemed big, but from up here I can see everything, and it is *huge*. We had only walked a fraction of the bottom floor I realize and could probably spend hours here going through the rest. I turn around and see him sitting on a couch in the middle of the floor.

He sweeps out a hand and smiles. "Take a look around."

The second floor has bookcases just like the bottom but there are more glass cases holding artifacts and tapestries on the walls than there are down below. I ignore the books and go to the cases and tapestries. The first case holds a bejeweled dagger. My first thought is to break the case and take the weapon then fight my way out of here, but for some reason that urge is not as strong as it might have been a few days ago.

Another case, sitting along the wall, has a stone statuette of a deformed wolf/man, as if the being was in mid-shift. The man part looks to be in pain and the wolf part is snarling and ripping at the man to be free. From what I have seen of their shift, it is more fluid than that. Then again, maybe it is a representation of what a made-wolf shifter feels. I shudder and move on. Stretching across a large part of the wall is a large tapestry. I study it and move slowly down the length and realize after a couple of steps it is telling a story.

I look back at North and point at the tapestry. "Can you tell me about this?"

He unfolds his crossed legs and stands from the couch smoothly. He walks over, his eyes flitting across the tapestry and taking in the artwork. "It has been a while since I looked at this."

He stands next to me and we both stare up at it for a moment, taking in the markings and color, the immense detail someone put into it.

"It shows the different ways to make a wolf," he says quietly.

I snap my head around to him and stare, trying to see if he is serious. He did not want to tell me how a wolf is made the other day, but he seems fine to let me see it for myself in this tapestry. I turn back to the cloth and study it, reading it like a picture book. In one part, a woman is giving birth and instead of a human, a wolf pup is held aloft.

"Is that really how you are born?" I twist up my face in barely suppressed horror. "You come out all furry like that? Claws and fangs bared?"

North chuckles and shakes his head. "No, the artist was just trying to make a point. That some shifters are born. But we do come out human looking and shift within our first year."

I shake my head slowly in wonder. "Wow, a werewolf baby. I cannot imagine it."

I look at the next part and see it shows another way to be changed into a shifter. I cringe and back up a step as if the wolf in the image would leap out and tear into me as it is doing to the human in the tapestry. The next scene is that human shifting into a wolf and a look of pain crossing his face as his body contorts and breaks apart to let out an animal.

The first image of born wolves had been happy, this one was full of pain and terror. "Is it really like that?" I ask and nod to the gruesome attack.

North hesitates then sighs and nods. "Even if the wolf wanted to make it easier for the human, a deep bite is what it takes and it is not always pleasant the first shift after."

"D-do you make new wolves often?" I was not sure I wanted to know the answer. Is this why Dorian wanted me to take out North? As a message to leave the humans alone? But why North? He does not strike me as the sort that would take pleasure in hurting people to add to his pack that way.

"Me personally, no. But my father, yes. He has initiations and ceremonies that induct new members each year."

I imagine a ceremony where the guests get torn apart by wolves, blood everywhere, screams filling every space. I shudder at the thought.

"It is not like that," North says quickly with a nod to the scene before us.

"What do you mean?"

He studies me for a moment, as if deciding whether he should tell me or not. He nods to himself as if deciding he can trust me then guides me farther along the tapestry and nods up at it, letting me see for myself.

The scene shows three humans facing a man with a gold cup raised above them. No, not a cup, a chalice. *The* Chalice. I look to North with wide eyes.

His lips are set in a grim line and he pinches my chin and guides it softly to look back at the scene.

"Keep looking? What does it show you?"

The next scene shows one of the humans in the line drinking from the Chalice as the man in front of him holds a colorful stone against his forehead and a full moon shines brightly above them. The next scene shows those three humans now as wolves, still in the same line facing the man before them with bowed heads. That is where the tapestry ends.

I face North with a raised brow, still not understanding what it is showing. "So, you're telling me a cup and a stone can change a human into a wolf? Without all…that?" I wave toward the part of the tapestry where the wolf is attacking the human.

His tone is completely serious and his gaze bores into mine as he says, "Yes. The Chalice you stole is one of two items that let us change our new initiates peacefully and without harm."

I stare open mouthed at him then turn back to the tapestry, looking at all three stories of how to make a wolf shifter. I cross my arms and continue staring.

I know why he let me see this. Why he told me what it meant. Why he explained each section. I cross my arms and dig my nails into the skin where they touch.

Suddenly I turn to him and slam the side of my fists on his chest. Not to injure, but to show my frustration with him. With this whole situation. To show my struggle and what he is doing to me. I let all of it out and beat his chest again. He grabs my wrists in both his hands and holds me there.

"What do you expect me to do? I can't just...I can't..." I deflate and lean my head against him, in between my fists that he still is holding.

He releases one and strokes the back of my head. It is surprisingly soothing, and I relax. He senses it and releases my other hand. I let both drop to my sides but continue resting my head against him, letting him pet my head.

"I understand your sense of loyalty to your Order," he says quietly. "It is the same sense I have to my father despite our...disagreements. But I also want you to know how important the object you took from us is to our packs."

"Why would D— my boss, want your Chalice?" I mumble into his shirt.

He is quiet for a moment then answers thoughtfully. "Well, back in Arthurian times, it was known as the Holy Grail. Thought to give the owner immortality."

I lean back and his hand drops from my head to let me. "Is it true?"

A few days ago, I would have laughed at the thought of a cup that gives immortality, but...well, I've seen things, so what the heck?

He purses his lips and stares at me, studying me. He does that often and I cannot help wanting to be a person he could trust without thought rather than have that look of hesitation in his eyes. But then again, he has only known me for a few days and two of those days I tried killing him.

Then he bobs his head side to side as if to say *yes and no* and gives me a half smile. "It does not give you the kind of immortality where you cannot die at all, it creates a weakness, but it does stop the aging process and gives the drinker self-healing abilities."

"Whoa." I shake my head at the enormity of what he just told me.

Before I could ask more questions, the doors to the library slam open and a woman's voice floats up to us.

"My *Lord*!" she sings out.

I arch a brow at North who rolls his eyes before stepping away from me and going to the railing to look down at who entered.

"Danika, what is it?"

I come over, not quite to the railing but just enough that I can see who this Danika person is. She is petite and has long, dark, styled hair and is wearing an elegant red blouse and black skirt. She takes a couple steps forward once she realizes North is upstairs and I see her skirt is actually flowy pants made to look like a skirt. She moves to just under the railing so I cannot see her anymore and have to step closer to North where I end up hovering behind him awkwardly.

"You have guests," she says, grinning up at him.

"Who are these guests?" He asks warily.

She ignores him, having spotted me, and stares at me with a suspicious glare. She props one hand on her hip and arches a delicate brow. "Who is that?"

North turns to find me right behind him and tenses slightly. If I was not so close, I would not have noticed it. He glances from me to Danika and back again and clenches and unclenches a fist before forcibly relaxing and plastering on a fake smile.

"This is the woman I told you about."

My head jolts back in surprise. He told people about me? I roll my eyes at myself. Of course, he told people about me. I am the assassin, the prisoner in his castle.

People had to know to keep an eye out for me in case I escaped.

Her eyes narrow and her lip lifts in a silent snarl. On anyone else that would look ridiculous, but she pulls it off and I am almost intimidated by it, knowing what power lurks beneath, but I stand straighter and arch a brow at her as if I find her little display silly. A low growl emanates from her.

"Enough," North barks and I sense a thread of that power he has go through the room.

She immediately stops the growl and lip snarl, and her narrowed gaze snaps to North. "Is it wise," she grits her teeth as if holding in her wolf, "to let her out of her…room?"

"That is none of your concern, Danika. Now about these guests?" He positions his body, so it blocks me from her view and I have to tilt to the side to see around him.

She closes her eyes and takes a deep breath through her nose then lets it out slowly through her mouth before plastering on a smile. "Your brothers are in the Main Hall."

He stiffens and I look up to see his eyes are wide. "Why are they here?" he mumbles to himself then says to Danika, "Tell them I will be right there."

She nods her head, shoots me one last glare, then struts out with a little extra wiggle to her step than natural.

I resist an eye roll and step back as North turns to me.

"So…your brothers, huh? As in the other Alphas of the other quadrants? As in the other Princes of the world's werewolves?" After each question, my eyebrows rise higher, and my voice becomes much less casual and more fearful and in awe.

He eyes me, doing that considering thing again.

I shake my head. "Well, I guess I will find my own way back," I joke and hook a thumb over my shoulder toward the stairs. I know he would never let me find my own way back and that he will probably call some guards to escort me before I even leave the library.

I start to step away and head to the bottom floor, but he grabs my hand and tugs me to a stop. "Would you like to meet them?"

"What?" I squeak and spin around.

He is completely serious. No hint of a joking glint in his eyes or murderous intent, which is the only explanation I can think of for why he would want me to meet his family. His family that will not be too happy to have an assassin who tried killing their brother in their presence.

He nods to himself, feeling more confident in his decision, and starts tugging me to the stairs. "Yeah. I want you to meet them. C'mon it will be fun."

Chapter 14

Jessie

It will be fun he said.

Staring at the three men in the Main Hall makes me doubt his definition of fun. Fun for who? I should have asked.

They form a line, unintentionally blocking anyone from passing them without squeezing past at least one and making contact.

The one on the far right is a bit shorter than the others but wider in the shoulders. His skin is also a bit darker as if he is in the sun all day, but his hair is light blond, shorter on the sides and longer on top, and his eyes a dark green which both stand out against his sun-kissed skin. I believe he was the one I saw with North in Peru, though the cave was dark, so I did not get a good look at his features back then.

The one next to him is the tallest of the bunch. He has very short, dark brown hair which differs from his brothers, and dark eyes which are the same eyes as the other brother to his right. He is the only one without stubble along his jaw as well as the only one wearing a suit. The way he holds himself makes it seem like he is a reserved sort of guy.

The last brother to his right, with the same dark eyes, is about the same height as North but has long, light brown hair just a shade darker than North's. His skin is the lightest of all of them as if he does not go outside often.

When they see North, they break ranks and take turns hugging their brother. North gives back just as enthusiastically, forgetting me for a moment. I eye the door behind the brothers wondering if I could make a break for it, my instincts automatically thinking of escape. The door is about fifteen feet away and since this is the Main Hall, that means that door leads outside to the front of the castle. It is tempting, but with five werewolves (five because Danika decided to stick around), I would not get far. In fact, I would not get two steps toward it before one of them noticed.

I try to slink back, to hover against the wall but my movement catches the eye of the tall, suit wearing brother who freezes me in place with his piercing stare.

North notices his stare and turns back to me. He comes closer and steps to my side, rests a hand on my back and introduces me to his brothers.

"This is…um, the woman I told you about." His eyes flick to Danika who is still hovering nearby, absorbing every word said, every move made. Then he looks to the sun kissed man and raises his eyebrows. "From Peru."

The brothers suck in a breath and share knowing looks with each other.

North points to the man in the suit. "This is Wesley, we call him West. I am sure you can figure out what quadrant he rules over." I nod my greeting to the man who continues to stare at me with his intense, dark eyes.

North moves his finger to the next brother, the one with the long hair and similar dark eyes but his are more welcoming. "This is Easton, or as we call him—"

"East?" I guess and grin up at him.

North chuckles and shrugs. "Yeah, you get the theme." He sweeps his hand out to the last brother but before he can introduce him, the man steps forward and grasps one of my hands in both of his.

"Sutton," he says then kisses the top of my hand, "but everyone calls me South." He straightens, continuing to hold my hand, and gives me a sly smile. "That was a nasty little trick you pulled in Peru. Are you really North's m—"

"Ok!" North claps his hands, interrupting whatever South was about to say. "I think that's enough introductions. Why don't we head to my office and we can discuss whatever it is you came here for."

That sobered them all up and they straightened, ready for business.

"It was nice to meet you…" South trails off realizing I never gave my name.

I only stare at him, not willing to give them my name, or any name. Because while I do not want them to know my true identity, I also do not want to lie to them.

"Call her Moonfire, or if you are so willing…Luna."

Danika gasps and I turn to see what caused the reaction. She is standing there with her mouth hanging open, glancing between North and me with wide eyes. North and the others look to her as well and North calmly tells her, "Danika, we can discuss this later. Not now." He says the last two words commandingly, and I sense a bit of power in the words.

She snaps her mouth closed, sends me a hateful glare, then tells North, "Later," as if there is no room for argument then walks away at a rapid pace with her hands in fists at her sides and muttering something in German.

When she is gone, I face North with a brow raised. "What was that all about?"

I look to the others expecting them to be just as surprised, but their expressions range from curiosity, to annoyance, to guilt. Why guilt would be among their emotions I am not sure.

To me North says softly, "It's nothing. Don't think much on it."

I do not like that they all seem to know what just happened and are not clueing me in. I narrow my eyes at him, and he purposely looks away, avoiding me.

"Let's go," he tells his brothers. To me, without looking directly at me he says, "I am sending some guards to escort you back. You can go to the garden, the library or your room. I will send for you later for dinner."

Two wolves step into the hall from seemingly nowhere and growl low at me. I roll my eyes at them then wave to the brothers.

"It was nice meeting you." I give them a tight smile then head down the hall toward what I assume is the direction of the stairs that will lead me to my room.

My focus is still on those behind me which is probably why I hear Sutton say, "Why haven't you told her yet? You cannot just throw around the title of Luna when she does not know what it means."

I turn the corner before I hear a reply, but my curiosity is piqued and a little desperation seeps into my body. I am tired of all this secrecy. What is North keeping from me?

I intend to find out one way or another.

Not ready to be locked in my room, I grab the tome about wolf shifters and bring it to the inside garden. My two wolfy guards station themselves at the exits so I cannot escape but have the illusion of privacy as I venture among the trees and flowers.

Instead of a bench, I find a patch of grass off the trail and settle among the flowers before laying out the book in front of me. I wish this book had a table of contents like the other tome, it would make searching for things a lot easier, even if I do not know yet what I am searching for.

I flip past the sections of their history I had already read and then slowly skim the others for information. I am hoping something will pop out to me. It takes some time but finally something catches my eye.

The Moon Goddess.

I stop skimming and read the page carefully.

The Moon Goddess is who the wolf shifters contribute their existence to. She grants them their wolf, determines their level of dominance, and makes them so they need companionship which is why there are packs. For companionship and protection. She also creates mates which briefly explains that they are two souls that are drawn together and complete one another. The line about mates has a notation to see page 120 for more information then continues on about the Moon Goddess. The rest is about her various names throughout history and in different cultures such as Selene and later Artemis for the Greeks, Khonsu in Egypt, the Hindu Chandra, and in the Aztec region she was called Coyolxauhqui. Some cultures thought her a man, but they are technically all the same deity, or so this book claims. It states that the reason wolf shifters are drawn to shift on a full moon is to worship her and show acceptance of her gift to them when her light is brightest.

I am not a religious person and this part makes me want to snort in disbelief but I stop myself, knowing that they believe it and I should respect that. Also, I cannot discount it is as myth because werewolves are real so this technically could be too.

On the opposite page, there is an artist's impression of the Moon Goddess. She is floating, the moon bright behind her and illuminating her. Her long, pale hair flows around her head, and she is holding a wolf pup in her arms as she smiles down at it. She looks so peaceful and loving.

I look for anything else, but it is just more history and mythology, so I backtrack to the part where it talks about mates and flip to the page it notes for more info.

I get to the page but do not get more than a sentence in when the silence of the garden is interrupted by a female voice near one of the entrances.

"Do not growl at me. I can go where I please." The voice follows that up by speaking something in rapid German then she goes back to English when she calls out for me. "Assassin! Where are you? Come out now."

I know that voice. It is the woman who came to get North at the library. Danika, I think.

I stay still, wondering if I should reveal myself or stay where I am at.

"I have a great sense of smell. Do not think you can hide from me."

I am not hidden where I am sitting but her words spark something in me, and I stand from the grass and step out onto the path, needing to show her I am not afraid of her. I dangle the book loosely by my side and wait for her to find me.

I wonder if she is coming to get me as an order from North or if this is personal. She seemed upset during the meeting with his brothers and her tone sounds personal.

First, I hear the crunch of the dirt path as she approaches then I see her figure appear through the trees just before she rounds the bend and spots me. Her brows instantly drop into a frown as she glares at me and storms over. She does not look happy that I made her come to me rather than the other way around.

I quirk a brow at her, and my lips tilt up on one side in a subtle smirk. I do not say anything but wait for her to reveal her reason for this visit.

She looks me up and down and, finding something lacking, curls her lip in disgust. "So, you are his Luna? Impossible. A disgrace."

Danika comes closer and circles me as she speaks. I know it is a mistake to give your back to a predator, so I turn with her, keeping her in sight the whole time.

"I don't know what that is," I admit. The way she says it sounds like it is insulting to her though.

She barks out a dry laugh. "You are supposedly his Luna and you do not even know!" She scoffs and stops abruptly.

She steps forward until she is only a foot away. Too close but I do not back up because that will make her feel as if she has power over me. Her head barely reaches my shoulder but that does not stop her from being intimidating.

She looks down at the book in my hand. "Have you not read about it yet? Figured it out?" She shakes her head. "He must be mistaken."

Frustration rises and I snap at her, "What is a Luna?"

Satisfaction pulls her lips up into a smirk. She steps back and crosses her arms. "I am almost tempted not to tell you. Let you walk around like the ignorant human you are."

I scowl at her and shake my head. "Then leave." I wave my hand toward the entrance to the garden and turn to go back to my grassy patch. If it is begging she wants she will be disappointed.

"But..."

The word stops me though and I face her again, a mixture of anticipation, dread, and annoyance filling my body. My fingers tingle from the emotions roiling inside and I wiggle them to get rid of it.

"I think your reaction to it will be better than your ignorance. Especially if it comes from me rather than him."

I narrow my eyes, wary about what it would be if she thinks my reaction will be that bad.

"You two are mates." She smirks at me and waits.

The term is something I saw in the book and was about to read more about but other than what I have seen on TV and that fact that apparently the Moon Goddess creates mates, I am not sure what it means for me. So, I just stand there and stare at her blankly.

She sighs and rolls her eyes. "You know? Mates. As in soulmates, his soul is the other half of yours, yada yada?" She puts a hand on her hip and stares again, waiting for my reaction.

Again, I stare at her blankly although my heart is beginning to race. Soulmates? That's impossible, isn't it? There is no such thing. Yet…I do…feel things for him. But that does not mean we are mates. Wouldn't I know if there was that kind of connection? I need to read about it so I can know everything about this term Danika has just used that could potentially change my life forever. For better or worse I do not know but it does not sound like it would be good for me despite my heart giving a little happy dance in my chest.

She growls, annoyed that I refuse to give her a reaction. "Ridiculous." She waves a hand in the air as if to dismiss the possibility that I am his mate. "It has to be a mistake. You are not even a shifter. Yet, he believes it is true." She stalks closer and points a red polished finger at me. "This is what you are going to do. The next time you see him, you are going to reject the bond and demand to leave."

"He will not let me leave," I counter. Mate or no, I am still an assassin who knows too much.

"Make him. He will not hurt you." She sneers at that. "If you are convincing, he may do as you say."

I arch my eyebrow at her. "I am guessing you have an ulterior motive for telling me this and wanting me gone. Does a certain someone have a crush on their boss?" I say it cutesy-like which earns me an angry hiss from the petite wolf shifter.

She steps even closer and I have to wonder if she thinks this is intimidating, which it totally is, or she just likes being in people's personal spaces.

"Unless you want to be tied to him forever, subject to whatever whim he might have, never to leave this place or have your own life, to be turned into a shifter by his bite, you will reject the bond and leave while you can." With that she stalks off the way she came and a minute later I hear her speak in German to the guards before leaving.

I am still standing in the path, staring ahead without actually seeing. Her words repeat over and over in my mind and that racing heart that was more of a happy beat is now a stampede of panic. *At his mercy. Never to leave. Never to have my own life. Turned into a shifter.*

It sounds awful. Like a prisoner just of a different sort. The image from the tapestry of a human being torn into by a wolf and changed painfully flashes before my eyes. I clench my fists only to realize I still have the book in my hand and am now digging my nails into the cover. I loosen my grip and bring it up to eye level. I stare at the front of the book. Did he expect me to read about mates and figure it out for myself? Is that why he gave me this book?

I make a disgusted sound and decide I will demand answers from him, make him tell me face to face, rather than read about it and let him be a coward.

I stomp toward the entrance where my guards are waiting only to see Elias coming through the door. I glare at him, then realize he probably knows about me being North's mate and glare even harder. Elias scowls at me then speaks in German to the guards. The wolves nod and lope off to wherever they go when they are not guarding me, leaving me alone with the Beta.

"I need to see Norden. Now."

Elias arches his brow but says calmly, "This way." Then he turns and leads the way to his cowardly friend.

Chapter 15

Elias is already in my office when my brothers and I arrive. I texted him as we left the Main Hall to meet us and now he sits against the edge of my desk with a concerned frown.

"Good to see you all," he greets them. "It has been a while. Yes?"

They nod and spread out among the room. Sutton is the only one to come greet Elias with a pat on the back before moving to lean against the wall. Wesley takes one of the available seats in front of my desk and Easton stands behind him.

I sit at my chair on the other side and lean my arms on the desk as I ask, "Not that I don't love seeing you all but is there a reason you came without notice?"

Sutton speaks up from my left trying to be casual. "So, that is her, huh? She is the one to almost kill you twice?"

Elias corrects him with a smirk and a dangerous gleam in his eye. "Three, actually."

My brothers raise their brows in surprise and look to me for confirmation.

I frown at Elias who cannot see because his back is to me. "I would not count the fork."

Sutton snickers and Easton and Wesley share amused looks.

"A fork?" Sutton asks, trying to reign in his humor.

I shake my head and steeple my fingers. "Is that why you came? Curiosity?"

"In part," Easton says.

"Father told us about the second assassination attempt," Wesley says.

"We were concerned," Sutton adds, but his tone makes it seem like that was secondary to their original reason.

I arch a brow to show them how much I believe that.

Easton sighs and shifts the topic. "Father is going to go through with this year's initiation."

I gape at him though I should not be surprised.

"We were wondering…" Easton trails off and looks to Wesley and Sutton.

"How far are you in getting the Chalice back?" Wesley finishes.

I look between all of them. We all know how serious initiation is. With the Moonstone, our father can change a human to a wolf on the full moon but without the Chalice he will still need to bite them to tie them to the packs and even then, that does not give the wolf a longer life so they could possibly die from the bite. I doubt he will avoid the bite. A wolf not tied to the packs makes it easier for them to betray or defect, to rise up against his rule or to go off alone. Our father is too controlling to let that happen.

I sigh and sit back in my chair. "Elias?"

Elias stands and starts to pace as he gives us an update. "The team is still having trouble tracking where she went after leaving Peru. Like I told you before," he says to me more than the others, "they narrowed it down to the States. The Chalice has not shown up on any markets, legal or otherwise, so we have to assume the Order still has it."

"What about the woman?" Wesley asks carefully.

I frown and purse my lips, but I know she is the key to finding it and cannot fault them for wanting answers from her.

"I am working on it," I say but do not elaborate. "Anyway, you could have just video conferenced us about all this. Again, why are you here?" I have a suspicion but need them to confirm it.

Sutton grins and pops off the wall to put his hand on my shoulder. "Alright, so we are curious. We knew as soon as Father told us you 'took care' of the assassin that she was the same one from Peru and that you would not let her go that easily."

I snort. I knew their curiosity was more than 'in part' of the reason for them being here. I grin and shake my head. "Don't you guys have anything better to do?"

They all shrug and Easton leans forward. "So, tell us about her. Has the mark appeared yet?"

I scoff. "It has only been a few days. I have not gotten that close with her yet." I mutter the next part, "I don't know if I ever will." I shake my head of those negative thoughts and say louder, "Plus, she is new to all this." I wave my hand in the air to encompass all our supernatural-ness.

"I think you should tell her. She deserves to know everything," Wesley says softly.

The other two brothers nod their agreement. Even Elias, who has not been Moonfire's biggest fan, nods.

I look between all of them then shake my head. "I can't yet. I left her ways to find out for herself…in books." I sound like a coward, but I cannot help it. This is an area I never had to deal with before, and the possibility of her rejection sends terror through me. Plus, with her fiery personality, she will probably try to kill me again if I claim her.

They do not push me, but I see the disapproval in their eyes. I stand up and walk to the door. "Come. Let's run. I do not wish to speak of this anymore."

They follow me and we head to the forest where I chased Elias a couple days ago. Elias splits from us to go do some work, leaving the four of us alone.

When we get back an hour later, they all head off to their suites that are readily available to them anytime they wish to visit, and I go off to do some work. Around dinner time, I send someone to get my brothers and send Elias to bring Moonfire while I get our dinner set up in the private dining room.

Their looks in my office earlier have stuck with me and Wesley's words have spun around in my mind. He is right, they are all right. She deserves to know. I decide as I am arranging the plates, glasses, and eating utensils that I will broach the topic with her tonight after dinner.

My brothers are the first to arrive, loud and energetic as usual. Except for Wesley, who comes in with his hands in his pockets, acting causal but a smile lights up his face at the sight of us all.

Wesley and Easton sit near the windows, Easton closest to me, and Sutton sits on my left on the other side of the table. Since I am at the head of the table, that leaves Elias and Moonfire to sit at the other end of the table when they come. My brothers talk among themselves, and I try to participate but my responses are reduced to one word comments because all I can think about is how nervous I am and how she might take the news.

"North. North, earth to North." A hand waves in front of my face.

I shake my head and follow the hand, up the arm, to the person it is attached to. "What?" I ask Easton.

"We asked you what is for dinner."

They all give me funny looks and chuckle at my absentmindedness.

"Oh, uh, I asked the chef to prepare—"

The door slams open bringing all our attention to the doorway where my mate is fuming and sending figurative daggers at me with her eyes. I would not be surprised if flames erupted from her, or actual daggers started flying.

I sigh and joke, trying to lighten the mood, "Uh oh, what did I do now?"

I spot Elias behind her with wary eyes focused on her, ready to protect me if she attacks.

"Hello, Luna," Sutton greets but his smile falls fast when she shoots him a sharp look.

She clenches her fists then closes her eyes as she takes a deep breath, holds it, and lets it out slowly, visibly relaxing as the air leaves her body. When she is calm, she opens her eyes and looks to me with a forced smile.

"Is everything ok?" I ask and stand.

Her eyes widen and she tilts her head. "Oh, everything is just...*peachy.*"

I frown and take a step toward her, but she is faster and before anyone can blink, she takes three steps and crashes her fist into my cheekbone.

Exclamations are shouted from my brothers, partly shocked and partly laughing. Elias is the only one who takes it as a threat and growls, fur rippling along his arms.

I hold up a hand to him to stop his progress and hold the side of my face with the other. I frown down at my mate who is glaring at me and breathing heavily. The pain is already disappearing, and I know there will not be a bruise due to my quick healing. I drop my hands to my sides.

"What was that for?" Quieter I ask, "What happened to our deal?"

She scoffs. "Our deal? This whole time you were using that weird werewolf magic on me. You broke it first."

"What are you talking about? I have not used any...magic, on you." I do not glance at my brothers, but I know they are hanging onto every word we say. This is prime entertainment for them.

"Then what do you call marking me as some love slave?"

My face screws up in confusion. Marking? She can't mean her mark appeared. We haven't kissed. And what does she mean love slave?

"What are you talking about?"

"Danika told me everything," she hisses in a low, angry voice.

I meet Elias' eyes behind her and we share a knowing look. My brothers whisper to each other having come to the same conclusion we have.

I cross my arms and look my angry mate in the eyes, and calmly say, "Danika has a way of twisting the truth."

She mirrors me by crossing her arms. "So, you're saying I am not your mate?"

There it is.

She knows.

And it was someone else who told her.

The room goes silent as everyone waits for my reaction.

Guilt gnaws at me and shame warms my face threatening to turn my cheeks red. I continue staring at her trying to think of the words that will not end up with me losing her or her trying to kill me…again.

However, I take too long, and my silence is answer enough for her.

She looks down at the table and reaches for a knife, one that would have been used with our steaks but now seemed to be for murder. I grab her wrist before she can reach it then take her other one and maneuver her away from the table to the wall.

She glares at me and struggles in my hold.

"Let me explain."

My brothers soundly wince at my words and I shoot them a quick glare before focusing on my mate again.

"There is nothing to explain. Danika told me everything and frankly I refuse!" She shouts and continues struggling.

My heart clenches at her words, but I need to explain everything to her. Danika surely warped the truth and scared Moonfire into this reaction.

"I highly doubt she told you everything. Please, just stop fighting and let me explain."

She quits trying to get out of my hold but continues glaring. Her eyes are filled with so much hate and terror, like a trapped animal's, it hurts me to witness it. Even more so because it is caused by me.

I slowly release her, waiting to see if she is going to fight or make a run for it but she stays still. Her eyes flit around, most likely marking the exits and possible weapons in the room. Elias stays by the entrance, leaving the double doors at the other end of the room as her only possible escape but that would mean getting passed four shifters. Seeing that escape is impossible, she slumps against the wall.

"Why would you do this to me? I don't want to be a love slave."

Snickers from behind me make both of us scowl at Easton and Sutton. They pull their lips in to hide their smiles and reign in their humor at her words. I realize then, we should have this conversation in private.

I look to Moonfire and softly say, "Let us go to your room—" At the panic in her eyes I quickly hold up my hands and amend, "to my office. I will explain what a mate means both in our lore, literally, and for you, because a love slave is immensely inaccurate. Do you have the book about shifters? It is all in there too, we could look at it together."

She studies me and I wait, leaving this up to her. If she does not want to talk then I will leave her alone to read about it without my presence, but I would really like to be there to help her through this. Anger at Danika simmers in my veins. Our discussion with her will have to be soon. For now, this takes priority.

She gulps and looks to Elias. She surprises us all by saying, "Only if he is there."

Elias' eyes widen and flit to me before going back to her. He gives her a single nod and that seems to calm her. I hate that she does not feel safe with me alone anymore, but I am hoping I can fix that, no matter how long it takes.

We leave my brothers to eat their dinner without us, Easton and Sutton giving me apologetic looks on the way out. I send a mental message down the pack link to one of Moonfire's guards to get the tome about shifters from her room and bring it to me while we settle into my office.

I want to sit next to my mate, but she seems to want space, so I sit on my side of the desk and leave her and Elias to take the seats on the opposite side. She sits perched on the edge of a seat and twists her fingers nervously in her lap.

"Ok, first thing I should mention is yes, you are my mate and I have known since you shot me in Peru."

She stiffens and seems ready to bolt but I hold up a hand and plead using my eyes and pressed lips for her to stay.

"A mate in our culture is a destined partner sent by the Moon Goddess, a perfect match, an equal. In no way would I ever use you in the way you suggested before." My lip rises in disgust at the thought. Hesitantly I add, "In fact, it is your decision whether you accept or not."

"It is usually a blessed day when a shifter finds their mate, because it means completeness, love, partnership, unending happiness," Elias says softly.

It is surprising to see him taking a calm and peaceful approach to her when he has been nothing but distrustful and annoyed. But he knows the importance of what we are saying and that our words could tip her over the edge one way or another.

"If it is such a good thing then why didn't you tell me days ago?" She asked me, the anger returning to her face in the form of a frown and hard-set eyes.

I twist my mouth and tilt my head at her then ask, "Would you have believed me?"

She sighs and her shoulders slump. "No."

I nod. "You had just found out about our world and was scared."

"And you tried to kill him. Twice," Elias adds, never willing to give up that fact.

I roll my eyes at him and Moonfire's lips tilt up just the tiniest bit.

"What if I do not want to be a mate?" she asks, sending a spike through my heart.

I take a deep breath but before I can answer there is a knock at the door. Elias goes to the door and comes back with the tome I asked for. He lays it out on the desk and I grab it, immediately flipping to the page about mates, then turn it around for her to see.

She runs her fingers down the page but does not read it, waiting for me to answer her first.

"As I said, you can reject the bond, but it will always be there. It is not like I put it there and can remove it if you do not want it. The Moon Goddess did it when she created you. Whatever your decision may end up being I will never reject it. You are my mate, and I am willing to give us a try and get to know you more if you are."

She gapes at me although I do not know what part of what I said shocked her or offended her.

She shakes her head and holds up a finger. "Hold on, I am not even a shifter, how could the Moon Goddess have created this bond between us?"

Elias and I share a look. He shrugs.

I answer for us both. "It should not be possible, but the Goddess must know something we don't. Maybe she knows you will one day become one or...how much do you know of your family history?"

Her eyes are wide but at my question she laughs. "If you're suggesting I have a shifter blood somewhere in my family then you're insane. I would know it, wouldn't I? Like, feel a beast in my body or something?" She sounds less sure now.

I mimic Elias' earlier motion by shrugging. "I really do not know, but we could research it and find out together."

She shakes her head and looks to the side as she asks, "What if it is a mistake? What if I am not your mate like you think I am?"

"There is one way to find out," Elias suggests.

I shake my head, "No, we are not doing that. Not while she is so new to this."

She looks from Elias to me. "Do what?"

I continue to stare at Elias, mentally telling him to drop it but he presses his lips together and turns to Moonfire anyway. "When mates kiss for the first time, a mark appears on both of them. A matching mark unique to them alone."

"Kiss?" She squeaks and looks to me.

I see a mixture of emotions cross over her face in the span of three seconds.

Shock, horror, fright, curiosity, embarrassment, and something that makes me lean a little closer…excitement.

Chapter 16

I must admit, the idea of kissing North is…intriguing. My body heats at the thought and something in my chest tugs at me to give it a try.

I shake my head. "If, and I am saying *if,* we kiss and this is all true then I will have a brand on my body and lose my freedom." I shake my head more forcefully. "No, I am not going to give everything up."

Hurt flashes across North's face but it is hidden behind a stoic face in an instant.

"Being a mate does not mean losing your freedom. Like I said before, mates are equals and a good mate would not treat their partner as a prisoner or slave."

I arch my brow and wait for him to understand. Elias gets it first and places a hand on his forehead. He must say something to North through their mindspeak because North suddenly winces and shakes his head trying to backtrack. "No, your situation is different. I am not holding you here in the castle because you are my mate."

I scoff. "Aren't you though? If I was not your supposed mate, then you would have killed me already. Instead, you are holding me here as a prisoner." I waggle my finger at him. "You know, I have been wondering why you haven't killed me or tortured me." I throw my hands in the air and let them flop down on the armrests. "Now I know."

North opens his mouth to say something but I keep going.

"So, what? Mates aren't prisoners so in order to get my freedom back I have to accept the bond? Yet it is 'my choice,'" I use my fingers to make air quotes, "to accept or reject it. But do I really? Ultimatums do not sound very equal and loving to me." With my tirade over I slump back in my seat.

"No, that's not—" North growls to himself and stands up. "You do get—" He sighs and runs a hand through his hair, making some of it fall into his face. He paces back and forth behind his desk, and I watch him, waiting to see what nonsense he will say next.

I can't believe I was thinking about going through with the kiss. I mentally shake my head at myself and patch up the walls around my heart which had been crumbling without me knowing it.

Finally, he stops and leans down, placing his fists on the desk to brace himself. "It's complicated."

Elias jumps in before I can retort. "You stole a relic from us. Though he does not wish to treat you as a prisoner or torture you as I have suggested—"

I snort. "Gee, thanks."

"—he also cannot let you go while it is missing and everyone thinks you are an assassin and thief and nothing more."

I look to North and his eyes are pleading for me to understand. He looks like he is in pain, and I have the realization he truly does not wish to do this to me, and it even hurts him, but he has duties just as I do.

I can understand that. I do not have to like it, but I understand it.

I press my lips together and look at both of them. They wait for my response but I do not know what to say. Their explanations have helped me understand a bit more, but I still do not know if I could accept it. It is a dream to have someone who loves me unconditionally and settle down with them, no worries. But that is just not my life.

I take a deep breath and let it out slowly. "I need time."

North nods and stands up straighter. "Take the book, read more on it. I will not rush you or force you."

I nod and stand, Elias following. I take the book and slowly head out the door. Before I leave, I turn around and ask, "What does Luna mean?"

North gives me a small smile. "It means moon in Latin. It is a term of respect for a female mate, basically calling her the moon like our Goddess is."

My cheeks heat at the compliment, but I turn away before they can see how it has affected me.

In my room I sit cross legged on my bed with the book open in front of me. I stare at the page about mates but do not read it.

What North said about mates does not seem as bad as Danika made it out to be. I should have known better. I knew Danika wanted something and my rejection was the key, but I didn't stop to think she would twist the truth. Or maybe North was the one twisting the truth.

I groan, not knowing who to believe, but I do know one way to find out, and it is the book in front of me.

I spend some time, carefully reading the page then rereading it. It is basically everything North and Elias said but with a bit more information such as mates, once marked, can sense each other's presence and emotions. Some can even speak mentally to one another even if they are not of the same pack if the bond is strong enough. According to North though, everyone is part of the same pack under his father, the King of Shifters, thanks to the Chalice. This page must have been written before the packs of the world united.

I try to imagine what mark would appear on me. According to the book, a mark appears after a single kiss and typically spreads along one shoulder blade to the other and up the back of the neck. It has been known for marks to appear on the arms too but is not common and there is no known reason why it happens. Elias said marks of mates represent both of them to form one unique marking. What would represent me?

I shake my head. No use pondering it if it is never going to happen.

I shut the book and my stomach chooses that moment to growl, reminding me I had skipped dinner. I look to the door and wonder if I could get one of my wolfy guards to get me some dinner then I think better of it. I would not put it past them to spit in my food or poison me.

North said I could move about the castle as long as I had an escort. Well, technically he said to the library or garden. It couldn't hurt to try elsewhere.

I step carefully to the door and knock softly. It is silent so I crack open the door, still surprised to find it unlocked. The guards growl but I have gotten used to it by now and it does not bother me as much as before.

"I'm hungry," I state.

Neither of them does or says anything so I open the door wider.

"I want to go to the kitchen."

They stand and face me, but I hold my ground. After watching me a moment to see if I would change my mind then realizing I wouldn't, one of them turns and starts trotting off to the left. The other one growls and I take that to mean I should follow.

They lead me downstairs and around a couple halls before coming to a set of double doors. They look back at me but do not enter.

I point to the doors. "That's the kitchen?"

They do not indicate either way, so I peek through one of the doors. It is the same kitchen I had been in when I first got here and helped Janie with her food. Which means the ballroom must be near.

I step into the kitchen and just as I remembered there is another door on the left that will lead into the ballroom. I look for the other door and find it in the back. I know that one leads outside. Before I can even think of moving toward it, one of the wolfy guards trots in and takes up position in front of it, eyeing me like he wants me to try for it anyway.

Instead, I poke through the fridges and under lids of things set out on the counter. I find a cake with some missing pieces so I figure it will not hurt if one more piece is taken from it. I find a plate and a fork and cut myself a piece then eat a bite. I moan at the flavor and texture and quickly stuff another bite into my mouth.

I am so invested in that slice of cake that I do not hear someone enter until they speak.

"Tell me that is dessert and not your dinner?"

I shriek and fling my fork at the intruder. Only after it flies through the air do I realize my guards would not have let a stranger approach me and that I recognize the voice.

It is one of North's brothers. The playful, sun-kissed one. The brother I saw in Peru with North. I forgot his name though.

He dodges the flying fork and arches a brow at me in amusement. "Do you always try to kill people with cutlery? Is that your thing?"

He walks over to me and picks up the lid to the cake dish, eyeing the contents within. Then he grabs a plate and two forks, handing me a new one, and slices himself a piece.

"Only shifters with the same bloodline as North," I joke.

He chuckles. "So, he told you about our nicknames then?" he asks through a mouthful of cake.

I nod. Then wave my fork at him. "Something about you naming yourselves after the cardinal points you were placed in by your father, the King. Though, I forgot which one you are," I say, unashamedly.

He points to himself with his fork. "Born Sutton, nicknamed South. You can choose which one to use."

We stand there in silence, contentedly eating our cake. When we are done, South grabs both our plates and cleans them up in the sink. When he finishes, he dries his hands on his pants then turns and leans against the sink and crosses his arms. He stares at me, seeming to study me just as his brother often does.

I walk round the island until I am directly across from him then lean against it, mirroring his pose. I refuse to be intimidated by him or any of the others.

After a moment, he grins. "You will fit right in with us."

He drops his arms and suddenly hugs me. I stiffen. He does not hold on for long and quickly steps back after a couple seconds.

"You know, you scared us all. We were not sure North would make it after Peru. Thankfully you did not use silver, so he was able to pull through."

Guilt pierces my heart and I wince and look away. "I had a job, and he was in the way." I say plainly but my gut churns.

South holds up his hands, palms facing me. "Hey, I never said you were wrong, I understand why you did it. I'm just saying…" he put his hands down slowly. "You scared us." Suddenly he laughs. "Then I find out you tried to kill him again at a party and again with a fork.

Girl, you are either a bad assassin or that is just your kind of foreplay."

I reach out and smack him on the arm. "I am a great assassin thank you very much."

He wiggles his brow and smirks. "So, it was foreplay then."

I smack his arm again, this time harder which only makes him laugh. I can't help grinning too. Something about South makes me feel at ease and this playfulness between us is like that of good friends or even siblings. It's nice.

"Hey, we are all going out tomorrow for a bit of fun before we leave the next day. You should join us," he says suddenly.

I shake my head and my smile dims. "That sounds nice, but his Lordliness will never let me leave. Not if there is a chance of me escaping."

Sutton tilts his head. "Oh, I don't know." Then he sings, "Never say never."

A laugh bursts out of me and I cover my mouth to hold back more but I can't help giggling. "Did you just Justin Bieber me?"

He raises his brows and holds his hands to his chest. "Of course, I did. Justin is my boy. He's Canadian, you know."

We both laugh and I wipe a tear from my eye after I feel it slip down my cheekbone. I have never laughed this much in…well, ever.

Once my laughter dies down, I say, "Well, I should get back to my room. I have a lot of reading left to do."

He snorts. "Have fun with that."

I start to walk away but he calls out, "Luna," stopping me in my tracks. "It was nice to meet you."

I nod. "Same." Then walk away, my two guards following behind.

Chapter 17

I toss and turn all night. My mind keeps playing out different scenarios where Moonfire rejects or accepts the bond. Then it replays the very real images of us in the dining room and in my office when she was discovering all of it.

When the first light breaks through the gap between my curtains I am up and already shifting to go for a run. I need to release some of this tension or else I will be snapping off heads for the smallest offense.

I urge myself faster until I am a blur through the woods. I gratefully lose myself to my wolf for the next hour or two until I feel calm enough to go back.

There is a bin next to the side doors of the castle, the one that faces the woods, for shifters to pick out some temporary clothes to put on when they shift back to their human halves. I grab a pair of sweatpants and put them on. When I open the door, four sets of eyes stare back.

I push past them and run a hand through my hair. "Wouldn't it have been more enjoyable to join me rather than stand there like some lovesick puppies waiting for their mommy?" Ok, so maybe I didn't release all my tension and it seems like I will be snapping some heads off anyway.

Sutton raises his hands. "Whoa man, so I am guessing our answer is that you are not ok?"

Wesley places his hand on my shoulder from behind and turns me to face him. "We are sorry for taking enjoyment in your predicament during dinner."

I shrug him off but nod, accepting his apology.

"Yeah, plus I met her, and she seems cool. I think she will come around," Sutton adds.

I spin to face Sutton and step close to him. "What do you mean you 'met her'?"

I cannot help it. My wolf rises and must show in my eyes because he pales at the sight. The fury and protectiveness in my wolf at the thought of him going to her room last night bleeds through and I start leaking Alpha power.

Sutton's other half responds and now he shows wolf eyes. He stands straighter and steps into me, pushing against me with his own Alpha power. "Back off man. I only mean, I met her in the kitchen last night. We had a piece of cake and got to talking."

I stare at him for a moment longer than force my wolf down and back away a foot. Taking the hint that there will be no fight, Sutton pushes his wolf back and steps away too.

I forgot we did not eat before leaving the dining room and I did not send dinner to her after she left. Guilt pinches my heart.

I breathe deep a couple times, enough to calm myself, then ask, "What did she say?"

Sutton shrugs. "She did not say much, it was me who did most of the talking…and teasing."

I growl at his insinuation, but he chuckles and waves me off. "Chill." He shakes his head still smiling and says, "We should invite her on our outing today."

"I don't think—" Elias starts to say, speaking up for the first time but he is interrupted by Sutton.

"It will be a good chance for you to show her your town, your family, and your true self away from the castle."

"Plus, she will probably not feel so much like a prisoner," Easton adds.

I snap my mouth shut at that. I look to all my brothers then Elias. I understand my Beta's concerns, but I also understand that she needs to get out and see the people, see me, in a different light.

"I'll think about it," I say and walk away before either of them could convince me one way or another.

For the next few hours I work, trying to lose myself in the details and business of the castle and pack but eventually it is lunch time, and my brothers are waiting in the Main Hall. Elias comes to collect me for our excursion and then it is decision time. I already knew what I was going to say as soon as they brought it up, but I wanted to think about all the risks and benefits before committing to it fully.

"I will be there in a second. I have someone I want to come with us."

Elias purses his lips but does not argue and leaves to tell my brothers while I go invite my mate.

At her door I nod to the guards who bow their heads then look straight ahead again. I knock softly on the door and, remembering our discussion about privacy, wait for her to invite me in.

A few seconds go by but eventually I hear her move around inside and then the door cracks open and one beautiful brown eye peers through at me. When she sees it is me, she opens the door wider and steps aside. I walk in and take a quick look around. I note the book lying on her bed and the others still lying on the dresser. The bathroom door is open and the faint smell of soap and lingering steam wafts from it.

"Are you here to invite me out?" she asks and walks over to her backpack at the foot of the bed. She pulls out a brush and starts combing it through her hair which is a little damp.

I am surprised for a second that she knows why I am here but remember Sutton saying he saw her last night. He must have told her about our outing.

"Yes, I would like you come out with us into town." My eyes widen and I hold up my hands. "Only if you want to," I quickly add.

The corner of her mouth tilts up but I do not get to see it for long because she turns away to put her brush back in her bag the second it appears.

She spins around and places her hands on her hips. At first, she looks confident, but I can see the slight bite of her lip and her darting eyes, so I know she is nervous, probably as much as I am at the moment.

"Only if we stop at Janie's bakery."

I grin and nod. "Deal."

In the Main Hall, we meet up with my brothers and Elias who scowls at Moonfire. She returns his look with a scowl of her own which seems to be their greeting for each other these days.

Her face changes into a smile when she sees Sutton and he tips an imaginary hat to her making her chuckle. My wolf threatens to growl at my brother, but I stamp it down. Showing jealousy for something so simple will only push her away more.

"Shall we?" I say and gesture to the door.

The walk into town is a short one but it seems like it takes forever today. My awareness of Moonfire is so high that every movement she makes sends my breath faltering and my arms twitching as I am tempted to reach out to her. I catch her stealing glimpses at me which makes my wolf preen inside. She talks with my brothers on our way down, asking them about themselves but deflects every personal question they ask of her.

When we reach the first set of homes and shops the conversation turns toward the wares sold and the people moving about. My brothers break away and start perusing the shops. I take up the empty place on Moonfire's left, my side warming with her proximity.

"So, we did not get a chance to have our book club meeting today. Read anything interesting?"

"Nope." She pops the P at the end and continues staring straight ahead.

I sigh but do not push her. "Shall we?" I gesture to the street ahead.

She stalks off without another word and I follow her a little more slowly.

She stops in front of a window to a jewelry shop. She looks at the pieces on display but does not give any indication whether she likes them or not.

Trying again to spark a conversation I point to the displays and ask, "Do you like these? Any catch your eye?"

She crosses her arms and walks away toward the other side of the street.

I roll my eyes and mutter, "I will take that as a no then," before following.

Next, we end up at the door to a crystal shop. Various colored rocks and gems are displayed in the window and a waft of incense reaches my nose from the cracked door. Again, she looks at the displays and I am almost afraid to ask. But her silence is ridiculous, so I try one more time.

"Do you like gems and crystals?" I read a card next to one of the crystals claiming it has healing energy. "Do you believe in the energies they claim to have?"

Again, she ignores me and moves on to another shop a little way down the street. I groan and run to catch up to her.

"You cannot keep ignoring me. It is quite rude."

She snorts but continues on.

"What do I have to do to get you to talk to me?"

She shakes her head and I am about to reach out to stop her so we can talk but she stops on her own and faces a shop with way more interest then she showed for the others. I look to see what has caught her attention and laugh when I see it.

"Of course, this would catch your interest."

She glares at me as she enters the shop.

I am mostly amused and partly concerned. Should I fear for my life once again?

I go after her into the weapons shop, deciding I am willing to risk it.

She is near the counter looking down into a glass case at the knives and throwing weapons. On the wall behind it hangs large axes, swords, and chain maces. On the wall to the right are various sorts of guns and in the display in front of it are handguns, some simple and some with styles printed or engraved on them.

The shop owner asks in German if he can help her, but she waves him off. He sees me next and opens his mouth to ask the same but realizes who I am and freezes with his mouth hanging open. Then he gives me a nod and steps back to let us browse.

I peruse the weapons but do not give them too much thought as part of my attention is on my mate. When she leans closer to inspect something I draw nearer and peek through the gap between her arm and body to see what it is.

I reach my hand out and place it on the case next to her to get a better look which presses my body closer to her. Moonfire sucks in a breath and jerks back. I instantly hold my hands up to show her I did not mean any harm, but she eyes me warily. I sigh internally, my wolf and I both sad at the distance she is keeping.

She takes one last glance at the weapon she admired then walks out of the store.

The shop owner hesitantly steps closer and, in German, asks, "Can I help you? I can offer you a discount."

I hold up my hand. "No need," I say in German. I start to walk away but at the last second turn around and approach the counter again, pointing to the weapon in front of me. Sticking to German, I say, "Actually, could I get that? Full price please. You are running a business after all."

He nods and smiles gratefully then rings it up and bags it. When he hands it to me, I stuff it in the back waistband of my jeans and speed-walk out to find where my mate has run off to.

I sigh with relief when I see she is with my brothers across the street. They are sharing their stories of what they saw in the shops. Elias sees me first and raises his eyebrows silently asking me how it's going. I bob my head side to side which makes him shake his head and smirk.

When I approach my brothers they give me pats on the shoulder or punches to my arms but Moonfire ignores me. So, I suggest the one thing she will not ignore.

"Want to go eat? Janie's bakery has some good stuff."

She instantly perks up and turns to me with a smile. Then she remembers she is ignoring me and crosses her arms and hides behind Sutton. I roll my eyes but cannot help a little smile as I lead them to Janie's.

Chapter 18

Nerves have me fiddling with my fingers the closer we get to the bakery. I am excited to see Janie again. She was so kind, and I owe her a huge apology, but I am afraid she will not accept it. What will I even say? *Sorry I used you to kill your Alpha but look, I failed, and he is alive, and you are free so it's all good now.* I have never been good at socializing let alone apologizing.

North's brothers race inside when the smells reach us leaving North, Elias, and me outside. North nods his head at Elias to go in first. The Beta shoots me a warning look to which I roll my eyes. I think I see a little smile on his lips at my eye roll before he leaves us. Aw, I am growing on him.

Sensing my hesitance, North steps in front of me to speak face to face. "We do not need to go in. I can have Elias get something for us to eat later. Your choice."

My choice, huh? I want to snark at him for his comment, but he looks at me earnestly, and I can see he really does care. I guess it isn't fair to ignore him all day.

"No, I need to do this."

He studies me for a second more before moving to the side and gesturing to the door, waiting for me to go first.

Swallowing then taking a deep breath, I enter the shop and take in the homey feeling.

North's brothers and Elias are at the counter ordering, but they are so tall and broad I cannot see the person they are talking to. When they finally move away to find a table there is nothing standing in the way anymore and I have my first look at the friendly baker.

Her smile dims when she sees me, and she glances quickly at North behind me then around the room. Probably to check if she or anyone else is in danger. Or maybe she is looking for an exit. My heart hurts at that look, but I understand it.

I approach the counter slowly, half expecting Janie to make a run for it, but the baker stands up straighter and watches me. She still has not smiled at me, but she also does not look wary anymore.

Progress? Maybe. We'll see.

"Hello, Janie..." I look down at the counter as I fidget with my fingernails.

"Hello, Jessie. Oh wait, that is not even your real name, is it?"

Her tone is one of hurt, not hateful or cold like I expected it to be but hurt. That strikes me deeper than her hate would have.

I ignore the name thing, not ready to tell anyone that Jessie is in fact my real name. I can feel Wolf-man behind me tensing and readying himself for my name, but he will just have to wait a bit longer.

"I want to apologize. It was nothing personal." There. Apology done.

Janie does not say anything, so I look up to see what she is thinking. Does she accept it or not?

"And...?" She prompts.

Ok, apology not done.

Just as well though, she deserves more.

"And you were kind to me and went above and beyond for me when you thought I was just a NYU student." I make sure to keep eye contact as I speak, wanting her to know I mean every word. "And you did not deserve to be seen as an accomplice or used like that. And you bake delicious treats." I add the last part when the oven in the back dings, letting everyone know something is ready to be taken out. "I really, truly, am sorry and hope you can forgive me."

She studies me a moment then walks away without a word.

I deflate. I should have known. I am an assassin and thief. A destroyer of lives. No one would want to be around me. Well, maybe except North.

I look behind me at my supposed-mate and he gives me an encouraging smile. He places his hand on my shoulder and I find comfort in the warmth it provides.

Janie comes back with a pan in one oven-mitted hand and places it on a prep station counter against the wall. Then she turns back to me with a smile, one she used when I first met her. It is so different than the look she gave me when I came in that I take a step back.

"Sorry about that. I had to take the cookies out of the oven."

She flips the top of the counter beside the register and comes out and gives me a hug. I freeze, not having ever expected or imagined this.

"I can see my Alpha has forgiven you which says much about your character, and I am not one to hold grudges. I saw something good in you the first time we spoke, and I still see it. So, I forgive you. Just do not let it happen again." She chuckles and pulls back.

I am too stunned to speak.

North leans down and whispers in my ear which sends tingles along my neck and cheek. "I think you mean to say, 'thank you, Janie.'"

I nod quickly and repeat, "Thank you, Janie." Then I add, "I hope we can be friends or at least friendly acquaintances."

Janie purses her lips in thought. "Hmm, we will see. I would like to be friends, but I think we have some trust bridges to repair first."

Janie goes back behind the counter and opens the glass case beside the register. She pulls out a few treats and plates them up before handing them to North. He nods his thanks and heads over to where the others are. I start to follow but Janie stops me.

"Wait, here." She hands me a plate too.

It has a cherry Danish on it, and a smile instantly forms on my face.

"I do not know what to call you."

North, somehow having heard her, shouts from the table, "Call her Luna, until such a time as she deigns to give us her real name."

Janie's mouth drops open and her wide eyes look me up and down. "You..." she points to me. "...and him?" She points to North.

I roll my eyes and shrug. "Supposedly."

I leave Janie standing there gaping and take a seat between North and Elias.

Sutton *oohs* and *aahs* over all the food then his eyes land on my Danish. "That looks great. Mind if I have a bite?"

He starts to reach for it so I do my best impression of a growl. "Touch it and I will stab you."

Everyone starts laughing and Sutton raises his hands in surrender before choosing something else.

We stay in the bakery for a while longer, even after all the treats have been eaten. The conversation and comradery are easy going. I can almost picture myself as part of their group and life permanently. Almost.

Something outside catches my eye. A flash of red. I sit up a bit straighter to get a better look, but the guys are still too tall and broad. I stand up and move closer to the windows.

There.

Red hair.

Usually that would not be anything of concern, but I feel as if I recognize that red hair. Her back is to me so I cannot see her face.

She lifts her phone, takes a couple pictures of the surrounding area then crosses the street and disappears around a corner. Before I register the movement, I am already out of the bakery and on her trail. I run across the street then peek around the corner before moving on. I tail the redhead around another corner then she suddenly darts into an alley.

I wait before following and peer around the corner to see where she had gone. Did she know I was following her and was trying to lose me? Or is this a shortcut to where she is headed?

The woman stands in the middle of the alley, back to me, but she stands still.

I inch my way into the alley but keep my distance.

"So, you're alive," she says then turns so I can finally see her face.

"Little Red. I thought I recognized you, er, your hair I mean." I cross my arms and arch a brow at her. I am showing confidence and bravado even though my heart is pounding, and my mind is racing. Why is she here? Does Dorian know I failed? Has he sent her to finish the job? My gut twists at the thought. "Are you here alone?"

She smirks and one large dagger slips from the sleeve of her jacket to land in the palm of her left hand. With her right hand she whips out a gun from a holster that had been hidden by her jacket.

If she did not look like an enemy right at that moment, I would be impressed. Ah, who am I kidding? I am impressed either way. I make a mental note to practice that dagger trick later.

"I have come to see what has become of the newbie and if you have completed your mission. Seeing as you are alive and wandering around, I guess you have not finished the job." She arches a brow. "Unless you have defected, in which case…" She holds up her gun, aiming right at my head.

My heart skips a beat and a flood of adrenaline sparks my fight or flight response but I choke it down and smirk instead. "My business is none of yours. I will come back when I am finished here."

"An elite would have already had it finished and been on their way back by now."

That cuts me deep. She smirks at the flinch it causes.

I mimic running with two of my fingers as I say. "Run along and tell Dorian I got this. You do not need to be here."

She starts twirling her dagger while her other hand keeps her gun aimed at me. "No, I don't think I will do that. He sent me to help you, Newbie. He does not think you can handle this on your own after all."

And the cut keeps getting deeper. I suck in a shaky breath.

"You can step aside now. The Alpha will be dead by the day's end."

"No!" I shout before I can think. I try to cover my outburst by calmy adding, "It is my job. I will do it."

Her mouth twists to the side as she thinks about what I said. Eventually she nods and puts her gun away. "Fine. I will give you until midnight. If he is not dead by then I will kill you both." She gives me a dark smile. "And you will never see me coming."

She turns and runs down to the other end of the alley and disappears around the corner. I do not follow this time. I sigh and shake my head, standing there a moment trying to figure out what to do. I could either kill him and live or do noting and doom us both. Again, the thought of North dead twists my stomach into knots.

Neither of those options are good.

I hear my name distantly and my head jerks around to the noise. It comes again, this time closer, so I walk to the mouth of the alley where I had come in and look up and down the street.

I see North across the road at the same time he spots me. He frowns and stalks across the street.

Oh man, I only now remember that I had walked out of the bakery without warning. They all must have thought I attempted to escape. Come to think of it, why didn't I escape when I had the chance? The thought never crossed my mind.

When he is on my side of the street and only a few feet away I hold up my hands in front of me. "I wasn't running away, I swear. I—"

I am suddenly crushed in a hug with my hands trapped between us and my face smooshed into his shoulder.

Ok, not what I expected.

He pulls back but keeps his hands on my shoulders. Warmth spreads into my body from his touch. He looks at me, relief and worry swimming in his eyes.

"I thought you left m—us." He clears his throat and drops his hands from my shoulders. "South was very worried." I smile a little at his concern and his attempt to hide it as someone else's. "Where did you go?" he finishes.

I look behind me at the alley and he follows my gaze, his brows drawing down in confusion.

I press my lips together in a thin line and make my decision. "I have something I need to tell you."

Chapter 19

Norden

I relay her story to my brothers and my Beta who insist we go back to the castle immediately. The four of them surround us as they escort us back, each one of them keeping an eye out from each direction they face. I grumble at their protective circle but do not fight it too hard since it keeps my mate safe.

I remember the bakery. I had looked up from the table to find her gone, I panicked. Had she run away? Had something bad happened to her? I had searched the streets for her, my wolf raging inside wanting to be let free to help, but my senses as a human worked well enough. I tracked her scent and was looking around for the exact location when I saw her across the street. The sight of her helped calm my wolf but not completely until I held her in my arms and saw she was okay for myself.

Her words ring through my mind as we walk back to the castle. *I wasn't running away, I swear.* She hadn't been running from me. She had plenty of opportunities to do so but she didn't. What does that mean? Not only that but she also told me about the assassin. She could have done what the assassin said and kill me or let the other one kill me and either way be free. Instead, she informed me. To protect me.

We are both in danger now and my wolf will not stop flinching at every sound, growling at every possible threat even if it is something innocuous. The need to keep my mate safe is overriding rational thought.

When we are back in the castle, I send Elias to alert all the guards and raise our security. When he is gone, I turn to Moonfire and grip her arm.

"I am trying really hard right now not to restrict your already limited freedom here in the name of safety. But knowing you, you will rebel against it, hate me for it, and possibly even kill me for it, so I will not do that. I trust you know how to stay safe. But *please…*" I stress the plea, "watch your surroundings and find me if anything happens."

She stares at me with wide eyes.

"What?" I ask feeling nervous the longer she stares. I let go of her, thinking maybe she is bothered by my touch, and cross my arms.

"I— Nothing, just...I did not expect you to say that." She clears her throat and looks away. "Thank you."

"Yeah, yeah, my brother is a decent wolfy. Now let's talk about hunting this assassin down before she can do any harm," Easton says, reminding me we are not alone.

"What do you know about this woman?" Wesley asks Moonfire in a low, serious tone. His eyes are flashing from his normal brown to his wolf's yellow and back as he attempts to restrain his other half.

She shrugs. "Nothing much. I have only met her once and in that time she attempted to stab me."

I growl, which makes my mate frown at me.

"Calm down, she intentionally missed."

That does not make me feel any better.

"She is an elite of the Order." She shrugs again and looks at each of us apologetically. "That is all I know, really."

"That is not much to go on," Sutton says, stating the obvious.

I turn to my brothers. "You guys do not need to stay. I have excellent security and I would rather you not be here while this danger is present. Who is to say she will not try to kill you guys too?"

Sutton scoffs. "She could try but she would not get far."

Easton snorts at the same time then says, "We are not leaving."

Wesley nods his agreement and the three of them stand in a line against me with arms crossed. I do not argue anymore. I would do the same for them if the situation was reversed. Sometimes I love my brothers.

"Fine. We have about twelve hours until midnight. We need to make a plan. First, I need to speak with Moonfire." I point to the woman next to me for emphasis.

I turn to my mate and open my mouth but notice that my brothers have not left so I look at them and raise my brows. "Alone," I add.

"Is that safe?" Easton asks.

Wesley nods at me then guides the other two away presumably to the security room but I can confirm that after this talk.

Moonfire watches me warily. "You are not about to go back on your word and restrict my movement around here, are you?"

I breathe out a sigh of frustration and roll my eyes. "No. You can still move about freely and I trust you to keep yourself safe although the guards who will still be trailing you are more to keep an eye on you." I hold up my hands apologetically. "There is only so much I can do until you give up the Chalice's location." I see her about to protest so I wave away her not-yet-spoken-words and beat her to it. "I know, I know, you are not going to tell me. That is not what I want to talk about right now anyway."

She quirks a brow and her lips pull up on one side in amusement as she waves her hand signaling for me to go on.

My words a few minutes ago show I trust her and I even said it just now but there is one more thing I want to do to show it.

"I planned to give you this before the whole assassin business came up," I say and reach for the item in the waistband of my jeans. I hand it to her and wait for her to unwrap it. "It just so happens that it is currently useful too."

Her brows nearly reach her hairline, and she gasps. She gapes at the item in her hand then looks to me with the same surprised look and back down at it.

"A dagger? You…You're giving this to me?"

"I saw you looking at it in the shop." I clear my throat and shift my feet nervously. "Do you like it?"

She is still gaping at it, but finally she closes her mouth and smiles up at me though a small, confused frown takes place. "I love it of course, but…why?"

"I wanted to do something nice for you and…I trust you." I chuckle humorlessly and add, "And as I said before, it also turns out to be useful right now, you know, in case you come upon a certain assassin."

She twirls the dagger around in her hand then grips the handle, stilling its movement. "What if I use it to kill you instead?" She suggests calmly.

I maintain eye contact and smirk. "We are back to this then?" I chuckle and shake my head. "I trust you," I repeat and take a step forward. We continue to stare at one another, and a sudden heat fills the space.

Her calm bravado falters and energy crackles between us. Her dagger is still aimed up, pointed slightly toward me, but I take another step closer anyway. I hear her breath catch and she licks her lips.

My pulse starts racing a bit faster. My fingers twitch, wanting to reach up and hold her. I get lost in her eyes. Goddess, I want to kiss her so much. I want to watch our mark spread across her skin. I want the world to know she is mine and I am hers. Hers since that day in the cave.

Her body leans forward, and I cannot help but reach up and touch her cheek. Her head leans into the touch and now it is my turn for my breath to falter. I lean down slowly but something pokes me in my chest and I wince.

Her eyes widen and she pulls away suddenly. "Oh, I'm sorry," she chuckles awkwardly and tucks a strand of hair behind her ear.

I look down at her other hand and see the dagger. It must have been what poked me. Thankfully it was not a silver dagger or else it would have stung a bit more.

"No worries."

"Are you hurt?" She reaches out with her free hand and pats me on my chest looking for any injuries. I reach up and trap her hand against me and her wide eyes shoot up to mine.

"I'm fine," I assure her.

With her hand against me, her body is now as close as it was before. This time she makes sure to keep her dagger pointed down and at her side. We gaze at each other, and I start to lean down again, the heat and energy between us building back up. My lips tingle in anticipation and my heart thrums happily when she does not move away.

"Bam! Now you're dead!"

Moonfire and I spring apart. She drops into a guarded stance and raises her dagger, aimed at the threat. I start to shift, fur sprouting on my arms, ready to tear into the person who dares try to harm us. My shift halts halfway when I see who it is.

I shake my head and curse.

"Whoa now, watch the language. There is a lady present," Sutton says, laughingly.

In one quick move, Moonfire is standing in front of Sutton, her dagger tip only an inch from his throat. "This *lady* does not appreciate your surprise."

Sutton raises his hands and looks to me. "So…you gave her a knife."

Moonfire twirls the dagger then holds it at her side pointing down again. She steps back until she is standing next to me then gasps as she takes in my half transformation for the first time.

"Now I see where werewolf movies get their image," she says. I can't tell if her tone is fearful or curious.

I look down at myself and see my arms covered in fur, my nails turned to claws and I could feel my lengthened teeth in my mouth. I would bet my eyes are bright yellow too, the color of my wolf's. I breathe in and close my eyes. I reign in the wolf bit by bit until I feel human again then open my eyes and glare at my brother.

I point my finger at him angrily. "We will have words about this later."

He shrugs, unconcerned, then waves for us to follow him. "C'mon, the others are waiting."

I share an exasperated look with Moonfire who shakes her head and smiles before following him to the security room.

Wesley and Easton sit at the small table in the room to which Sutton saunters over and plops into the other available seat.

Elias sits at the monitors and raises a brow questioningly at me when I come in. Then his eyes slide to Moonfire and note the dagger at her side. He shoots up out of his seat and points at it.

"Why does she have a weapon?"

Wesley and Easton look to it but sit calmy in their seats.

"Calm down, I am not going to kill any of you," Moonfire says and takes an open seat against the wall.

Elias looks to me, alarmed, but I wave his concern away.

"Don't you think I would be dead by now, well maybe not *dead* since it is not silver, at least injured, if that was her plan?" I ask my Beta.

Sutton snorts. "She almost made me into a shish kebab."

I snort back. "Yeah, and you would have deserved it."

Wesley and Easton look between us confused but we do not elaborate. Instead, I walk the length of the room and lay out what we know.

"Ok, so, we have until midnight before the red haired, elite assassin starts her hunt. That is unless Moonfire here kills me herself by then."

She shakes her head. "Not going to happen."

I nod, already knowing that was her choice but I think she said it for Elias' benefit.

"So, we must find her first or draw her out," I conclude.

"Finding her will be nearly impossible without alerting the whole pack to the issue and getting their help," Elias points out.

"What about our security?"

"They are aware but that only covers the castle."

I nod and pinch my chin in thought. "Then we draw her out."

"How?" Easton asks.

"Well, she wants me but will not interfere until midnight, so we set up a trap in the ballroom and show her Moonfire will not act."

"Why the ballroom? That is not a secure area," Elias points out.

Moonfire nods her agreement, remembering that is how she got to me before.

"Exactly," I say, then elaborate, "Draw her in then close the trap around her. Trust me. It will be fine."

Chapter 20

An hour until midnight.

Setting up the logistics had taken some time, but Sutton had broken the tension with an involuntary, loud stomach growl. We ordered some food, ate like nothing was wrong in the security room, then parted ways to prepare.

In my room I start to pace as I twirl my new dagger. One more hour.

I still cannot believe he gave me this.

I smile down at the weapon and run a finger along the smooth top. It is not a silver dagger, for obvious reasons, rather the blade is made of steel and the grip is yellow with a twisting design. On the cross guard is a snarling wolf and an image of a bleeding heart rests on the pommel.

I start pacing and twirling it again when my eyes land on my fedora. I place my dagger down on the dresser and go to pillow on the bed to grab my hat. I know what I will find but I still run my fingers along the band around the hat.

Yup, nothing. I wonder if North would give me back my shuriken if I asked.

I place my hat on my head, feeling a bit like my usual self now and go back to the dresser to grab my dagger. My hand freezes above it when my eyes land on the book next to it. Instead of grabbing the dagger I shift an inch above it and grab the black leather journal. I have been putting this off out of loyalty but it will not hurt to see what is inside.

I flip through a few pages and read short passages, taking note of the dates at the top. Some of these are from seventy or eighty years ago. Locations where members have been spotted. Items taken and people assassinated. Observations and speculations. One thing that is never clear is who wrote the passages and collected the information. I know that a little over seventy years ago the packs had their war and became united under one leader. Since this book is in Germany, does that mean a German Alpha had written in this journal? But why would the information not be in German then?

I keep flipping through but accidentally go too fast and make something fly out of the book. At first I think it is a loose page, the book is old after all, but when I go to pick it up I see it is a photo.

After picking it up, I start to put the picture back inside the journal but something, or rather some*one,* in it captures my attention. It is an old black and white photo but nothing gives away exactly what year it was taken. I look on the back but it is blank so I study the two people in the image again.

How is that possible? Maybe it is not as old as I thought, and it is just a filter to make it look black and white. However, I have retrieved enough artifacts and studied enough history to know it is a legitimately old picture. I would guess from the thirties or forties based on the way the two people are dressed. However, there is no way that person could be in it if that is true.

A knock at my door breaks the silence and nearly makes me jump. I do not have a clock in the room so I do not know how much time has passed since I started reading through the journal, but I assume it is North at the door ready to take me to the ballroom/formal dining room.

My assumption is confirmed when his voice carries through the wood. "May I come in?"

"Yes, come in," I call out. I do not wait for him to enter all the way before I cross the room and shove the picture in his face. "Who are these people?"

He leans back and takes the photo from me then holds it at a reasonable distance so he can see it clearly. He frowns at it then flips to the back looking for words or dates then looks at the image again when he does not find any.

"That's my father. He looks different. I am not sure who the other one is." He lowers the picture and looks at me. "Where did you find it?"

I ignore the question but take the picture back from him instead and walk over to the dresser. He follows.

"I know who this is," I turn to him and shake my head. "But it is not possible."

He frowns and crosses his arms before looking down at the picture. "Who is it?"

"It is my boss, Dorian. The leader of the Infinite Order."

He sucks in a breath and takes the picture from me to look at it closer. "What is my father doing with the leader of the Infinite Order?" He looks at me and shakes the picture. "Where did you find this?"

I answer by picking up the thin black journal and shaking it like he did with the photo. "That cannot be my boss."

"You just said it was." He shakes his head. "Now I am confused." He takes the book from me and hands me the picture. I stare down at the image of Dorian shaking hands and smiling with North's father. If that really is

Dorian, then he has not aged a day. How is that possible?

"Where in the book did you find it, maybe there is a notation that explains it," North suggests as he flips slowly through the book.

I shrug. "I don't know. It fell out." I sigh, realizing I am about to give him more information than I should. "North, this man looks the exact same today."

He frowns at me over the book. "What do you mean?"

"I mean," I turn the picture around so he can see it. "He looks the same. He has not aged at all."

North shrugs and continues flipping through the book. "So, he aged well. My father looks about the same, maybe different haircut and clothes but otherwise the same."

I shake my head. "Yeah, but your father is immortal. but Dorian looks the *exact same*. How is that possible if he is human?"

North's brows rise higher as realization dawns. "Unless he is not."

I look down at the picture again and study Dorian's face. It is him aright. I have spent my entire childhood around the Infinite Order. I would know him anywhere. I always thought he looked infinitely young as I grew up, but I never would have thought he was immortally young.

"Did you find anything?" I ask after I notice him stop on a page.

"Maybe? Here look at this and tell me what you think."

I take the book and read where he points. It is a small notation in cursive under the date April 14, 1945.

Mission success. New pack order in place. Mr. Gray paid but debt remains. Unknown future payment.

The next passage is for a different date one year after the last.

Pack order successful. No need for further services. No debt collected yet. Unknown future payment.

The notations are so simple and small I would have flipped right passed them without another thought. If this had been in another book I would assume it was for something else but the fact it is in here and came with a picture, means…

I look up at North and softly state what we are both thinking. "Your father used the Infinite Order to get his new pack order."

Which means, his father had the other leaders assassinated and swooped in to take over. I thought Dorian hates supernaturals. Why would he work with them and help them get more power? My first thought is he did it because it caused chaos among the packs and put the new King in his debt. That sounds like something Dorian would do.

"It appears so." North shakes his head and crosses his arms. "I knew he had to have help, but I did not think he would hire the Infinite Order. They hate each other." He gently takes the picture from me and stares down at it. "So, this is your boss, Dorian Gray, then?"

"I never knew his last name, but it seems likely that Dorian is the Mr. Gray spoken of in the book." I frown and tap my chin. "Wait a minute. Why does that name sound so familiar?"

North quirks a brow at me and smirks. "Maybe because he is your boss and we just read his name?"

I shake my head and flap my hand in the air. "No, the name Dorian Gray. I have heard it somewhere before. I just can't…" I sigh and give up. "I can't remember. Anyway, do you think your father ever paid the debt?"

North slowly shakes his head. "I…am not sure. All he ever said about the Order was that he dealt with them years ago. I always thought it meant he shut down the Order or made it so they would not bother us again but…maybe he meant payment." He shakes his head harder. "It is no use speculating about it now. We have—"

I gasp loudly and swat at his arm in my excitement. "Oh my gosh, I think I know what happened. Or at least I have a guess. *Ohhh*" I flap my hand in the air again.

He grabs my hand, stilling my movement and gazes down at me with a mixture of concern and amusement.

"Care to share?"

"Think about it." I place the book down on the dresser so I can use my other hand to express my thoughts by flapping them around as I speak. "The book said a debt remains but nothing ever said it was paid. What if Dorian wanted to be made immortal and he asked for the Chalice but your father refused."

North nods, catching on to my train of thought. "That must be why he asked you to steal it. Dorian must have gotten a lead on its location and decided to take what he thought was rightfully his." North frowns. "But why would he want to drink from the Chalice when it seems he is already immortal, based on what you said."

"Hmm, I feel like there is an obvious answer, but I just can't get it. Something about his name…Gah! I don't remember."

North squeezes my hand that he still has trapped in his and places the picture down on top of the book. "It is ok, we will figure it out. Right now, though, we should probably go."

I suddenly remember why he is here so late in my room. "Right. Let's go deal with her first."

I take one last look at the photo and lead the way from the room. I am highly aware of North's hand around mine, but I do not try to take it back. It feels warm and right.

We arrive in the ballroom/dining hall, five minutes before midnight. No one else is here but I know there are guards stationed around the perimeter, upstairs and on our level. It is strange to be back in this room, not trying to kill Norden Kane from the balcony but standing by his side instead where I am about to turn against a member of my team to save his life. A weird turn of events that I never would have seen coming.

While we were planning, North explained that this room is usually very dark during the night. On one hand, it would be good to keep it that way in order to draw her out, but on the other it would also give her too many places to hide. So, we compromised and turned on a few lights, so each section of the room is lit but it is still dark enough for an assassin to feel comfortable creeping up on us.

"How do we know she is going to attack at midnight?" North whispers, after a few minutes passes and we are facing the one-minute mark. "Wouldn't that be too predictable? Wouldn't she wait until a later time when our guard is relaxed?"

I shrug. "That would be smart, but from the limited interaction I have had with her, she is too prideful. If she does not attack us now, I know she is at least watching and will hear me as I taunt her out of the shadows."

North frowns down at me. "You think that will work?"

I shrug again and resist the urge to look around the room.

Our plan requires us to only face each other and not look around the room for the assassin. That way she will be more confident in coming out to kill us. We are hoping that as soon as she steps out of the shadows, a guard will take her down before any shots can be fired. We are the bait and, as North nods to let me know it is officially midnight, we have to see if she will take it.

"Anything?" I ask, wondering if his wolves are doing that mindspeak thing to update him.

He shakes his head. Even though his face is pointed down to me, his eyes flit around, trying to spot any danger. His eyes keep flashing from green-gold to a bright wolfy yellow. His wolf is near the surface, but he knows it is better bait to be in human form. Not for the first time, I wonder what it feels like to have that animal right under your skin, pushing to get out.

Two more minutes pass without any sound or movement. Time to taunt.

"I told you she wouldn't be able to infiltrate your castle and kill us. She is too weak. That is why Dorian gave *me* the assignment." I speak loud enough that she would be able to hear me even at the far sides of the room.

North raises his brows at my sudden volume then gets a faraway look. It clears and North whispers, "Elias thinks you are making a mistake by taunting her."

Ah, so the faraway look was him speaking to Elias in his mind.

"Eh, he will get over it," I say.

North smirks and shakes his head.

Suddenly he straightens and turns to the left, facing the direction we came in from.

I touch the brim of my hat with one hand and lightly feel my side where my sheath is. On our way here, I convinced North to take a detour to where they kept my weapons and loaded myself up. The familiar feel of the blades in my boots and sheath by my side settles me.

I wait for Little Red to step closer so I can see her and tense, ready to move if necessary.

"It's not her," North says, surprising me.

"Then who is it?" No one was supposed to show themselves until after Little Red did. They are going to blow our operation.

My answer comes in the form of a petite brunette in a silk night gown.

"Danika?" I ask, bewildered.

"What are you doing here?" North asks at the same time, a hard edge in his tone.

"My lord? What are you doing out here so late?" Danika asks, ignoring our questions. She briefly looks at me but focuses on North again and sashays over. The Nightgown she is wearing does not hide much and I scowl, knowing she is wearing it for North.

I turn to him and whisper. "We cannot have her here. Get rid of her."

Danika gasps and places her hand on her decolletage. "Excuse me?" Her eyes flash yellow so I know her wolf is right at the surface. Sometimes I forget that she too is a dangerous shifter.

"Danika, you shouldn't be here. Go back to bed," North tells her gently. I am surprised by the softness.

Instead of going back she moves closer. "My lord, I could not possibly leave you alone with such a…" She looks me up and down and scrunches her nose, "*Depp.*"

North growls and steps closer to her with a clenched fist. "Watch what you say about her."

Danika smirks.

I wanted to ask what it means but that will only make Danika more satisfied. Plus, we do not need this right now.

"North, we should focus."

North continues glaring at her but eventually backs off and turns to me. "You're right, my Luna, let's—"

Danika shrieks in outrage beside us. "Do not call her that. She is not your Luna. I am!"

Before either of us can react, Danika pushes me away and throws herself at North. She wraps her arms around his neck to bring him down to her level and smashes her lips against his.

"What the—" I stand there, shocked she would be so bold, then an unnatural rage takes over.

I move before I can think and grab her hair. I yank her off him then advance on her. Adrenaline is fueling the anger as I swing out and strike her in the nose. I hear a crunch and Danika shrieks, flinging her hands up to cover her nose.

"You b—" she starts to say but I cut her off.

"Do you have no shame? He obviously is not interested in you and more than that, his mate is standing right here. He is taken and you need. To. Back. Off." I go in for a kick this time but North grabs me and pulls me back.

"Moonfire, it is ok. I think she gets the message." He does not release me until I have calmed enough to think before I act.

Danika is still standing a few feet away, her head tilted back and hand on her nose. Blood seeps out between her fingers but I don't care. She is alternating between whimpering and growling sounding more animal than human though she is still in her human body.

"Moonfire," North says and waits until I am looking up at him. He is smiling and has a dopey look on his face. "You claimed me." At my wide eyes and panicked expression, he hurries to revise. "With your words. Not literally," he chuckles awkwardly and scratches the back of his neck. "Do you really think that?"

I open my mouth to ask what he means but he suddenly straightens and looks to the right where the Main Hall connects with this room. "She's here."

Just as he says it, a tall red-haired woman in a crimson hooded jacket enters with two guns held at her sides. She is still somewhat cloaked in shadow, but I can see enough of her to notice the sneer on her face.

Little Red smirks and steps closer until she is bathed in the lonely light lit in that section. "Mates, huh? Oh, this is good. Like mother like daughter. Now I have a better reason to kill you both."

Chapter 21

When Danika threw herself at me and kissed me, I was stunned for a moment. She had always flirted and made it clear she was interested but she had never gone this far. Probably because it was not appropriate, and I had always expressed I was not interested. Apparently, calling Moonfire Luna was the last straw. After my moment of surprise, I had grabbed her shoulders and started to shove her away but she was suddenly ripped away instead. Watching my mate attack Danika was both surprising and a bit heartwarming. It meant she cared.

My wolf was pretty proud of our mate in that moment. Then she told Danika that my mate was standing next to me and that I was taken. She essentially claimed me in front of Danika and whichever of my guards were listening in from their places around the room and down the halls.

And apparently in front of the assassin.

My wolf is growling on the inside, ready to burst into action, but I stare the assassin down in my human form and partially shift enough to extend my claws and teeth only. It is a skill not all could master but I am an Alpha and have more control than most. My brothers can do it too. Speaking of, where were my brothers? They should have circled her by now.

Moonfire gasps. "My mother? What are you talking about?"

The assassin ignores her and keeps speaking. "You call me weak? You couldn't even finish your first elite assignment. I have already called it in to the Order."

Moonfire tenses then looks up at me with raised brows. She seems to be silently asking what the hold up is. I check in with Elias and the guards mentally and get confirmation they are on the move. I give a tiny nod to Moonfire to reassure her.

"It doesn't matter," Moonfire tells the red-haired assassin, though I can tell she does not believe herself.

The assassin had just dropped a bombshell on her about her mother. I do not know the story behind her family life but from what I am hearing it sounds like her mother was an assassin and died and that maybe it was related to a shifter. I also do not think she believes herself because, although it seems that Moonfire warmed up to me and my family and she discovered Dorian is not who he seems, she still holds her boss' opinion in high esteem.

I should have let her go free days ago, then maybe we would not be in this situation.

The red-haired assassin raises her gun and smirks at her. "I think I will shoot you first. I never liked you, or your mother."

Moonfire scowls and twirls her dagger. She steps side to side, readying herself to move, though dodging a bullet is next to impossible even for a shifter.

Now I tell my wolves through our pack link.

Suddenly, four wolves burst out of the shadows and halls around her and four more make themselves known on the banister above. Two wolves, Elias and Sutton, creep up behind Moonfire, Danika, and me, and bare their teeth at the assassin.

I smirk. "Even if you get one shot off, you will not be leaving here alive. Surrender now, and I will make sure it is a quick death."

I wait for Moonfire to object to her coworker's demise, but she only glares and continues twirling her dagger.

The assassin eyes the wolves around her then moves at a speed that is almost supernatural. She takes a shot in our direction but the bullet lands in the throne behind me since she is not aiming too carefully and sends shards of wood spraying around it. She does not try again since she has to immediately move back to avoid the bite of a wolf. She turns and runs, making the wolves chase her but does a maneuver off the wall that flips her over them and puts her on the backside of her attackers. She aims her gun at them and shoots two before anyone can react.

Moonfire moves forward and tosses her dagger at the assassin's back. At the same time, I launch forward and shift into my wolf, jaws open. The assassin evades us by twisting so the dagger passes her then she does a flip to avoid my jaws. She is nimbler than I would have expected. Then again, there is a reason she is an elite.

I have always known the elites of the Infinite Order hunted supernaturals so it made sense they would be skilled at fighting them. That is one reason I suspected Moonfire was a newbie elite when she first arrived here. She had the silver but was not quick enough to evade us and had been too shocked by our shift.

The elite takes two more shots at approaching wolves, successfully incapacitating those that had surrounded her. Elias and Sutton split and circle around her looking for an opening while I stick to Moonfire's side, protecting her.

A wolf from behind leaps over me at the assassin, snarling. I forgot Danika is still here. Instead of running, she decided to help even though she had just gotten into that big argument with us. The assassin raises her gun and I have a moment of panic as I see what is about to happen. The assassin shot the other wolves in their shoulders or legs, just enough to keep them out of the fight but not kill them. Danika however is positioned in such a way that the bullet will pierce her belly or even heart and she will be less likely to recover.

Elias and I realize this at the same time and start to leap forward both of us aiming for the assassin's legs, but someone else moves less than a second before us. Moonfire jumps and pushes Danika which knocks her off course just as the bullet is released. Instead of hitting Danika in the middle, the bullet grazes her side. Sutton places himself just right so when Danika falls, his body cushions her. They all fall into a pile and Danika whimpers from the pain of the silver. Thankfully, it is not embedded in her and she will recover quickly.

Moonfire does not wait to see what happened to Danika and uses the distraction to kick the gun from the elite's hands. The elite does not bat an eye at her missing gun and raises her silver dagger instead. The two face off, trading blows and slashes and kicks. I circle them looking for an opening, but they are moving too much and I do not want to risk hurting my mate.

The wolves from the second floor finally make it down and circle us, some snapping their teeth and others growling. They are blocking any escape the assassin can make while Elias stands on my other side waiting for an opening to take her down.

The elite dodges an attack then smacks Moonfire's wrist hard enough so her blade goes skittering across the floor. Moonfire immediately reaches for her hat and produces two ninja stars. She tosses them in quick succession which the elite barely misses as she spins. Her spins put her close to Elias who snaps out and bites her calf. The assassin cries out and slashes down with her dagger, slicing a gash into Elias' shoulder. Elias yelps and pulls back. The silver will make his injury hurt for a long while but Elias growls through it and circles her once more though he takes extra care with his right side.

The elite hisses in pain as she spins around to face Moonfire again. I see then that she is not hissing at her leg pain but because there is a ninja star sticking out of her shoulder. The elite is much slower now but still manages to fend off most of my mate's attacks. I see an opening and go in for the bite. She sees me coming and slashes at me, but I avoid it and bite her wrist making her scream and drop her dagger. I jump back before it can touch me and watch as the assassin backs up from me holding her wrist. Moonfire appears behind her back and smiles.

"You should have stayed home."

The assassin starts to turn around, startled by Moonfire's voice behind her but gasps and stiffens. Moonfire steps back and the assassin turns around, showing everyone what happened as she faces her coworker. The dagger I gave Moonfire earlier sticks out of the assassin's back, deeply embedded so only the yellow, twisting hilt is seen.

The assassin collapses but manages to rasp, "He will not let you live, you know." Then her body slackens, and I hear her heart stop.

Elias sniffs her then nods his wolf head at me to confirm what I already know. Moonfire killed the assassin. A member of the Infinite Order.

I look at Moonfire to try and gauge how she is feeling but her face is blank, even as she reaches down and retrieves her bloody dagger. She wipes it off on her pants, face still blank even as her clothes get ruined from the blood, and slips it into the sheath at her side. She takes one last look at the red-haired assassin then steps over her body and heads toward the hallway.

"Well, that's that then. I think I am going to go to bed now," she says, nonchalantly.

Elias makes a rumbling sound and chuffs. I look at him but he is staring after Moonfire. Then he turns to the other wolves and begins giving them instructions using our mindspeak.

I look to Sutton who is standing next to Danika, both of them watching me. Sutton nods his head in Moonfire's direction then his voice enteres my mind.

"Go. I will tell East and West that it is over and see if they can pick anything up from her scent trail."

Easton and Wesley were assigned to the tracker team to try and hunt down the path the assassin had followed today and to check if there were any other *visitors* in town.

I leave them to it and follow after my mate. I shift once we are in the hall and catch up to her in my human form.

"I think we should talk first," I say.

She keeps walking. "Or, we could do that tomorrow when you're more…" she glances at my bare chest then quickly looks away, "decent."

I chuckle and keep pace with her. "I can have someone send me some clothes if it bothers you that much."

She just grunts and keeps going.

"Plus, it is tomorrow already," I add, trying to draw words from her rather than grunts.

She frowns. "Fine." A warm, happy feeling fills my chest until she adds, "tomorrow, tomorrow then."

I shake my head. "Are you ok?"

She snorts. "Why wouldn't I be?"

"Hmm, maybe because you just found out something new about your mother." I am assuming it is new based on her reaction earlier. "Maybe because you killed a fellow assassin you worked with, or because your boss may try to kill you now."

Her frown deepens and her pace quickens but it is easy to keep up with her with my long legs and shifter stamina and speed.

"Or maybe because you said I was taken, practically shouting your love for me to everyone."

I smirk when she stops and spins around to jab her finger into my chest. I knew that would get a reaction.

"I did no such thing."

I place my hand over her finger, trapping it against me. "It is ok, it was bound to happen." I use my free hand to circle my face. "I am irresistible."

She snorts but a small smile plays at her lips, even as she tries to fight it.

My heart warms at the sight and my nerves settle a bit. Her complete emptiness she displayed moments before in the face of everything today worried me. I did not know if she was hurting or angry or happy.

"I see what you're doing," She says and shakes her head sadly. "You don't need to, though. I'm fine."

I squeeze her hand before letting go so I can wrap her in a hug. She squeaks at the suddenness of it but I hold on.

"I know that now. Just know if you ever want to talk, about anything, I will be there for you."

She stiffens so I let go and lean back to look at her face.

"Why do you care so much? I am an assassin. I tried killing you multiple times. Is it because some weird werewolf voodoo says you have to?" A hurt look passes over her face.

I gape at her a moment, completely taken back that she would think that, then I shut my mouth and sigh. I understand why she would think that, but she needs to understand now.

I grip her shoulders, not too hard, but with enough pressure to let her know I am serious. "I honestly think our meet-cute is adorably funny. I think your background makes you tough and interesting and I can tell you care about others despite what you would like everyone to think. You are protective and funny and fierce. What is not to like?"

She blushes and looks down to avoid my intense gaze then snaps her head up when she notices I am still naked and stares fixedly at the wall as her blush deepens.

I chuckle and release her. "Can I walk you to your room?"

She nods and spins around, so her back is to me and she does not have to look at my nudeness anymore. My grin is plastered on my face the whole way there.

At her door, I nod to her bloody clothes. "If you leave those outside the door, I will make sure they get washed and returned."

She looks down at her clothes and raises her brows in surprise. Did she not know there was blood on them? Seems unlikely since she was the one to wipe it there.

"Um, thank you, North. For everything, you know despite being a prisoner."

I wince but she waves away the reaction letting me know she is joking.

"Good night."

I nod and step away from her door, turning to head back to the ballroom and help the others. "Good night."

"North?"

I stop and turn back to her. She is half hidden behind her open door now and biting her lip nervously.

I frown. "What is it?" I grin wolfishly. "You want me to stay with you tonight?"

Her lack of a grimace or snort makes me straighten. Whatever she is going to say is serious enough that not even my flirtations will distract her.

She takes a deep breath then on her exhale she rushes to say. "The Chalice is in New Jersey." Then she shuts the door loudly before I can do or say anything. I stand there for a moment, stunned by her words.

The Chalice.

New Jersey.

One step closer.

Chapter 22

Jessie

A few days pass since I killed Little Red. I warned North that Dorian might send more assassins when he finds out she is not coming back. He assured me they would be on the lookout for others which did not really reassure me. Both Little Red and I were able to infiltrate the castle and get close to North. He claims to have excellent security in place, but I am having doubts.

Things between us were awkward but we had breakfast and dinner together in his private dining area every day and I was given a bit more freedom (no more guards at the door and I could take trips to town as long as I took someone with me). I noticed on the occasions I left my room that I had an escort, but they always seemed to be watching the area around me rather than me personally. It made me feel like I had a bodyguard rather than a prison guard. I never knew how to bring it up to North without sounding weird, so I let it go.

It is one of those times I find myself in now as I make my way to Janie's bakery. My escort for the day, Ralf I think, watches the people passing with suspicion and demands to go first around every corner lest we be ambushed. He was one of the wolves that night that Little Red shot. I see that he is still healing even now as he tries to hide a limp as we walk. Silver really does a number on these guys. Since that night though, some of the guards had warmed up to me and even greeted me in the halls or when they were my escort for the day.

I had spent the last few days pouring over the little black journal for any hints about the Chalice or Dorian's past but did not come up with much. Next step was the library, but I am putting it off. I do not like books, and I have already read more in the past week than I have in years. My mother was an avid reader so she would often read to me growing up, but I never picked up the same hobby. If I am being honest, I am using the bakery today as an excuse not to go. Last night, North urged me to check out the library since he would be busy today and could not hang with me. He and my mom are a lot alike in the sense that if you have a question or are bored, pick up a book.

I smile at the memory of the night before. We had spent most of the night hanging out in my room talking and sharing stories over some wine and dinner (Apparently in Germany, the legal drinking age is 16 opposed to America's 21. Which means I can drink all the wine I want. Not that I ever respected the law before, but with three more years until I am 21, it does not hurt to drink where it is legal.) I told him about my mom and growing up under an assassin and he told me about growing up a shifter under the King and Queen of wolves and moving to Germany to become Alpha. It was the most I had ever opened up to someone, yet I still could not bring myself to tell him my name.

I have tried not to think about the little revelation Little Red shared before our attack. *Like mother like daughter,* she said. Does that mean my mother had a mate? There is no way to know for sure or even if the assassin was lying, trying to make me lower my guard. North never brought it up either even as we talked about our families last night.

The bell jingles over the door when I enter Janie's bakery. The Baker herself pops up from behind the glass display case and shouts a greeting in German. Then her eyes widen when she sees it is me and switches to English.

"Good day…um, Luna." The name sends a jolt through me. It is strange to hear people call me Luna knowing it means they are acknowledging me as North's mate.

"Hi, Janie." I approach the case and make a show of looking at all the pastries and sandwiches on display even though we both know what I am going to get.

"Three cherry Danishes please and…." I turn to Ralf. "What do you want?"

Ralf holds up his hands and shakes his head. "I don't need anything." I give him a stern look and put my hand on my hip. I frown at him until he gives in.

Ralf sighs. "Ok, a coffee and bear claw."

I turn back to Janie and nod.

I wait for her to package them up and hand Ralf his coffee before adding one more thing. "And maybe a friend to talk to?"

Janie's head snaps up. She stares at me a moment but when I don't retract my question or back away, she smiles and flips a piece of the counter up to walk through. "I would love to talk to you." Then she adds with a little growl, showing the wolf underneath, "No lies."

I smile and follow her to a table. I give Ralf his bear claw and he finds a seat farther from us to eat it so we can have some privacy even though I know he will be able to hear everything we say with his shifter hearing.

"How have you been?" I ask Janie when we settle into our seats across from each other.

"I am fine. Same as always. Actually, that is not entirely true. I have been very curious about what has been going on in the castle." Janie's raises her brows, waiting for me to explain.

"Did you hear about the assassin?"

Janie nods. "Everyone in town was shocked that another assassin snuck into our most secure building."

I snort. "I am starting to believe it is not as secure as everyone says."

Janie ignores my comment and continues, "I have also heard you saved Danika and killed the assassin."

I nod. "I wouldn't say I saved Danika, she still got hurt, but the other part is true."

"She saved all of us that night," Ralf calls from the other side of the room.

I frown at him. "Eat your bear claw."

He chuckles and goes back to acting like he is not listening.

"It must have been hard killing a fellow assassin from the Order like that," Janie says sympathetically.

I shrug. "Not really, I never liked her." I take a big bite of my Danish and moan as the flavors hit my taste buds.

Janie's jaw drops and she stares at me, trying to figure out if I am serious about being so casual about killing the assassin or just hiding my pain. She slowly shakes her head and decides to move on.

"What are you going to do now? Have you decided to stay here?"

Now that question is a tough one to answer. As far as I know, North has kept the missing Chalice under wraps. The only ones who know of it is North, his family, Elias, and the few trackers who were assigned to find it. Now that everyone knows I killed the assassin to protect the wolves that night and the news of me being North's mate is starting to circulate it would be weird to say I am still a prisoner. I do not feel like one anymore, but I doubt North will let me leave that easily.

Do I even want to leave?

"I don't know what I want to do," I say honestly.

It is the first time I have ever doubted my life. Should I go back to the Order? Should I stay? If I stay what will my life look like? I am not an idle person.

"My boss, Dorian Gray, will probably send more people to kill North. I think…" I sigh knowing the truth of what I am about to say. "I am going to have to face him sooner or later. The longer I wait the more danger I put everyone in."

Janie laughs. "Dorian Gray is his name? Like the book? Oh, that is funny. His parents must have loved the story. As for the danger, my Lord is Alpha of the Northern Packs, he is protected and can handle a little danger."

Her first words catch my attention. "Book? Story? What are you talking about?"

Janie frowns, trying to remember what she said then brightens. "Dorian Gray, from *The Picture of Dorian*

Gray? My mother used to say some people thought it was based on a true story. Maybe your boss is the original." She laughs at her own joke, but I do not join in. I am too stunned to speak, and her words trigger a warning in my mind.

"Can you tell me how the story goes?" I ask, seriously.

Catching my tone, Janie's laugh fades away and she studies me in confusion. "Um, sure. But it is just a story you know. His parents were probably just fans of Oscar Wilde."

I raise my brows, wanting her to hurry. Understanding, she clears her throat and gives me a summation. "According to the *fictional* story," she gives me a pointed look but continues, "he was obsessed with his youth and the pleasures it brings so when his friend painted a portrait of him, he claimed he would sell his soul to stay as young as the portrait. So, a wish was made and he stayed forever young, only his portrait showed the true age and sins he made as time went on."

She shrugs as if that is the whole story.

I frown down at my Danish before taking a bite and chewing it slowly to give me time to think. When I swallow the piece I ask, "How does the story end?"

Janie twists her mouth to the side in thought. "If I remember correctly, Dorian stabs his own painting, and it kills him."

She looks at me and shakes her head. "I can see what you are thinking, but it is impossible. The only supernatural beings are fae, shifters, witches or sorcerers, and vampires. Dorian Gray does not fall under any of them."

"He may not be, but what about the being who made his wish come true? The one who enchanted the painting. Could a witch or fae have done it?"

Janie thought for a moment. "Maybe? It is such an old story and I do not know much about other supernatural races. The library probably has more information and the story of Dorian Gray."

I groan. "Great, more reading."

Janie chuckles. "Lord Kane may have some knowledge of it too. Why are you so interested anyway?"

I tell her about the black journal and what I found inside. Then about my boss who seems to have always owned the Order and no one knows who came before. She listens intently and nods to show she is following along. After my explanation she sits back in her chair.

"I see. I mean, it is possible, I guess. But even if it is true, what are you going to do about it? Kill him? If you want to kill him, you will need to find his portrait."

I shake my head. "I do not want to kill him."

Janie shrugs. "Then this realization is pointless."

I shake my head again. "Oh, Janie, knowledge is never pointless. Knowledge holds power and gives you an advantage."

Janie rolls her eyes. "Yet you are against reading."

I chuckle and eat the rest of my Danish, letting the subject go for now. I will tell North when I see him again, and we will come up with a plan. Although, I do not know what that plan will entail. We are not going to kill him, and I will not tell them where the Order resides. I already gave them enough information about the Chalice that would deem me a traitor. I could go back, but what would I do? What would I say? More importantly, could I leave North after everything I have learned and started to feel?

Too many questions.

I end up eating two Danishes and ordering a few more to take back before leaving Janie's bakery. It was nice to talk to her. Once we got away from the assassins, Order, and mate stuff we talked about random things like hopes, dreams, hobbies, etc. Stuff I assume regular friends talked about. It was a nice change from my everyday life, and I am even more grateful she has forgiven me.

I walk slowly back to the castle, savoring the peace of the little town. Ralf leads the way still, keeping an eye on our surroundings, but he lags back enough to be practically by my side.

"Janie seems to like you," Ralf says after a few minutes of walking in silence.

I raise my brows, surprised he would strike up a casual conversation, then nod. "Surprisingly so, especially after everything I did to her."

Ralf may not know exactly what I did but it is not too hard to figure out the gist of it. He knows I am an assassin. He has been one of the wolves to guard my door and was there when I fought my fellow elite. Now I hinted that I did something to her, so it is not a big leap to figure out it was assassin related.

"She is a nice girl, not a dominant wolf, very trusting." There is an edge to his words that makes me stand straighter.

"I have figured this out, yes. What is your point?"

Ralf shakes his head. "I would just hate to see her hurt is all. The pack is very protective of those who are less dominant. Not only that but Janie is dear to the town."

I know a thinly veiled threat when I hear one. "I will not hurt her. Not again."

Ralf harumphs but seems pleased by my response. We turn the corner and I accidentally bump into someone.

"Oh, sorry," I say, righting myself and grabbing the man to make sure he does not fall. I look up to ask if he is ok but he mumbles that he is alright then shrinks away around the corner where we had just come from before I can get a word out.

I stare after him with a small frown but shrug it off and move on. I notice then that Ralf is frowning in the direction the man walked off to. He seems a bit confused and much more guarded.

"What is it?"

Ralf waits a moment then shakes his head. "Nothing. Come on."

We travel in silence, Ralf continuing to watch our surroundings even though there is only forest and rocks around now that we are on the path back to the castle.

I start to feel tired the longer we walk, and my mouth begins to go dry. I must be worn out after walking all day. I am going to need to lie down for a nap when we get back. My muscles are starting to ache, and a tall glass of water seems like the best thing ever right now.

Ralf turns back after a few minutes and tilts his head in a classic wolf-be-confused move. When did he get so far ahead anyway?

"What is wrong?" Ralf asks.

I pull my head back and smirk at him as if he is silly for asking. "Notin'. Why you assssk?"

Hmm, that is weird. Why am I talking like that. Let's try that again.

"Nothing." I nod when I get out the word successfully this time.

Ralf comes back to me and places his hands on my shoulders. Then he looks down at my arm. "Why do you keep rubbing your arm?"

I look down, confused because I hadn't been rubbing my arm. My eyebrows rise when I see my left hand rubbing furiously at my right bicep without my knowledge. I stop and drop my hand to my side.

Ralf sucks in a breath and raises my arm for closer inspection. I follow his gaze and gasp when I see a large red welt. As soon as I see it, I hiss and raise my other hand to scratch it. I did not feel it before but now it itches like crazy. Ralf swats my hand away and probes the area then to my shock he sniffs it.

I try to pull away from the weird shifter guard. "Wha' you do-ing?" Ok my speech is all messed up again. Something is not right.

As soon as I have the thought, my legs give out. I would have fallen to the dirt path if Ralf did not catch me.

"Luna? Luna!" Ralf shakes me a little, but I am no longer able to answer him.

What is going on? My tongue feels like a hundred pounds, too heavy for my mouth. My arms and legs do not want to cooperate. My mouth is dry. I swallow a few times, trying to get saliva to coat my tongue but nothing comes. Maybe if I just close my eyes everything will work itself out. Like restarting a computer.

"Luna, don't close your eyes," Ralf says, then curses and lifts me into his arms. "I need to get you back." He starts running but I barely feel it.

He sounds so concerned.

Am I going to die?

Chapter 23

Norden

A voice pierces my mind urgently, causing me to wince.

"*Alpha, emergency, Luna has been hurt.*"

I am halfway to the door to the secondary security room, where the trio I assigned to hunt the Chalice had been briefing me on their progress, after the words *Alpha, emergency, Luna.* The rest of the sentence registers after I am already partway down the hall. *Hurt.*

Great Goddess, what now?

"Lord Kane, where are you going?" One of the trackers asks, coming out of the room I abruptly left.

I ignore her and walk quicker.

My wolf pushes against me, urging me to go faster or let him take over so they can reach our mate. I push him down but cannot help the claws that extend from my fingers and the teeth lengthening in my mouth.

"Where are you?" I ask Ralf, the guard I assigned to her today and whose voice spoke to me.

"Infirmary."

I call Elias in my mind to meet me and race to the infirmary on the first floor. It is farther from the kitchens and ballroom and on the opposite side of the castle from Moonfire's room, so the fact he is taking her to the infirmary must mean it is serious.

I sniff the air when I reach the hall where the infirmary is, but I do not smell any blood which is what my active imagination was picturing. Blood everywhere. But my nose says differently so maybe it is not as bad as I think.

I burst into the room and scan every inch for my mate. The beds were full earlier in the week with the injured packmates after we battled the assassin. Silver bullets can mess a shifter up. Thankfully all have recovered or are on their way to a full recovery which means there is no one here now. Except I spot three people in the back of the room.

I stride over and growl an order at Ralf to tell me what happened. My heart skips a beat and my wolf howls inside at the sight of our mate, motionless on the bed. The doctor ignores us as he hurriedly checks her vitals and tries to figure out what is wrong with her.

Ralf is panting as he runs his hands through his hair. "I do not know." Then he slips into his native German language and proceeds to explain what happened.

"Did she touch anything, eat anything?" The doctor asks in English. He checks her arms then straightens and points to a spot. "Was she stung?"

A red bump that looks like bee sting or bug bite sits high on her bicep.

"Nein, nein." Ralf shakes his head and takes a deep breath. Then his head freezes in the midst of another shake. "Wait," he says speaking in English again. "She was itching that spot before she collapsed. The only time she encountered anything before that was when—" He stops midsentence then curses.

I grip Ralf's arms and turn him to me. Elias enters the room at that moment and I only spare him a glance and a single nod before looking back at Ralf. I know Elias will be able to hear everything across the room so I do not wait for him.

"What is it?"

"We ran into a man. Nothing out of the ordinary except I did not recognize him. She bumped into him, but it was only for a second then he was gone," Ralf explains.

"Did she recognize him?" Maybe it was another assassin from the Order.

Ralf slowly shakes his head. "I do not think so."

I turn to the doctor. "Could something have been injected?"

"I will run some tests," the doctor says and gets to work quickly.

I listen for her breaths to make sure she is still alive. It is shaky but there. Her heart rate, though, is fast. I relay that to the doctor who nods.

"Yes, Alpha, I can hear it too. I will do what I can. Please stand back." The doctor ushers us back a step so he can access her on her other side.

I curse and spin to Elias. "I want everyone looking for this man. He may not be at fault but with everything going on recently I do not want to chance it. Ralf," I call, turning slightly to include the guard in our huddle. "Can you describe him? Did you get any distinct scents?"

Ralf scrunches up his face as he tries to remember. Eventually he shakes his head. "He had brown hair, average height. Wore a brown jacket and khaki pants." He purses his lips and snaps his fingers repeatedly as he tries to recall anything else. Finally, he shrugs and throws up his hands. "He just looked like an average guy. No distinct markings and…hmm."

I am going to throttle him if he goes any slower. "What?" I almost shout.

"Now that I think about it. He did not have a scent."

Elias' head snaps back and I frown.

"No scent, what do you mean by that?" I ask at the same time Elias whispers, "Impossible."

"I mean he did not have a distinct scent. I would not be able to track him or even spot him in a crowd, human or wolf."

I curse and slap the curtain next to me making it swing on its metal rings. "Send out that limited description to the others. Keep eyes on any stranger in town." I say to Elias who nods and both he and Ralf stalk from the room.

"Doc, anything?" I ask and place myself next to Moonfire again. If we were bonded, then I could share my healing energy with her. Shifters can heal from almost anything thanks to the Chalice and natural abilities. But alas, we are not and now I have to watch her weak frame lay motionless on the medical bed.

"I do not know for sure, but it seems she has been poisoned," The doctor relays as he continues to check out her body and inputs data into a laptop next to him. "I will have to get these tests done to determine what it is so I can get a cure."

"How long will that take?" I ask in a strained voice.

He looks at me grimly. "It depends"

"On what?" I nearly shout.

The doctor does not even flinch. "On whether it is a common poison or not. Now if you will let me pass, I can run these," he holds up a couple vials of her blood then nods his head in the direction I am blocking. I step aside, though my hands clench, and he passes. I want to force the doctor to hurry but I know it will not do any good to hinder his process further.

When he is gone, I step to Moonfire's side and grip her hand. "Moonfire. Can you hear me? I am right here, Luna. Hang in there. We will figure this out. Then together we can kill the devil who did this."

I wait, expecting her to respond in some way. A few seconds pass but nothing happens. I sigh and squeeze her hand.

My cell phone rings, and I pull it out to silence it, but the caller ID has me answering it instead.

"Yes?" I growl.

"Excuse me, who are you growling at?"

I take a deep breath and close my eyes to calm myself before answering. "I am busy. What do you need?" Hey look at that, no growling. Progress.

"That is no way to speak to—"

"Father," I interrupt, "What. Do. You. Need?" I have no patience today, not even for the King.

He splutters for a moment then decides to ignore my behavior and moves on to the reason he called. "I heard you had another assassination attempt. This is getting serious. Do I need to send some forces there?"

I grip the phone and nearly throw it at the wall. "Danika, I swear, I am going to—"

"It was not Danika," Father says. "It was Wesley, actually."

West? Why would he…?

My brothers had gone back to their own homes and packs the day after the attack. We were close, and we all hated how controlling our father was. So, why would West call him and tell him about the attack when it was handled.

"Well, he told your mother who told me." Then he grumbles, "I should not be having to hear things like this second hand."

"It was handled," I say.

He snorts. "You said that last time and yet I hear you have had a special guest staying at your castle. A certain assassin from the Order?"

I hold in a gasp and take measured breaths to calm myself. My silence must say more than words because he laughs.

"Don't tell me you have fallen for her. She is an *assassin*. She is luring you in so she can kill you easier. She is also most likely the one who is drawing these other assassins to your doorstep. Have you ever thought of that?"

"Did West tell you about her?" I ask.

Father grumbles unintelligibly then says, "No, I have other sources."

I roll my eyes. Great, now I have more moles in the pack. After all this Order and Chalice stuff is dealt with, I need to have a serious talk with my pack and root out the moles.

"You need to get rid of her, Norden. She is dangerous to you and the pack."

I laugh, humorlessly. "Dangerous, yes, but not to me."

Father sighs. "See? She already has you under her spell. That is it. I think I need to send some people to you."

"No," I say firmly.

"Norden—"

"I said no. You do not know anything about what is going on here even with your moles so do not try to act like you do."

He is quiet and I realize I am breathing hard, and my claws have extended. I pull them back in and take a few calming breaths.

Finally, in a quiet voice, he says. "I care about you, Norden. I only want to look out for you."

I shake my head, even though he cannot see it. "I think you care about power and want to look out for your control over the packs. That is why you placed moles here, right? That is why you are worried about my safety, right? That is why you are trying to force Danika to be my mate, right? Well, I already have a mate and right now I need to be with her."

Father gasps but before he can say anything I hang up. Immediately it rings with Father's name on the screen. I silence it and toss the phone to a nearby medical bed then turn my attention back to Moonfire.

I stay by her side for the next couple hours. In that time, the doctor comes in and out checking her vitals and giving her fluids through an IV, then rushing off to do more tests. I perk up each time the door opens only for him to give me a shake of his head letting me know he has not figured it out yet.

"Anything yet?" I send out to the pack.

Immediately I hear lots of voices in my head all saying the same thing. *"Nothing, Alpha."*

I growl and stand up to pace. Movement from the bed catches my eye and I spin to my mate, a smile forming on my face. She is awake, thank the Moon.

My smile falls and panic replaces my relief.

Her body is seizing, and her eyelids are half open showing her eyes rolled back.

"Doc! Get in here now."

I hover my hands over her, wondering what I could do to help but not wanting to make it worse.

The doctor bursts into the room and rushes over to me, quickly taking in the situation. He pushes her on to her side then stands back until we are both staring down at her convulsing body.

"What are you doing? Do something."

"I can't. We have to wait."

A few seconds pass then her body finally stills. She is so motionless I wonder if she is dead. Immediately I listen for her heart and nearly collapse in relief when I hear a steady beat. I reach over and brush some of her hair away then squeeze her hand.

The doctor reaches around her head and places an oxygen mask over her face then tilts his head and listens to her heart and breaths just as I had done a moment ago.

"I think she will be ok, I have discovered the poison used on her, now I just need to get a cure..." He hesitates and I turn my head to see an anxious expression on his face.

It is never good when a medical professional is anxious.

"Doc?"

"I do not have access to the cure."

I face the doctor fully and advance on him until I am only a few inches away. "What do you mean?" I ask through gritted teeth. I let out some Alpha power causing him to lower his head and hunch his shoulders. "What do you need?"

The doctor takes a step back and swallows before speaking. "The poison is a mixture of wolfsbane and cyanide. I-I will give her something to help combat the wolfsbane, but I cannot be sure it will work with the other poison running its course."

I step back and run a hand through my hair.

"I know a hospital in the next city that has an antidote to cyanide but..."

I shake my head. "But it may be too late by the time it gets here," I finish. I curse and clench my fists, wanting to punch something but not having anything nearby that would be satisfying.

"If she were a shifter, it would be much easier. Anyway, I will make the call and maybe we will be lucky." The doctor rushes off before I can say anything.

I look down at my mate and feel my whole world falling apart. I just met her and started to picture what a life might be like with her and already it was being torn from me. My heart aches and my wolf howls inside. I hate the Infinite Order. What is their issue with me and Moonfire anyway? I swear I am going to find them and kill Dorian Gray.

I cannot sit here and do nothing. There are two options. Mark her or turn her, both of which may give her a chance to heal or at least hold on until an antidote can get here. However, turning her would risk her life even more, especially without the Moonstone and Chalice to help the process along. No, turning her is my last option so the next thing I can do then is mark her and hope I can share my healing energy and that it will be enough.

I take off her oxygen mask and lean over her, ready to press my lips to hers but hesitate when I am a breath away. She does not want to have her mate mark. She thinks it will bind her to a life she is not ready for. Maybe I should not force this on her.

I start to pull back, but my ears pick up something from her.

Her heart.

It is slowing.

No, no, no. I grip her shoulders and shake a little. "Moonfire, hey, don't give up now. Just hold on a little longer."

Her heart continues to slow, and I know she will be gone soon if I do not do something.

"My Luna, my everything. I cannot think about life without you. I refuse to let you leave me like this. Please let this work." The last line I send up as a prayer to the Moon Goddess before leaning down the rest of the way and pressing my lips to my mate's.

It is a soft kiss. A light touch of our lips. I am getting real Sleeping Beauty vibes and I always found it kind of creepy that the Prince kissed a sleeping woman without her consent, however, in this moment I feel a kindred spirit in Prince Philip. He was only doing what he could to save his love just as I am trying to do now. Though I know better than to linger longer than necessary because that would be pushing some boundaries that I know would get a silver dagger in my heart if she ever found out.

I pull back after a moment and stare down at her. What will happen now? Will we get our marks at the same time? Will it hurt? Can I start sending my healing energy now and how does that work? I have a moment of panic and dread that nothing will happen because maybe she is not my mate after all.

I nearly growl at all the unknowns.
All I can do now is wait.
And hope.

284

Chapter 24

Jessie

The first thing I notice is the silence.

I do not think I have ever been around such silence.

I try to open my eyes, but it is a monumental effort. My eyelids are so heavy, and my mind is in a fog. *Go back to sleep* it seems to say, pulling me down.

What time is it? Have I been asleep long or can I sleep in for a little longer?

Oh, what does it matter? I am in a castle with no responsibilities. I can sleep as long as I want to.

With that in mind I snuggle down into my pillow and heave out a contented sigh before letting my body pull me into a sleeping void again.

Something tugs inside my chest. It is a heavy feeling. The more I focus on it the more my heart starts to race. I feel helpless and worried. What is that? They are not my own feelings. It feels foreign. Then it starts to swirl around. Part of it is still heavy and sending worry through me but the other part is warm and fluttery.

My eyes shoot open and I sit up, wondering what the strange energy is. The first thing I notice is the bed I am in. It is not the same one I have been staying in the past week. The next things are the walls and the window next to me. It is daylight outside but dark clouds cover most of the sun and rain pelts the glass. I look around, wondering where I am and spot a body on the bed near mine.

Oh no.

North!

I leap off the bed and stand so I can go check on North but my legs nearly give out under me and my head spins. That strange feeling inside me surges and worry pounds my insides mixing with my own. I lean against the bed to get my bearings before moving to the bed North is in.

I touch his shoulder and the feeling inside me soothes. The worry is still there but not as heavy. Instead, the fluttery feeling swirls and sends heat throughout my body. I feel happy and content, yet again those feelings feel foreign.

What is going on?

The door at the other side of the room opens and I look up to see a man in a white coat walk through with a clipboard.

He spots me and his steps falter before he plasters a smile on his face and makes his way over to us.

I sense something in him. It is a sort of…wildness. Danger. It contradicts the smile on his face and his easy gait.

A moment later a word whispers through my mind. *Wolf.* I know then that this man is a wolf shifter. I do not know how I know but I do.

He stops next to me and glances down at North then focuses on me. "Maybe you should sit." He nods to the bed behind me.

I take one last look at North then do what he says. As soon as I am sitting, I ask, "What happened?"

"What is the last thing you remember?" He counters.

My eyebrows scrunch together and my mouth twists to the side as I try to think of the last thing I remember before this place.

I gasp.

The doctor leans forward, concern pulling his brows down. "What? What is it?"

"My Danishes." I look around but the white bag is nowhere to be seen. Ralf better not have eaten them.

The doctor straightens with a chuckle. "I don't know anything about Danishes, but do you remember anything else?"

I remember leaving the bakery and heading back to the castle then…

"I had a terrible itch," I reach up to the spot on my arm that had felt like fire but am met with a bandage. I look down and suck in a breath. So, it had been that bad? "Then I felt my mind and body shutting down and all I wanted to do was sleep." I shrug, letting him know that was all I could recall.

The doctor nods and writes a couple things down on his clipboard. While he does that I look past him at North. I am finding it hard to keep my eyes off him ever since I woke up and spotted him on the bed.

"What happened to him?" I ask.

The doctor glances behind him then back down at his clipboard. He answers as he finishes writing his notes. "I will explain that in a little bit but first I have a couple more questions for you."

He looks up with eyebrows raised in question and I nod, letting him know I am ready.

"So, you were poisoned. Do you remember coming into contact wi—"

"Poisoned?" I shout.

The doctor nods. "You were injected with wolfsbane and a little cyanide. Do you remem—"

I gasp and place a hand on my chest. "Cyanide?" I have used that to assassinate certain individuals in the past but never dreamed it would be used on me. "How am I alive?"

The doctor sighs and crosses his arms. "Yes, and I will get to that in a minute but please, for now, answer my questions."

My shoulders slump and I look to him apologetically.

"Now," he says, uncrossing his arms, "Do you remember coming into contact with a man in brown. Ralf says he may be the one who injected you."

His words bring the memory to the forefront of my mind. I nod enthusiastically. "Yes, yes, I remember. I never would have thought of him if you did not say anything. We bumped into each other when rounding a corner."

"Did you recognize him?"

I frown and look down at the floor. After a moment I gasp and look up at the doctor with wide eyes. "Yes, I do. I did not before but now that I am focusing on it…" I shake my head, unnerved at how beneficial being average looking is for assassinations. "He is an elite assassin for the Order."

The doctor pressed his lips together and made a note on his clipboard. "We thought so, but no one has been able to find him."

"How long have I been here?" I should have asked that earlier.

"36 hours."

Over a day. If they haven't found him by now, then they won't. "Why target me instead of North?" I mutter to myself, thinking about his motivations.

Does that mean he is still around, waiting to get North next? Or was I his target all along? The thought sends a shudder through my body.

The doctor notices and rests a hand on my forehead. "Are you okay? Feeling dizzy or nauseous?"

I push his hand away. "I'm fine. Just a little weak."

Once again, my eyes stray to North. "What happened to him?" I nod my head toward the prone form of his Alpha.

The doctor sighs and places the clipboard on a side table then faces me with his hands clasped in front of him. I feel immediately uneasy and want to bolt yet a small part of me is excited. When I focus on those feelings, wondering what is causing them when all he did was put down his clipboard and face me with a serious expression, I realize they are foreign feelings. Not my own excitement or uneasiness but they are coming from somewhere else. I nearly growl in frustration. Maybe I am not okay after all. I should probably tell the doctor about these strange feelings. I open mouth to do so but he speaks before I can and I decide I will tell him after.

"I was told to approach this delicately," he starts.

I refrain from interrupting him knowing he will get upset if I did and knowing it would only delay his answers, however I wish he would hurry.

"We were able to push back the wolfsbane in your system but I had no cure here for cyanide. A hospital in the next city over had it and I was able to call and have it transported here but by the time it got here you would have been dead."

Thrown by the turn of conversation I blinked at him and tried to process his words. "So…you're saying I should be dead right now. And it has something to do with him?" I point at North as realization begins to dawn on me. I gasp and look at my hands. "I'm a werewolf now? Is that what that strange feeling inside is?"

"Wha— no, wait, what feeling? Oh, you must mean— Ok, let me explain." The doctor's face goes through many emotions before I see understanding in his eyes.

So, he knows what is happening to me. I sigh internally, glad that I am not hallucinating and that there is an explanation for it, but if I am not a shifter then what does my rapid recovery have to do with why North is passed out on a medical bed?

I raise my brows at him, waiting for his explanation.

The doctor looks around for something then grabs it once he spots it on the side table nearer to North. He hands it to me and I stare down at it. My own face peers back up, with my brows drawn together and circles under my eyes. I look at the doctor and hold up the handheld mirror questioningly.

He stares at me, seeming to measure how I will take the news, then rushes to lay it all out before I can react, "North had to kiss you and make you his mate officially so he could transfer his healing energy to you so now you have a mark. Congrats by the way. Now he is suffering from exhaustion since he gave so much to you, against my professional opinion." He muttered the last part before turning to North to check on him.

I sit there staring at his back, wondering which part of his explanation I should freak out about the most. *Kiss. Mate. Healing energy.* My mouth opens and closes, unable to find the words to express my shock and apprehension.

My mind registers the mirror in my hand and I lift it to look at the mark he said is on me now. I did not see it before when I looked into the mirror because my hair was covering it. My hair is normally braided, but someone must have undone it. I gather my hair in one hand and hold it away from my neck as I use the mirror to try and find the mark.

It is not hard to find. Once I have my hair out of the way, the mark is obvious. It wraps around the back of my neck, from the base of my skull to just between my shoulder blades and stretches until parts of it peek around the sides of my neck. I drop my hand with the mirror to my lap and look up to the ceiling, holding in an avalanche of emotions. I breathe deeply to keep them all in and take another look at it. It looks like a tattoo of black ink. One I would find really cool on anyone else. It swirls and branches throughout my skin, the swirls each ending in sharp points.

I do not realize the doctor turned back to me until he speaks.

"It is a beautiful mark."

He is smiling down at me and his gaze flicks to the mark on each side of my neck as if to emphasize what he is talking about.

"Thanks?" I have no idea what to say to that. It is not like it was my choice to get it. I drop my hair letting it cover the back though parts of it still peek out.

"May I?" He asks, reaching out to touch it but hesitating before making contact.

I frown but nod. It feels wrong to let him touch it. Something inside urges me to lean away or threaten the man for trying to touch my mark, but I do not know why I would think that. He is a doctor, maybe he just wants to check that it did not give me a rash or something.

The doctor steps around me and moves my hair to the side. I hear his indrawn breath and turn my head to look at him over my shoulder. "What? Is everything ok?"

"It is remarkable," he says breathlessly. A second later I feel his fingertips graze over the mark.

A growl rips through the room. My eyes immediately go to North, thinking it was him, but he still lays motionless on the bed in front of me. The doctor's fingers freeze then abruptly retreat.

My eyes search the room for the source and finally see Elias glaring at us from the doorway. He stalks over, fists clenched, looking ready to rip us to shreds. I tense, expecting a fight.

"What do you think you are doing?"

Since he spoke in English, I assume he is talking to me. I open my mouth to defend myself though I do not know what I am supposedly doing wrong. Instead, when Elias reaches us, he pulls the doctor away from me and gives him the full force of his glare. My mouth shuts and I frown at the two shifters.

The doctor's eyes drop to the floor, not able to hold the gaze of his Beta. "My apologies Beta. I have never seen one and wanted a closer look." The doctor's words seem true enough but something inside me doubts he is telling the whole truth.

Elias snarls and my eyes widen at his anger.

What is the big deal?

"You know better than to touch the mark of a mate, male or female. And do not think I did not see the look in your eye."

What look? My eyes snap to the doctor to see his reaction to the accusation. Suddenly my skin feels tingly, as if ants are crawling on it. I shift on the bed and run my hands over my arms and neck, trying to get rid of it.

Elias notices my movement and sighs, some of the anger melting off his face. "I think you should leave us for now," he tells the doctor whose name I still have not gotten.

The doctor does not spare me another glance as he rushes out of the room. When the door shuts behind him, Elias faces me and the uncomfortable feeling disappears.

So strange.

"What was that about?" I ask.

Elias purses his lips and looks to the side. I roll my eyes, assuming he is not going to answer, then open my mouth to ask about North instead but Elias speaks before I can.

"You should not let anyone touch your mark…except North of course."

I stay quiet, feeling as if he will explain more if I wait.

"A mate mark is special and as Oskar said not many are seen in a lifetime, so it is tempting to look at it up close."

Oskar. That must be the doctor's name. Again, I wait silently, knowing there is more for him to say and knowing Elias, if I push, he will just give up on telling me anything. Stubborn wolf.

"However, sometimes our instincts can take over." Now he turns to look at me directly instead of the wall as he had been. His eyes flick to my mark peeking out on the sides of my neck.

"Some shifters, if too close to a mate mark that is not theirs, may start to act unnatural. Their wolves may start to take over and they may start to wonder if the mark is real. Their human minds would know it is but the wolves would sow doubt. They may bite it to mar the mark, try to claim it for themselves."

My eyes widen in horror at the images he is putting in my head. Would Oskar really have bitten me? I want to say no but I do not know him or the shifter life well enough. Instincts can be powerful.

"It was only a touch, I-I doubt he would have bitten me," I say though there is a hint of doubt in my tone.

Elias shrugs. "Who knows. Oskar is a good guy, but too much longer near your mark could change that. I would rather not risk it. Everyone knows not to touch a mate mark if they are not the mate."

"Great, so now I am going to have to be fending off pawing wolves?"

Elias surprises me with a laugh. "No, like I said, most shifters know better." He shoots a dark look at the door even though Oskar is long gone.

"*Okay,*" I say drawing out the word, "now tell me what is wrong with him. The doctor did not explain that part well."

I stand and walk over to North. It is only until I am near him, I realize how nervous and uncomfortable I was being away from him. I internally shake my head. If that is how it is going to go, then we are in for some trouble. I cannot be attached to him all day, every day. Especially since I have to—

I stop the thought before it fully forms. Instant dread and nervous energy fill my chest at the thought I almost had but I already know it is something I have to do. I can think about it later.

For now, an Alpha shifter is laying on a bed with a matching mate mark after having saved my life.

That swirling, light, happy feeling floats around inside me, dispelling the darkness I had before.

"Also, I have been…feeling things. Some of it is mine but some of it is…other. Is that a side effect from healing?"

Elias' eyes widen. "You can feel him already?"

Feel him? As in North? We both look down at the unconscious shifter.

"Fascinating," Elias whispers. He clears his throat. "As for your first question. He spent all of his energy healing you through the mate bond and is recovering. He has been out for half a day." He hesitates. "You know…he is sorry he had to complete the bond. He knows you were not ready for it, but it was the only way until the antidote could get here."

I nod. I know that but I feel like it is for me and North to discuss so I do not say anything.

"Now, as for those feelings," he says in a lighter, more excited tone that has me looking at him curiously. "You are feeling his emotions and yours at the same time. Usually, it is impossible when one is unconscious but maybe he is starting to wake or your bond is deeper. Your marks are bigger than some I have seen or heard of. What is he feeling right now?"

I look down at North then back to Elias startled. "I am feeling his emotions?" Ok, let's take a second to process that. And done. "How am I supposed to know what is his and what is mine?"

"Did you not say it feels other? Find the feelings that are strange inside."

He waits patiently but stares at me intently. I clear my throat nervously and start fiddling with the sheet near my fingers.

"Ok, well…" I focus on all the jumbled feelings inside me and try to sort them. "There is a light, fluttery feeling. It is mine, yet also…not. It is the same emotion but in me twice, if that makes sense."

Elias stays quiet, letting me figure more out.

I gasp when I find a feeling that is not mine but instantly has my heart racing and fingers twitching. "Panic. Worry."

Elias inhales through his nose sharply and looks down at North whose face shows none of this.

"Anticipation and nervousness, though some of that is my own too." I relax, done with trying to sort out mine and someone else's emotions. "Do you think we should wake him?"

Elias hums. "I do not think so. He needs rest. He will wake when he is ready."

Then all I can do is wait to talk to my mate.

Chapter 25

Norden

A nervous energy flits around inside me. Underneath the nervousness though is a bright, warm light. It calls to me and I drift toward it until it envelops me.

My eyes snap open and I quickly take in my surroundings. My wolf draws in all the scents around me until one overpowers everything else. Plants and soil after a rainfall. Floral. Spice. I latch onto it and follow it to its source.

Worried brown eyes peer at me from a bed next to where I lay. She is sitting on the edge, her fingers twisting around each other and her foot swings back and forth quickly. When she sees me awake her foot stops and she gasps.

That nervous energy I felt before intensifies and bits of apprehension seep into the mix. I wince, rubbing my chest to rid myself of the feelings. They are not mine which means…

My eyes widen when I realize I can feel Moonfire's emotions. My eyes immediately dart to her neck, looking for our mark. I did not get to see much of it before since I was focusing everything into keeping her alive but now, I see bits of it peeking out from under her loose hair.

Noticing my stare, she rubs at her neck, breaking my focus. I look back up into her eyes even though everything in me wants to make her move her hair so I can see all of the mark.

"Hello." *Wow, real smooth,* I chide myself.

"Hello," she mimics.

She stands from the bed and slowly walks over to stand at my side.

"I'm sorry about—" I start to say.

"I know you had to—" She says at the same moment.

We both chuckle nervously.

"Oh, just kiss already," a wry voice says from behind me.

I look over my shoulder to glare at my Beta but he is smiling which makes me soften my expression.

"Do you mind?" I ask and look pointedly at the door.

Elias grins and crosses his arms. "Well, actually I—"

"Leave," I growl at him.

Elias uncrosses his arms and walks to the door, chuckling as he exits.

I wait until he is gone before looking back at Moonfire. Her cheeks are red and she stares at the bed sheet below me with an intense stare. I feel a foreign emotion and it takes a moment to identify it.

Embarrassment.

I clear my throat before speaking. "So, I am guessing you know then?"

She snorts and gestures to her neck then circles her chest with a finger. "Kind of hard to miss."

My brows shoot up. "So, you can feel me?"

I was not sure she would be able to since she was not a shifter. Now I am rapidly going through the past few minutes in my mind wondering if I felt anything from my end that might embarrass me.

She nods then winces. "It is strange to feel someone else in here." She gestures to her chest again.

"I'm sure we will get used to it." I grin when I feel a leap of hope inside that is not mine. Maybe she will be more open to the bond than I thought.

I try to sit up and nearly fall back when my head spins. Who knew healing someone would make me so weak?

Moonfire rushes to help me, and her touch sends heat and awareness throughout my body.

"Thanks," I say when I am sitting up with my legs hanging over the side of the bed.

She starts to let go but I capture her hand and hold on. She gasps and looks down at our hands before looking up at me with a blush. She is so adorable. I just want to lean forward and kiss her.

The thought sends my gaze down to her lips which part slightly at my attention. I smile at her reaction and lean forward slowly, letting her know my intention and giving her time to pull away.

She doesn't.

I am only a couple inches away when her lips move. It takes me a moment to realize her lips are forming words not puckering up.

"What?" I ask, leaning back slightly to take in her whole face.

She bites her bottom lip drawing my attention to it, and I nearly miss her words again.

"I am going to New Jersey."

I frown and lean back more. I shake my head, feeling as if I misheard her. Her emotions swirl around with mine. It is hard to decipher whose is whose usually but right now I know the differences. Me: confusion and hurt, her: apprehension and determination.

"Why?" I try to stand, continuing to grip her hand, now more in desperation for her not to leave than fondness or support.

"More assassins are going to come and one of these days we might not be so lucky. We almost died! I need to end this. Now."

I hold back my immediate response of wanting to lock her away here and keep her safe. I force myself to override those protective instincts and remember who she is.

"I'm coming with you."

Moonfire shakes her head and pulls her hand away then takes a step back, trying to put some distance between us. I don't let her. I step forward until I am standing a couple inches away and she has to slightly tilt her head back to see my face. I notice her gulp and look away with flushed cheeks and I smile at her reaction to me.

"I am coming with you," I repeat.

Remembering what she was saying no to, she shakes her head again but stays close. I count it as progress.

"You are the Alpha here not to mention the Prince of werewolves and the top of the Order's hit list. You cannot just leave and put yourself at risk."

"I am not letting you go alone," I argue.

She sighs and looks to the side, thinking. Finally, she says, "Fine, then I will not go alone. I will bring Janie."

My brows rise at her words. "Janie?" I frown at her skeptically. "I don't know about that. She is not a dominant wolf. She has not had much training with battle. Take Elias."

She shakes her head again. "As much as Elias and me have grown to accept each other, he is your Beta and needs to be here with you. What if another assassin comes while I am gone? I cannot protect you."

I snort and shake my head. "Honey, I can protect myself. Plus, Elias and I have been separated before. I will feel much better with Elias by your side."

Moonfire sighs. "Fine. Elias and Janie then." She steps away and starts to walk toward the door before I can protest her decision about Janie.

I grumble and stalk after her. Before she reaches the door, I grab her hand and spin her towards me. She squeaks and reaches out a hand to my chest to steady herself.

"Aren't you forgetting something?" I ask in a low tone.

She frowns and peers around me toward the bed then gasps. "My Danishes. Did Ralf bring them here?"

I growl and pull her closer. "No, not your Danishes. Though I will buy you as many as you want after this. I mean, we should…" I lean down to whisper the last four words in her ear, "talk about the kiss."

She shivers and I feel curiosity and desire coming from her. Being able to feel her emotions is fast becoming one of my favorite things.

She leans back enough to look up at me. "What about it? You mean the fact you did not ask or that I don't remember it? Or about how you marked me forever because of it?"

Her words sound like she is angry, but her feelings are not as tough. Anyone else may think she is berating me and maybe she is but I know she has accepted what happened already and is more curious how it would be when she is awake.

Instead of answering her questions, I lean down and press our lips together.

She gasps, and I freeze against her, waiting for her to pull away, but she surprises me by leaning in and pressing her lips more firmly against mine. I reach up a hand to tangle into her loose hair and bring my other up to rest on her hip. I use my hand in her hair to angle her head so I can kiss her deeper. She moans against my mouth and I cannot help but smile at the reaction I cause in her.

Our emotions swirl inside me, causing my head to spin and filling me so much I think I will burst. I never thought we would end up like this after meeting her in Peru. I had hoped but three bullets to the chest quickly staunched that hope. Now, with her in my arms, and against my lips, I am eternally grateful she was assigned to assassinate me. I could have done without the scare caused by her almost dying though.

We break away after who knows how long, breathing hard and feeling hot all over. We have not moved from the place near the door but it feels like we just took a trip around the world.

"Now, *that's* a kiss," she whispers, causing us both to chuckle.

I place my forehead against hers and rub my thumb up and down the back of her neck.

She gasps and I feel her shiver as bumps rise on her skin. "Oh my, that feels…"

I search inside me and pause my rubbing when I see what it is making her feel. I grin and start rubbing it again. She leans into my hand and closes her eyes, humming contentedly.

"It is the mark," I explain.

"The mark? It did not feel this good when Oskar touched it."

My hand freezes and my whole body tenses. "He. Did. What!?"

Her eyes shoot open, feeling my sudden anger. I take my hands off her and move her aside then yank open the door. Before I get one foot out, her hand latches onto my arm and tugs me back.

"You do not need to be mad. Elias already took care of it."

It takes a moment for her words to register but they only diminish my rage a little. I reach out to the pack link and call for Elias before focusing on my mate once again. I place my hands on her shoulders and rub them, reassuring myself she is ok and mine.

"You know, I did not really understand why it was such a big deal—" I open my mouth to tell her why but she continues, "but Elias told me and I guess I can understand. Although if you get all macho, ragey-wolf on everyone who touches me I think we will have to have a little chat." She arches a brow at me, suggesting the chat would be of the fist-in-face variety.

I do not want anyone touching her, not even a friendly pat on the back but I tamp down my urges. She does not understand our life and does not have the same instincts. I have a feeling I will have to be reminding my wolf half of that much more than he would like.

I take a deep breath, trying to put the image of the doctor touching her mark out of my mind and nod. "Only if they touch your mark, got it."

"That's not what—"

I kiss her again, cutting off her words. She melts into it and I smile against her lips.

"Don't think this means you won," she mumbles against me.

I chuckle but do not argue.

Elias comes a few minutes later and smiles at seeing us awake and healthy. We had stopped kissing by the time he came in, but our faces must have shown something of it because he smiles slyly at us.

"I see you have been newly acquainted."

I roll my eyes and turn him around, pushing him out of the medical room and following him out. Moonfire follows after us, shutting the door behind her.

I take her hand and hold it in mine as we walk down the corridor to the security room. Her hand is warm and sends tingles of awareness up my arm. Her feelings swirl around inside me, melding with my own, in harmony for the first time.

In the security room, it is just the three of us. We sit at the table in the middle of the room and I immediately jump into the plan Moonfire and I barely put together.

"Moonfire insists on going to New Jersey to end this once and for all. Apparently, I am not allowed to go."

I pause and glare at my mate, but she holds my stare and gives me a single nod. Usually, my wolf would rise at the challenge but instead he feels proud of our mate for standing up to us. I on the other hand could do without it in this instance. I do not like the idea of being so far from her and letting her go into danger. Thankfully she will not be alone.

"So, I need you to go with her, watch her back."

"And Janie will come too," Moonfire adds. "Well, if she wants to."

Elias frowns at her addition. "Janie is not a dominant wolf and she does not have any battle experience."

"Let us leave that up to her," she counters.

Again, I am surprised at her authority which would usually be a challenge to a dominant wolf but Elias only nods then shoots me an amused smile.

"Are you sure you want to leave?" He asks, turning back to Moonfire. "You just connected with your mate."

She blushes and my hand is rising to rub her cheek where it is reddening before I realize what I am doing. My touch only makes her blush harder but a smile creeps on to her lips. I wish we were alone so I could taste those lips again.

Elias clears his throat, reminding me we are not alone.

I sit back and drop my hand.

"Yes, I am sure. Dorian will keep sending people to kill us if I don't meet him where he least expects. Since he will not be expecting me to show up at HQ, we can take him by surprise."

Elias leans forward and places his elbows on the table. "Are you going to kill him?"

I expect Moonfire to balk at the idea, but she calmly stares back. "Not if I can help it, but I will if it becomes necessary."

Sometimes I forget she is an assassin and can kill so easily.

"Alright then, Luna. When do you want to leave?"

I am pleased to hear him use the revered name. It means he finally accepts her and even respects her.

"Tomorrow morning." Then she looks between us nervously. "And I guess you should know my name now. My real name is Jessie."

As much as I like hearing her called Luna and as much as I love the nickname Moonfire, my heart soars at hearing her real name. It is as if it was a barrier keeping us from being completely open with one another and now that barrier is gone. She trusts me. She likes me. Maybe even loves me.

I grin at her and smooth my hand over her hair.

"Jessie."

Chapter 26

Jessie

My name on his lips repeats itself over and over in my mind. Each time the memory of it surfaces, little thrills explode in my belly and my mark seems to warm. I have to consciously stop myself from rubbing the mark on my neck when once again the memory of him saying my name in that soft, loving tone enters my mind as I am standing in the Main Hall waiting for the others to show up the next day.

Ralf hovers a few feet behind me, silent and more distant than he was before our outing. I wonder if he is mad at me or hates me all over again for the incident. But every time I attempted to approach him yesterday, he found some excuse to divert the topic to something else.

I look around but no one has arrived yet, so I decide to force Ralf to talk to me before I leave and lose the chance. I stalk over to him and put my hands on my hips. He raises a brow but otherwise does not move.

"Well?" I ask and wave a hand in the air.

His other brow goes higher which I did not think possible. "Well, what?"

I huff and shift my weight to my other foot. "Well, why are you not talking to me. I thought we were passed the whole I-hate-your-guts-because-you're-an-assassin thing."

Ralf chokes on air and coughs a couple times. "That's what you think?" He asks when he has his airways under control again.

I throw my hands in the air. "Well, yeah. Why else would you be so distant after the incident?"

Ralf steps closer and places a hand on my shoulder. "Luna—"

"It's Jessie, actually," I interrupt. The cat is already out of the bag, no sense in trying to shove it back in.

Ralf stares a moment, processing the new information, then begins again. "Luna," I roll my eyes but do not interrupt this time, "I am not avoiding you because I do not like you. I admire the fact you fought beside my Alpha and that you are his mate." His eyes flick to my mark for a second before meeting my eyes again. "I am avoiding you because I feel as if I have failed you."

My mouth drops open. "Failed me? You are crazy if you think that." I shake my head and place my hand over his which is still on my shoulder. "If it was not for you, I would probably be dead right now."

Ralf shakes his head, but I squeeze his hand to hold off his protests. "Seriously, Ralf, thank you for carrying me back to the castle."

Ralf stares at me, searching my gaze to see if I am serious then finally nods, accepting my words.

A low, familiar growl sounds behind me. Ralf instantly yanks his hand back and stands up straighter. I shake my head and turn around to see my mate glaring at Ralf. I walk over to North and smack him on the arm.

"Quit that."

North quiets and looks down at me, his face transforming from protective fierceness to soft fondness as he snakes his arms around my waist and leans down to nestle his nose in the curve of my neck. I blush and try to push him away, but he holds on tight.

"North," I whine. "People are going to see us."

He chuckles, the sound vibrating against my skin. His emotions swirl around inside me, humor and love.

"Let them see."

I push again, and this time he pulls back but keeps one of his hands around my lower back. I will not admit out loud that I love the contact.

His smirk tells me he knows though, and I have to wonder if this bond is going to be problematic. At least he cannot read my mind.

"Aww, you two are adorable."

Janie comes down the hall from the main doors, smiling widely with a bag around her shoulder.

I disengage from North and go to give her a hug. Before I reach her, she holds up a bag and my slow steps turn into a sprint. I grab the bag and open it, inhaling the delicious aroma of pastries, then hug her harder.

When I pull back my smile falters as the situation we are about to embark on comes to mind. "Are you sure you want to come? It is not too late to say no."

She frowns and tightens her hold on the strap of her bag. "I am sure. You are my friend and Mr. Kane is my Alpha."

"Janie, you can call me North." North comes to stand by my side and gives the baker a friendly smile.

Janie nods but it does not look like she fully agrees.

"It will take some time to drive to the airport, then our flight leaves this afternoon, so we should be going," Elias says from behind me.

North and I turn to meet him, but I frown at who is tagging along.

"What is she doing here?" I slightly position my body so it is in front of North as Danika comes closer.

She snorts, but there is no hostility in it. "I am coming with you."

"No!" North and I shout simultaneously.

Elias lets out a long-suffering sigh. "She insists. She claims it is payment for you saving her life."

I look to Danika again, wondering if Elias is serious. She does not deny it.

"But I barely did anything," I say.

"It was something to me," Danika argues with conviction.

I eye her up and down and notice for the first time that she is wearing simple jeans, sneakers, and a black long-sleeved shirt. I do not think I have ever seen her so casual.

I look to North and shrug.

"Danika, if you do anything to—"

Danika holds up a hand, cutting off North. "I am not going to hurt her. I can obviously see there is a bond between you and will not interfere." Her eyes flit to our marks and something akin to hurt flashes in her eyes but it is gone in the blink of an eye and she walks confidently past us toward the doors.

After a moment she turns back and puts her hands on her hips. "Well? Are you coming?"

North and I look to each other, and even though we cannot read each other's minds, I seem to know what he is thinking.

You can trust her. Be careful. I love you.

I reach up and kiss him. He pulls me closer, deepening the connection. After a moment we pull back and take deep breaths.

"I will come back. I promise," I tell him.

He leans forward and rests his head against mine. "I will be waiting."

I pull away before I change my mind about this mission and walk toward Danika. Steps sound behind me and Janie appears beside me. Elias comes to take position on my other side and together the four of us leave the castle in Germany to end these attacks once and for all.

I debate taking them directly to The Dressy Cleaners but decide some food and planning will be better. Plus, my guns and knives are at home, and we will need all the weapons we can get if we are going to go into the den of assassins.

We take an Uber from the airport, but I have the driver drop us off a block away from my apartment, in front of a pizza parlor. I wait until the driver leaves then turn to my group and gesture for them to go into the pizza parlor behind them.

Danika turns and looks the restaurant up and down before lifting her lip in disgust. "This is where the infamous Infinite Order is located?"

I scoff. "No, Danika. This is where pizza is located. I thought we could eat before going to my place."

She raises her nose in the air and sniffs as if taking in all the smells of the place before shrugging and marching into the parlor.

Janie and I look at each other and roll our eyes simultaneously which sends us both into a fit of laughter. It has been forever since I laughed with someone like that. Elias is already inside when Janie and I finally walk in. One of the waitresses in the back shouts for us to sit wherever we want so we choose a booth in the back where a little peace can be found in the hubbub of the restaurant.

"What is the plan?" Janie asks once we are situated and a waitress has taken our order.

Danika and Elias look to me for the answer too.

I grab the discarded wrapper to my straw and absently fold it and unfold it as I speak. "I think we should take a look at The Dressy Cleaners after we eat for you three to get an idea of where this showdown will be taking place and then we can scout the entrances and exits. Then we will go to my place to stock up on weapons and finalize any plans and head out in the morning to finish this."

"Why do we not end this tonight?" Danika asks, her fist clenching on the table.

"He may not be there. He is a businessman and follows business hours. Even though he is immortal he is still human, or I assume he is, and needs sleep. I have never known him to stay beyond closing time. I do not want to risk going in and getting caught before we have a chance to talk to him or kill him if it comes to that."

"Oh, it will come to that," Danika says assuredly.

I bristle at her words. Dorian may be the head of an assassin organization and an immortal who apparently keeps secrets but he is still the closest thing I have to family. I will not resort to killing him until I have a chance to convince him to drop the hit order on North and find out if there is any truth to Little Red's confession.

"We should go to his house. That way we can avoid…Dressy Cleaning altogether," Danika says Dressy Cleaning as if it is disgusting and beneath her to ever go to such a place.

"First off, it is *The* Dressy Clean*ers*." Danika rolls her eyes. "And secondly, I do not know where he lives. Everyone in my line of work is very secretive when it comes to things like that," I say.

Elias jumps in before Danika can suggest anything else. "Jessie is right, we will wait until morning, that way we have more time to stakeout the place and plan. I trust her judgement."

I stare at him, surprised by the support, but no one has time to say anything because the waitress comes by and drops our pizzas off with a bright smile and loud, cheerful voice.

"Here you go! If you need anything else, let me know! Our special dessert today is cheesecake."

We murmur our thanks and she flies off to the next table. We spend the next half hour scarfing down pizza and soda, dropping the subject of assassinations for now.

I eat quite a bit, but it is nothing compared to the wolves around me. They finish two and a half pizzas together and still order cheesecake to go. I try not to stare at them though I am amazed by their appetite.

Once the check is paid for I guide them out of the restaurant and look around before heading in the direction of The Dressy Cleaners. The journey is longer than it normally would be since we are on foot, but the others do not complain. I watch everyone and everything, on guard even though the Infinite Order probably does not know I am here in New Jersey.

"Expecting trouble?" Elias whispers next to me, after I stop for the third time and look around before turning down the next road.

I shrug. "Never can be too careful."

He does not say anything, but I see the three of them tense and move in closer to me. The action warms my heart and I suddenly feel like I am part of their pack despite being human. I cannot help but smile as we continue down the street.

After a while I come to a stop near a shop selling crystals and buddhas. I feign interest in the displays in the window but focus my eyes so they see the objects in the reflection instead.

"The Dressy Cleaners is the shop there across the street," I say in a low tone.

People continue to walk past us oblivious that an assassin organization is right across the street from them. The Dressy Cleaners is one of the only shops on the street to have its own parking lot albeit a small one. I see three vans in the lot, each with The Dressy Cleaners logo on the side—A pink circle with DC written in fancy lettering in its middle and a suit jacket above the letters also inside the circle. The lights inside are off making it look like everyone has left but it is still early evening, so I know others are still inside, just not Dorian.

I wave for them to follow me and go inside the crystal shop. The shopkeeper shouts a greeting and I wave but otherwise we ignore each other as I walk to the items in the display window. Now that we are inside, I look across the street at the building of The Dressy Cleaners and the others line up next to me doing the same.

"There are cameras on each side of the building and some at the edges of the property," I say. "I can probably disable them, but I will need to do it when we are ready to go inside."

"Then what are we supposed to do now if we cannot get close?" Janie asks.

"I just wanted you to see the location and get an idea of what we will be up against. The rest I can tell you at my place. I can draw some maps and we can plan there."

Elias grumbles but otherwise does not object. Danika on the other hand, of course, has an issue.

"That is it? We come here and do nothing?" She mumbles something in German but since I do not understand it I give it little thought.

I let them take one last look at The Dressy Cleaners before waving for them to follow me out. I walk right out of the store toward my apartment wishing for a moment for my scooter so I would not have to walk so far. Elias and Janie talk to each other while Danika and I stay quiet. We reach my apartment, but I continue walking past it and turn down a different street. I repeat the random turning and circling back until I am satisfied we have not been followed then finally stop in front of my apartment building and stare up at it.

"This is where you live?" Janie asks, stepping next to me and staring up at the brick building with me.

I look to her, not able to read what her emotions are about it. I look up at the building again and try to see it from her perspective. It is not that bad of a building. It is made of bricks and some are cracked and the door leading into the building could use a wash but otherwise the windows in front and their little balconies give the place a nice elegant look. It is the alley on the side that kind of ruins the look with the overfilled dumpsters and the questionable fire escape. However, that part cannot be seen from here.

"You are telling me this was your place the whole time? Then why did we walk past it three times?!" Danika shouts.

I turn to her, surprised. "You noticed?"

She snorts and crosses her arms. "Of course, I noticed."

I look her up and down, taking in this new side of Danika, impressed by her observation then nod and turn back to the door in front of me.

I have to resist the urge to go around to the alley and climb up the fire escape to my apartment. I lead them through the front door, which feels odd because I think I have ever only gone through the front door a handful of times, then up the stairs.

I look around once more before entering my apartment on the fourth floor, quickly ushering everyone in before locking the door and listening for suspicious sounds on the other side. Satisfied no one is there I sigh and turn to the others. The three of them stand in the middle of the room looking around at my minimal possessions. Elias walks to the windowsill where my succulent is placed and looks out at the alley below.

Janie walks to the fridge and opens it then grimaces at the smell that comes out from the probably-moldy Chinese food left in there. Danika walks to the other doors and opens them, first finding the bathroom then my bedroom in which she goes into, probably to snoop around.

I leave Elias and Janie and follow Danika into my room, trusting her the least and because I need to grab a few things.

Danika is scowling at the room when I walk in and I take a moment to look around from her perspective. My bed with its thick blue-gray comforter askew and a laundry hamper in the corner that probably needs to be emptied soon. A single nightstand with a lamp but no personal items displayed. Dark curtains covering the window leaving the room in darkness. I shrug, not really caring what Danika thinks of my room, and go to the closet where my weapons are stashed.

I pull some out and find places to hide them on my body then leave the closet and grab some paper and a pencil from my nightstand before turning back to the door to get this planning started. I stop in my tracks when I see Danika staring at me.

"What?" I ask, trying hard to control the annoyance in my tone.

Danika shakes her head and turns to the door. "Nothing."

I shake my head at her back as she walks out and follow her, closing my bedroom door on my way out.

"Ok, now that everyone has had a chance to snoop, let's get down to business."

Janie looks up from one of the drawers in the kitchen and Elias comes over from my small desk in the corner. We converge around the sofa in the middle of the room and I place the paper on the coffee table.

I wait until everyone finds a seat whether on the floor or on the couch next to me before beginning.

"Ok so I am going to draw out the building," I start as I sketch the outline of the The Dressy Cleaners, "and mark the entrances and points of interest, from there we—"

A knock at the door interrupts me and all of our heads shoot up to stare at it.

"Expecting someone?" Elias asks in a low tone. His eyes flash his wolfy color as he stands and crosses to it.

I follow him, frowning at the door. "No, and none of my neighbors usually bother me."

When neither of us open it, the door handle jiggles. I suck in a breath and reach for a dagger in a sheath at my waist. Elias tenses and I see his fingernails shift into claws.

I hear Danika and Janie come closer and know they are probably doing the same thing as Elias.

Elias reaches for the doorknob just as foreign feelings pass through me. Impatience. Longing. Curiosity. Hope.

I frown at the strange feelings and wonder what it is from. Then I remember my new connection to a certain someone and reach out to Elias. "Wait—"

But Elias already has the door open and is grabbing the man by the throat.

Chapter 27

Norden

I feel my eyes shift to their wolf counterpart's and my Alpha power roll off me in waves until Elias lets go of me and the three wolves in the apartment are showing me their necks. When I am satisfied there is no danger and that everyone realizes who they were about to attack, I ease up on the power and stroll into the apartment.

My eyes instantly find Jessie and I feel her emotions intensify. Longing. Confusion. Excitement. A little annoyance.

I grin and hold my arms out to my side in invitation for her to come and hug me. "Miss me?"

She does not step forward but instead frowns at me. "How did you find me?" Then she shoots an accusatory glare at Elias.

Elias holds up his hands. "It was not me. I have not had time to call him."

She looks at me for an answer.

I shut the door behind me before moving further into the room and sitting on the couch. I take a quick look around, curious about where my mate has been living. The room is bare except for a couch, tv, and coffee table. I spot the kitchen from here and notice it is clean and tidy. I crane my neck further around and spot a desk in the far corner and a little succulent next to the window. I remember her telling me about the plant and smile at seeing it. There are no photos or personal items on the walls or shelves. I spot a couple doors off to the side, but they are closed. I focus back on the group who has moved closer and all stare at me with varying degrees of bewilderment.

Although they are all waiting for answers, I look to Jessie when I respond.

"Elias has been searching for your identity since you came to Germany, so I had the trackers finish his search and they finally cracked your location. Well as close to your location as possible. They narrowed it down to this neighborhood so when I arrived, all I had to do was follow the feeling." I tap my chest to emphasize what feeling I am referencing.

She frowns and places a hand over her heart. "Why did I not feel you?"

A pang of hurt flashes through me and her chagrin tells me she feels it. I push the hurt away and send feelings of reassurance to her before responding. "Maybe you were focused on getting here without being seen or maybe because you are not used to these supernatural things yet." I shrug letting her know I am only guessing.

"Wait, so you can track me with…" She waves a finger between us. "Our bond?" She crosses her arms and looks more like the Moonfire I know. "Well, I don't like that at all."

I laugh and move to stand in front of her. When I place my hands on her shoulders and look into her eyes, I feel her emotions turn from annoyance to something more heated. Before I can lean down and kiss her, Elias interrupts.

"But that does not explain *why* you came?"

I turn my head to look at my Beta but keep my hold on Moonfire. The touch calms me, reassures my wolf.

"I changed my mind," I say.

Elias growls. "You should not be here."

Danika surprisingly chimes in. "He is right. We have this handled. You should not be here putting yourself in danger."

I look to her then Janie who is staring at all of us with wide eyes then back to Elias. "I could not stay behind." I stare at Elias, hoping he will get my underlying meaning. *I could not stay behind without her.*

Elias sighs and runs his hands through his white-blond hair.

I look back down to Jessie who has not said anything in a while. "What do you think? Can I stay?"

She rolls her eyes and smiles. "It is not like I can really say no."

"Of course, you can," I say.

She snorts. "Yeah, but you would probably stay right outside the door like a lost puppy."

I laugh and draw her into a hug.

After a moment she hugs me back. I bask in her warmth until she pulls back and clears her throat. "Ok, we should probably get back to our plan."

She sits on the couch and looks up to me, waiting. I sit next to her, making sure our sides are completely touching. I feel a zing of heat go through me and know it is a shared feeling.

The others find seats around the table, whether on the floor or remaining space on the couch and look to the paper on the table. There is a shape drawn on it but otherwise has no markings.

"We were just talking about the building and what will need to be done when we get inside," Jessie informs me.

I nod and she grabs the paper and a pen to continue her sketch.

After some time, the sun is set and our plan is made. I lean back in the couch and stretch. I feel my mate's eyes on me, specifically the bit of skin I expose with my stretch and hold my position a moment longer, basking in her attention before righting myself. I look to Jessie and smile slowly. Her cheeks redden and she turns away and clears her throat. She stands up suddenly and claps her hands. "Well, I guess that is it for the night. I will grab some extra blankets and pillows." She grimaces as she looks around the room. "I am sorry, but I do not have much."

Elias stands next and shakes his head reassuringly. "This will do."

My wolf rises with the sun. Without thinking I reach through the bond to find Jessie and smile when I feel her peace and sleepiness from the other room. I scan the area around me and see Elias already awake and in the kitchen, frowning into an empty fridge. Danika sits up and stretches on the couch still half asleep. I am sure Janie is awake, but I cannot see her since she is still with Jessie behind the closed door of the bedroom.

Wolves usually preferred an early morning run and mine stretches inside me wanting out, but a wolf running around New Jersey is not a good idea so I have to tamper him down and promise he can come out later.

Elias shuts the fridge door with a shake of his head and heads for the door. I do not ask where he is going, trusting he knows to be safe and back in time. I stand from the floor underneath the window with the succulent just as the bedroom door opens and Janie slips out. Her eyes meet mine across the room.

At my raised brow she nods her head to the door behind her. "Still sleeping," she responds to my unspoken question.

I know that already, but it makes my wolf settle knowing someone else is looking out for her too. I walk toward the bedroom and ease open the door, peeking inside before stepping into the room and shutting the door behind me. I take a moment to watch my mate sleep, no worries bothering her, tangled sheets around her legs. Even in her sleep she looks beautiful and dangerous. How did I get so lucky?

A thought comes to me about testing to see just how dangerous she is and I grin wickedly. Without effort, I shift into my wolf and pad over to the foot of the bed. Her foot is sticking out and I lick it waiting with subdued laughter for her reaction. When nothing happens, my wolf huffs and I move to her left side where her face is toward the wall, away from the door. I put my front two paws on the bed and lean over her. I am about to lick her ear when suddenly her eyes shoot open and her arm is around my neck. Next thing I know she is flipping me onto the bed, my jaw and claws faced away from her and a knife is at my throat. My body freezes, though inside, my wolf is ready for a fight and I lift my lips in a silent snarl. Another part of me is smug and thrilled at how dangerous and quick she is. I have no idea where the knife came from but she seems to be ready for anything. Even a wolf in her bedroom.

I know the moment she recognizes me because the feeling in my chest lightens and a burst of happiness and playfulness fills me, settling next to mine. I yip like a pup and crane my neck back to lick her, unafraid of the knife at my throat.

She groans and pulls back, wiping at her wet face with the back of her hand holding the knife. With the threat gone, I turn back into my human self and laugh as I watch my mate's eyes go wide and cheeks turn red. She squeezes her eyes shut and throws her blanket over my body, covering my nakedness.

"North, what the hell? I could have killed you. And why are you in here? If I wanted you here I would have let you stay with me last night instead of Janie."

"Oh, come now, Moonfire. You would not have killed me. You *love me*," I tease, drawing out the last two words.

She grumbles and shakes her head as she climbs out of bed. "What time is it?" She asks, changing the topic.

She checks her clock on the nightstand and sighs. "I guess we better go soon if we want to get there before regular business hours."

Part of our plan is to be inside The Dressy Cleaners before the surrounding businesses open for the day. That way when we break in, there will be less witnesses and maybe even less assassins inside.

She leaves the room without looking back and before I can follow her she comes back to the doorway and tosses my bag at me. I catch it before it can hit me and she leaves before I can say thanks.

I hear her talking to Janie and Danika and smile as I dress in fresh clothes when I hear Janie's embarrassed squeak and Danika's laughter.

When I come into the living room, Jessie is nowhere to be seen but the shower running in the bathroom tells me she has escaped into there, probably still annoyed with me. I check into the bond and know it is nothing to worry about.

A while later, Elias comes through the door with a box in one hand and a carrier of coffees in the other.

Jessie comes out of the bathroom rubbing at her hair with a towel, a cloud of steam billowing behind her. She lets out a delighted squeal when she spots the box and coffee and holds out her hands toward them.

"Gimme, gimme," she says, practically salivating as Elias sets it all on the counter and opens the box to reveal doughnuts.

She moans when she takes her first bite of a doughnut. After scarfing down half of it she turns to salute Janie with it. "Not as good as your pastries, don't worry. But still good, so everyone come and eat. We have to go soon."

That was all we needed and soon we were all crowding the box and cradling a cup of coffee.

"Thanks Elias."

"Yeah thanks!"

"Thank you, Beta."

Everyone chimes in as they eat their fill in sugary food.

"Yeah, well, when I saw how empty and disgraceful Jessie's fridge was, I knew breakfast was going to have to be brought here." Elias says after swallowing a bite of an apple fritter.

"Can we keep him?" Jessie asks, her lips pouting as she looks to me with pleading eyes.

I chuckle, loving the way we are all bonding and hanging out like a family. It is almost as if we do not have a serious, risky mission in a few minutes. I hope after our mission today, we can have more moments like this.

All too soon, the mood shifts as everyone prepares to leave. Jessie has a bag full of weapons on the couch and straps them to her body in various places. Her fedora is the last thing to be put on and she turns to us with her hands on her hips.

"Ready?"

I sigh, my body suddenly tense and waves of nervousness course through me, both my own and Jessie's. We share a knowing look and I force a feeling of confidence to pass through me so she will feel it too. She gives me a small smile before leading us out the door and to the street below.

We are quiet as we traverse the city that is starting to wake up. Shops all around are closed but a few people bustle about trying to get to their first place of the day. Eventually Jessie slows and holds her hand out to stop us going further.

She turns and looks us each in the eye, bouncing on the balls of her feet and gripping the straps around her chest. "This is it. Everyone know their part?"

We all nod.

"Good." She glances behind her. "Then it is now or never."

She turns a corner and there, across the street, is a seemingly empty shop with a sign above the doors depicting it as The Dressy Cleaners. It is a plain, white building with barely any windows and a small, empty parking lot other than two white vans with the logo on the side. It is tiny compared to the towers and buildings around it, but it also makes it less noticeable. A good thing for a secret order of assassins.

We cross the street and creep up on the parking lot of the building. I immediately go to stand behind Jessie, my instincts wanting to protect her back as we go forward. She unholsters a gun from her side and aims. A second later she fires two shots, and a small spark lets us know she hit her marks. With the cameras on this side destroyed we are not afraid to run across the lot to the wall, taking us one step closer to the Order.

Jessie leads us to the back of the building and shoots once more at a spot above a door before coming around the corner fully. She yanks open the back door and waves us in. Inside is a long dark hallway with laundry bins by the doorway. They look like they had not been used in a long time and the smell coming from them was of dust. Jessie ignores the bins and moves slowly down the hall keeping her hands on her gun in a ready position. None of us talk, knowing the key is silence right now. I continue to keep close to Jessie's back and look around for any threats.

Eventually we come to a part of the hall that is actually lit and looks clean which means it is used more often, yet Jessie does not slow down. When we come across a section that veers right Jessie stops and finally turns to us.

In a whisper she explains, "Third door down there leads to the artifact room."

That is the signal we needed. Elias, Janie, and Danika nod then split from us to go in the direction she mentioned. Our plan is for them to search the room for the Chalice, which I had to let Janie and Danika know about last night, while Jessie and I distract Dorian.

Jessie waits a moment to watch them leave then waves me onward, back down the hall away from the others. It does not take long until we are near the front of the building and Jessie turns left. She puts her gun away and instead grabs two daggers from sheaths at her side.

Two women walk out of a room on the right oblivious to our presence until one looks up and gasps. She stops midstride causing the other women to look up and halt as well. They stare wide eyed at Jessie, all of us tense, waiting for the other to react first.

Quick as lightning Jessie tosses one of her blades at the woman on the right. The woman tries to dodge it, but it embeds in her shoulder before she can fully move out of the way. The other woman grabs something at her waist, but I growl, showing my wolf eyes, which makes her freeze. My claws extend as I leap forward, but she finishes grabbing the item from her waistband. She aims it at me but before she can get a shot off, I swipe at her wrist with my claws and she screams in pain as the gun goes flying. Jessie knocks out the woman with the knife in her shoulder then yanks it out before she collapses then turns to my opponent and tosses her dagger. The handle hits her in the temple, and she goes down. Jessie picks it up and cleans it on the fallen woman's shirt before standing and continuing down the hall. As we pass, I can see the room the woman came from is some sort of break room.

The only other door is on the left not too far from the break room. Jessie stops outside it and looks to me. Her face is masking her emotions, but I feel them as if they are my own. She is nervous. Betrayed. Yet still feeling love for the person on the other side of the door, a familial love.

I nod to her, letting her know I am with her and send reassurance through our bond.

This ends here one way or another.

Chapter 28

Jessie

I kick open the door to Dorian's office and rush in, daggers raised. Too many emotions swirl inside for me to sort but soon one comes to the forefront. Confusion.

"Where is he?" North asks from behind.

I growl in frustration and sheath my daggers. "I have an idea where he might be, but we should search here before moving on."

I move further into the room until I am behind his desk. North checks the hall before closing the door and going to a file cabinet near a bookcase to search.

I yank open a drawer in Dorian's desk and rifle through the contents before banging it shut and moving to the next. When I find nothing useful in the last drawer, I slam it harder than necessary and turn to see North's progress.

"It is not here. Have you found anything?"

North shuts the last drawer of the file cabinet with more care than I would have given it and shakes his head.

I press my lips together and go for the door. "Then let's meet up with the others and see how they are faring."

Before I reach it, North stops me. "Wait, let's look in one more place." Then he starts pulling at books on the bookcase.

I stare at him, confused. "What are you doing? I don't think the Chalice will be behind the books."

North keeps going, finishing with one shelf then moving to the next, his movements quick as he scans and pulls each book before putting it back in place.

"Dorian is old, like Victorian age old at my guess. Those kinds of people tend to have secret rooms especially when they are trying to hide something," North explains.

My mouth drops open. How had I never thought to check for a secret room in a secret order of assassins? No, this is not a castle or an old building that would have something like that. Dorian was not the one to have the building built. However, the location of HQ has been here as long as I have known, and if Dorian is as old as

North claims, a secret room would be nothing for him to install.

I move closer and watch as North works through the bookcase searching for a trigger. I am trying not to get my hopes up, but anticipation bubbles up inside me. It would be so cool to find a secret room in here. North pauses over a book suddenly and lets out a bark of laughter. I study the book, wondering what made him stop then laugh.

The Picture of Dorian Gray.

"No, it can't be that easy, can it?" I ask.

North shoots me a wide grin. "It is only obvious if you know who he is. Let's find out if this is it."

Slowly he reaches for the book. My fingers tingle wanting to reach out and grab it. I grip the straps across my torso to hold myself back and wait with bated breath as North finally touches the book and pulls.

We both tense, but when nothing happens, I let out a disappointed breath and my shoulders drop.

"Well, that was anticlimactic."

Just as I finish the sentence, North pulls the book completely off the shelf and instantly there is a clicking noise. One side of the bookcase slightly pops forward.

I gasp and let out a short laugh. "No way."

I reach for the side that moved and pull it toward me. The bookcase swings open like a door. North and I step back and peer inside, not yet wanting to enter it. It is smaller than I expected, more like a walk-in closet than a real room. I take in the artifacts set up as displays like a museum and gasp when my eyes land on something to the right of the opening. I look toward the office door, expecting someone to suddenly burst in, but when nothing happens, I step into the secret room with North close on my heels.

I approach the painting hung on the wall and stare at it, partly grossed out and partly amazed. "Is this what I think it is?"

North steps closer and brushes a finger over the image. "I believe so."

"No wonder he wants a secret room if it is to hide something like this," I say.

The image is grotesque. Almost like a zombie but it is undeniably my boss. My boss if he was wearing 18th century clothing and had his skin peeling off.

"So, this is how…" I can't bring myself to say it.

North nods, knowing what I am thinking. "This is how we kill him." He reaches around me and grabs the painting off the wall. "If it comes to that."

I gasp at what is behind the painting. "Whoa, another mystery hiding place? Dorian really likes his secrets. Thankfully I am good at breaking into safes." I crack my fingers in anticipation then move closer to the wall safe that was previously hidden behind the painting.

I press my ear against the metal and turn the lock, listening for a click. I turn it a few more times before sighing in disappointment and leaning back. I gesture toward the safe as I say, "Ok, usually, I am good at breaking into safes, but I can't hear anything without my tools."

North steps forward and crowds me. I gasp and try to step back but I am already against the wall.

"What are you doing?"

North smirks down at me, and I feel a pulse of satisfaction from him. "Don't worry I am not going to kiss you…"

I feel a pang of disappointment even though I know it is not the right time or place for such things.

"…yet," he adds. Before I can say anything he explains, "I can use my shifter hearing to listen for whatever it is you're looking for."

Super hearing. Of course. I nod and make room for him to take my place. He presses his ear against the metal like I had before then looks at me.

"What am I listening for?"

I twist the lock dial slowly and whisper, "Let me know when you hear a click."

We are silent for a few moments as I slowly twist the dial. I am staring so hard at North that I know the moment he hears something when his eyes slightly widen and he inhales sharply.

"There"

I nod encouragement then twist the dial the opposite direction and wait again for his confirmation.

He nods again and smiles. I feel pride and excitement in my chest but I know it is him feeling those things. The more I open myself up to these foreign emotions the more I can identify whose emotions I am feeling in the moment. His feelings have an underlying sense of Other and adrenaline. Mine feel more familiar and sneakier.

I twist the dial the opposite way and almost immediately he nods. I stop as the door clicks open a fraction. North straightens and reaches for the door eagerly.

North exhales in obvious relief as the dark interior is shown. He reaches in and pulls out the Chalice. The light from above causes the gold to shine and the jewels to sparkle.

"So, we have the Chalice and the painting. Let's go find the others," I say.

North takes a moment longer to inspect his relic then nods and turns to the door, gesturing for me to go first. I grab the painting and leave the small hidden room, North close on my heels. He closes the bookcase door gently behind us then gets a faraway look. Once it clears, he focuses on me.

"I told Elias what we found. They will meet us in the hall where we split up the first time."

We head out of Dorian's office and walk quickly down the hall. The two women are gone, which concerns me. We were in the office for quite a while. They could have alerted the whole Order by now. North gives me a worried look which tells me he is thinking the same thing.

We turn the corner that leads to the deserted back door hall but North freezes and tilts his head. "Incoming."

Just as the words leave his lips five people come from another hall to the left. When they see us, they spread out and aim various weapons at us. I see three handguns, two daggers, and the last person with a katana. My brows rise at the katana. Why did I not think to train with one, it seems so cool now that I see it.

North growls and hands me the Chalice. I grab it, though I am confused at what he expects me to do with it. His reason is soon revealed in the shape of his wolf form. As soon as he is shifted, he lunges for the first man off to his left. I watch all the other assassins' eyes in front of us widen and two of them race off down the hall they had come from.

Those two were not Elites then, but I already knew that. Possibly not even assassins. They could be artifact retrieval experts who felt way in over their head when they saw the wolf. I smirk and stalk forward to help North.

I place the painting down carefully against the wall and replace my dagger with my gun holstered at my side. I shoot the woman on my right who was aiming at North's back. She goes down to one knee and aims at me instead. I roll forward just as her shot goes off then pop back up and shoot her again this time in the heart, so I know she won't get back up.

The man North attacks screams as he goes down and tries to shoot the massive wolf, but North is faster and bites into the man's hand, making him drop his weapon. I feel a surge of excitement, the need to protect, and glee for the mayhem. I chuckle and shake my head without turning to check on the wolf the emotions are coming from.

The man with the katana is the last one and he eyes us both as he readies his blade. I hear the screaming man suddenly go silent then North appears by my side, growling and baring teeth at the last assassin.

The man eyes the wolf warily but does not back down. He would have made a good elite. I look to his weapon and notice it is not silver which means North should be relatively safe against it. I, on the other hand, should keep my distance. I raise my gun and get off two shots, but the man is fast and dodges them both, his katana spinning through the air in added defense.

Whoa. I really need to learn that.

He jumps and slashes at North's neck. If he were a regular wolf, that definitely would have been a killing blow but North is not a regular wolf. North races to the side just in time to miss the attack then swipes out at the assassin. The man jumps back and misses it. While he is distracted, I aim and shoot again, hitting one of his hands. The man cries out and releases part of the weapon, but his other hand is still firmly holding it.

The man does a flip off the wall and on his way down swings out at me. I reel back until my back is against the wall, but his blade keeps coming as he advances on me. I aim again, but he knocks the gun out of my hand and it skitters across the floor. He is quick and there is nowhere to run in time. He stabs toward my heart and I use the only other thing in my hand to protect myself.

The katana blade hits the Chalice instead of my body making it slide off to the side. I use the opening it makes and kick him hard in the chest. He stumbles back which is enough of a distraction for North to leap onto him and tear him apart.

My stomach twists at the sight and I turn my head and squeeze my eyes shut to avoid seeing the gruesome death. The man goes quiet and a moment later a hand lands on each side of my face. My eyes fly open and I gasp, readying the Chalice to bludgeon whatever enemy is touching me.

My heart calms when I see who it is and I lower the artifact. North has blood around his mouth and hands. I know it is not his since I do not sense any pain from him. I collapse against him and give him a hug full of relief.

He hugs me tightly then murmurs against my hair. "Did you block his sword with my pack's most prized possession and was about to hit me with it too?"

My head snaps back. "Well…yes, but—"

North chuckles. "As long as you're safe, I don't care."

He grabs the artifact gently from my hands and checks it over for damages. Only the smallest of scratches mar its surface where the blade hit it.

"C'mon, let's go. There are surely more to be on their way. Those two who ran off probably alerted the others to a wolf," he says.

I quickly grab the painting and he gently guides me down the hall with a hand on the small of my back.

I clear my throat and glance down at him before quickly averting my eyes. "Maybe you should stay in wolf form?"

North looks down at himself and chuckles. "What, you don't want me to walk around the Infinite Order naked? That will surprise the enemies more than my wolf at this point."

I roll my eyes and shake my head.

His smile is wide as he hands me the Chalice and shifts. His wolf nose nudges my hand until I give his head a pet. He yips then leads us down the hall until we finally come across his pack.

Janie sees us first and gasps. "My Lord!"

I smile at them and lay a hand on North's back. "It's ok. It is not his blood."

"The Chalice!" Elias says happily, his eyes fixated not on his Alpha but the artifact in my hand.

The others look my way at his declaration and to the gold relic in my hand.

I hold it up for them to see better and grin down at North.

"What is that?" Elias asks, pointing to the painting tucked under my arm.

I lower the Chalice and my smile drops. I glance down at the painting, obscured by my body and arm. "It is Dorian Gray's painting." I shake my head at it then look to the group. "We have the Chalice and the painting. I think we should leave now."

"Dorian Gray's painting?" Danika asks, ignoring my last statement.

Elias explains. "As in Dorian, leader of the Infinite Order."

"As in Dorian Gray the immortal?" Janie squeaks, sounding terrified. Janie looks at me, both of us remembering the conversation we had about Dorian Gray in her bakery.

I nod. "Yes, but we don't have a lot of time. We need to get out of here." I start to head toward the back door hall that we came in from but Danika stops me with a hand on my arm.

"You have the painting, we can end this now. We can kill him."

I turn on her. "It is too risky. We just fought a group of assassins, and more are surely to be on their way. Most likely the elites. You saw how hard it was just to take down one elite. Imagine four more of them plus Dorian. Our surprise is blown. We can use the painting as leverage for now." I shake my head and look to North. "Tell them we need to leave and try again another time."

Everyone looks to the massive Alpha wolf. His word is law and if he tells them to leave they will, no more arguments.

Janie, Danika, and Elias all get an unfocused look which tells me North is saying something to them through the pack link.

Elias crosses his arms and translates for me. "He says we should use the painting and kill Dorian."

I look to North stunned. "That is putting us all in danger."

"He thinks if we kill Dorian it will throw the Order into disarray and the assassins will back down."

I shake my head. "If anything, it will give them cause to hunt us even more!"

My hands shake with the stress of trying to get them to see reason.

As it turns out, our decision is taken from us.

"Well, well, well, what do we have here?"

We all turn, guards up and a growl from North, to see Dorian standing near the hall the artifact room was located down. And the elite room if I remember correctly.

Behind him are the four remaining elite assassins, each with some kind of weapon aimed at us that I would assume contains silver.

Dorian's eyes land on the Chalice and the painting in my possession, a hard, dark look entering his eyes. "My, my, you have been busy, Jessie."

Chapter 29

Norden

I watch the man in front of us and compare him to the image in the book Jessie showed me back at the castle. He is average in height and wears a dark suit. His hair is dark and long, nearly to his shoulders and his face is clean shaven. He stands with his shoulders back and exudes authority. It is remarkable. He does not look any different than he had all those years ago. As a shifter, we are immortal too, but only if we drank from the Chalice. This man is not a shifter and somehow has lived over 200 years, if the painting is any indication, without aging a day.

My focus lands on those behind him and my hackles raise at the silver in their hands. These must be the elites. The two on Dorians's right are men.

One looks older than the rest, with white streaked though his dark hair and lines on his forehead. He has a gun trained not on me but Elias with a steady hand.

The man next to him has dark, Asian set eyes and short blond hair with black roots growing out. His weapon, also a gun, is aimed at the women behind me and he smiles at them and gives them a wink.

The other two are on Dorian's left. One is a small, dark skinned, woman with long brown, curly hair and bangs. She has two daggers by her side, but I see the outline of a gun at her waist. She is not aiming at anyone in particular but she is eyeing Jessie up and down.

Lastly, a man stands next to her, totally unassuming. Brown clothes, brown hair and eyes. Dull expression. No weapon in his hand, but the way he looks at me as if waiting for me to move an inch tells me there is more to the man than I see. If I had to guess, this is the man who tried to kill Jessie in Germany.

Jessie widens her stance in preparation for a fight which makes us tense as well. Instead of launching forward to attack she holds up the painting as if it is a shield.

"Don't move, or I will destroy this," Jessie warns. To emphasize it she grabs her dagger and holds it up to zombie Dorian's face on the painting.

The elites' expressions don't change and it makes me wonder if they know about Dorian and the painting or if they are just professional enough not to show any hint of inner emotions about the situation. Probably the latter.

Dorian's eyes harden and his lips press into a thin line. It is gone in a moment and he is back to his relaxed smile. He spreads his arms out as if waiting for a hug and speaks directly to Jessie in a calm reassuring voice, completely ignoring the rest of us.

"Jessie, I've known you your whole life. I knew your mother. You wouldn't do anything to harm me would you?"

I feel Jessie's hesitation and turmoil of emotions. I step closer to her until my body is pressed into her side. Instantly her resolve hardens and warmth from our touch spreads through both of us.

Dorian must see something in her face because he shoots me a hateful glare. "Ahh, the Prince of wolves. Still alive I see. How unfortunate."

"What about me?" Jessie calls out, forcing Dorian's attention off me and back to her.

Dorian raises one dark eyebrow. "What about you?"

Jessie presses the dagger into the painting until the canvas bends back, not quite ripping but on the verge of it.

"You said it yourself. You've known me my whole life. Knew my mother. So why would you send not one but two elites after me?" She shoots a dark look at the man on Dorian's left, the plain looking one, confirming my suspicions.

"Oh that? That was just a bit of a misunderstanding," Dorian responds in his calm voice. "However, I was very surprised to hear of Veronica's death and you living with *him*." Once again Dorian shoots me a glare.

Veronica? Who was—?

"Little Red's name was Veronica?" Jessie whispers to herself then snorts as if the idea is funny to her.

That clears it up for me. The red-haired assassin. Veronica.

Jessie laughs, but it is obviously fake. "You know, *Veronica* told me some interesting things before I killed her." Dorian looks unimpressed but he stays quiet, encouraging Jessie to continue. "My mom fell in love and you disapproved."

Those were not the exact words used but they were implied.

Dorian's face twists into disgust and one of hate. His calm façade shatters and he shouts, "She fell in love with one of *them*!" He points angrily toward me and my pack. It is obvious he doesn't mean one of us literally but a wolf shifter.

"And you killed her," Jessie continues. "And you tried to kill me for the same reason. If you just left me alone, it wouldn't have come to this."

She shakes her head in disappointment then with one quick movement, she rips the dagger through the painting in a downward stroke. Jessie tosses the ruined painting on the ground in between our groups.

"No!" Dorian shouts and falls to his knees to grab the painting of himself, but it is too late. The middle of the painting hangs from the frame into two pieces and the Dorian zombie is whole no more.

We watch with bated breath for something to happen. Will Dorian dissolve into dust? Will his heart give out and he will just collapse where he kneels?

"No," Jessie whispers a moment later. "How?"

"Um, was something supposed to happen?" Danika asks from behind us.

Dorian suddenly starts laughing, a deep maniacal laugh. He stands up and tosses his painting aside. "It worked." He laughs again before continuing. "You know, I did not have the guts to destroy my painting, in the off chance it didn't work."

"What...?" Jessie asks but can't find the words to continue.

Dorian gestures to the Chalice. "You didn't think that I wouldn't try it, did you? Immortality! Of course I used it! Now I am not tied to that dreadful painting any longer and can truly fulfill all my desires." He grins maliciously at us. "Starting with killing you lot."

He gestures to those behind him and without any questions or hesitation, the four elites spring at us. I feel Elias, Danika, and Janie shift but don't look back to see if they are ready. My pack meets the assassins in the middle and chaos ensues.

A ninja star whizzes across the space, but the lady elite Jessie aimed at dodges it easily and it embeds in the wall behind her. I launch myself at the assassin just as she jumps in the air and is about to impale Jessie with a dagger. The assassin twists midair to avoid me and we fly past one another. Jessie pulls out another shuriken and throws it at her again, but the lady is fast and dodges it. Now she is trapped between us but looks unruffled to be so. She slowly puts one dagger away and pulls out a gun with one hand while keeping her other blade pointed at me.

Jessie does not wait until the gun is fully out before attacking. She kicks out at the assassin's stomach but she jumps back, taking her eye off me. I leap forward and manage to swipe her hand which causes the dagger to skitter across the floor. I yelp at the contact with silver but don't let it slow me down. The assassin does some kind of twist and is able to avoid both mine and Jessie's next attack. She aims the gun at me, no doubt loaded with silver bullets and shoots. I flatten against the floor and feel the bullet rush by. Jessie jumps at the lady and they start doing a series of fast attacks, punching, swiping, stabbing, kicking at each other until finally Jessie gets the upper hand and stabs the assassin in the stomach.

Jessie smirks at the assassin as she pulls the blade out. The assassin stares down at the wound, her hands holding it as if trying to close it up before she bleeds out. Then the assassin grins and moves her hands away to show the hole has disappeared.

Jessie and I stare at the assassin with unbelieving eyes.

I growl and look to Dorian who is watching the chaos with glee from the side lines. Noticing our dilemma, he tilts his head thoughtfully. "Oh right. I forgot to mention they drank from the Chalice too. Have to have my elites in tip-top shape after all."

"How are we supposed to kill someone who is invincible?" She asks me.

I don't have time to answer even if I could tell her. The lady assassin renews her attack.

While Jessie and I fight off the assassin in a seemingly endless battle, Elias' voice hurriedly speaks through the pack link. *"They drank from the Chalice which means they will have the same vulnerabilities."*

"Silver," we all say at once.

For the first time I notice each of the assassins wearing leather gloves and taking extra precaution not to touch the silver in their weapons.

I look to Jessie and try to relay the emotion, the desperation I feel, since I cannot speak to her like I can to the others. She glances at me, and I pointedly look at the silver dagger that is still on the floor.

She nods then feints to the left before rolling past the assassin on the right. She picks up the silver dagger and throws it at the lady, this time hitting her heart.

The lady assassin screams and scrambles at the weapon but her hands blister and she screams some more until finally she collapses and does not get up again. I listen for a heartbeat but do not hear any from her. I give Jessie a nod and a happy yip.

Jessie grins at me then reaches down and takes the gun and dagger, exchanging her weapons for the new silver ones.

We turn as one to observe the others and find the best way to help. Elias is fighting off the older man who is grinning as he twirls and ducks out of the white wolf's reaches. They seem evenly matched but it is only a matter of time before one of them makes a mistake.

Danika is fighting off the young assassin with the blond and black hair. Every time he dodges he makes a quip, either flirting or suggesting a way she could fix her attack, all of which causes Danika to growl and try again. He holds his gun down at his side and only seems to play around rather than fight. I know he is baiting her, making her angry so she will slip up.

Janie is fighting off the last man, the one all in brown but he does not seem to be holding any weapon. His face is deadpan and he makes no sound as he moves. Yet somehow he has the upper hand against Janie. He makes a move which causes Janie to yelp, though I cannot tell what he did to cause that reaction.

Janie slumps to the ground whimpering and staring up at the assassin. She does not look like she has enough energy to fight anymore. Whatever he did to her, it is slowing her down. He places a foot on her stomach and presses in as he leans over the gray and brown wolf. Something glints as he reaches for her neck and I notice it is a syringe.

I do not wait to find out what it is. I start racing toward them, my jaws open, my powerful legs pushing me to reach her before he plunges that syringe into her neck and injects her with whatever substance is in it. No doubt something deadly.

Janie's eyes flick to me and he goes still, hovering over her. Just as I am about to chomp down on his arm he dives to the side and I miss him by a few inches. The man pops back up and faces me, his face as stoic as ever and not a hair out of place.

"Be careful. Don't let him close to you."

I don't need Janie's caution to know he is dangerous at close range, but I appreciate the warning.

Just as I am about to launch myself at him, a shot rings out, followed by two more in quick succession. I freeze, fearing one of the assassins got through to my pack and turn to see who had been shot.

All three of the assassins are frozen then they look around before spotting Jessie who still has her gun raised. All at once, the three of them drop, leaving the rest of us standing in the middle of the hall safe from the elites.

Jessie smiles at me from across all of the bodies but my attention is fixed on what is behind her. I shout through the pack link as well as howl a warning. I start running just as the others do too, all of us seeing what Jessie cannot. Elias is closest but even he does not reach her in time.

Dorian had somehow snuck behind her while she was focused on all of us and with her own dagger, the yellow one I gave her in Germany, he stabs her through the back. Jessie gasps at the sudden impact and shock. She drops the gun and turns to look at Dorian, the dagger still sticking out of her.

He stares at her triumphantly and spreads his arms wide. He had a chance to escape while everyone was distracted. Instead, he took the chance to stab Jessie and therefore forfeit his life.

"If I go down, you go with me," he says to her just before she collapses in a heap on the ground in front of him.

Elias and Danika leap over her and tackle Dorian. His screams fill the hall as the two wolves tear into him. Elias and Danika make sure there is no way he can come back to life. I ignore their frenzy and shift so I can grab Jessie and clutch her to me.

Janie whimpers and limps her way to us, her body still weak from the assassin's attack before. When she reaches us she nudges her nose against Jessie's face which has suddenly gone very cold. Water drips onto

Jessie's skin and I startle, wondering where it came from, then realize when my vision blurs that I am crying.

When finished with Dorian, Elias and Danika crowd on either side of us and stare down at Jessie. I feel my soul ripping in two. I do not know how I will come back from this. No, I know that I *won't* ever come back from this. In such a short time, Moonfire has become my everything. Without her there is no point to life. Everything feels like it slows down: the world, sound, my heart.

Elias sniffs Jessie then abruptly looks to me.

"Her heart is still beating."

His words sound muffled to the buzzing in my ears. I look up at my Beta. "What?"

He repeats himself and soon we are all crowding in, silent, until we hear the faintest beating of a heart from the woman in my arms.

I grip her tighter. "Moonfire?" I choke on a sob.

"She is fading fast," Danika notes.

"The hospital is too far away and we have no way to stop the bleeding if we pull the dagger out," I say. "I'm going to lose her." I squeeze my eyes shut and a vision flashes behind my lids.

Water being poured into the Chalice. A circle of wolves gathered around a human man under a full moon. A robed figure holding the Chalice out to the man. It is a vision of the Changing ceremony. The moon seems to brighten in my mind's eye until it covers everything in its light. The vision fades and a strange voice whispers through my mind.

Drink.

"Drink?" I whisper out loud, unsure of what I saw and heard.

Drink, the voice repeats, accompanied by an image of the moon. For the briefest moment I think I see a woman in the moon's face but it, and the image in my mind, is gone just as fast as it appeared.

"Where is the Chalice?" I ask urgently and look around for the gold artifact.

My pack spreads out to look, not questioning my motives.

A moment later Elias trots over with it gently in his mouth.

"Get some water," I order and wave him away.

Elias speeds off down the hall, Danika close on his heels and I can only hope they find a place to fill up the cup and bring it back in time.

Janie whines and nudges Jessie's arm then looks at me. I don't need the pack link to know she is worried and asking if we can save her in time.

"I don't know if it will work," I tell her, "but we have to try."

I remember how I sent her healing energy in Germany. It was enough to keep her alive until a cure could arrive. I have to try it now. I search inside for the bond, but it is slippery and thinning fast. It feels like it will break at any moment and she will be lost forever. I grit my teeth and grab hold of the fading bond with a tight mental grasp and shove everything I have down it to her.

Janie lays down next to us, her head on her paws, and whimpers softly.

I lean down and whisper against Jessie's skin. "Hang in there Moonfire, just a little longer. Don't leave me. I just found you and we are finally mated. It can't be your time to leave just yet. The Goddess would not do that to us. I promise you if you hold on for just a little longer, I will buy you all the knives you can ever want and you can throw them at me any time I displease you."

I send her my warmth and love through our bond with the healing energy, but I have no idea if she feels it. The bond is hanging on by a thread. Any moment now and it will break for good, and me along with it.

Janie's head suddenly pops up and she looks down the hall. I follow her gaze and see Elias in his human form carefully holding the Chalice, making sure not even a drop spills. Danika trots next to him, still in her wolf form.

Elias quickly kneels next to us and brings the rim of the Chalice to Jessie's lips. I prop her up with an arm and open her mouth with the other hand. He quickly pours liquid into her mouth slowly yet steadily. Some of it dribbles out the side of her mouth but we keep going, making sure it goes down all the way.

I start to feel faint and weak, my energy still pouring into her. Soon I will not be able to hold on to consciousness.

When it is all gone, Elias sits back cradling the Chalice in his hands and I release her jaw. I tip her to the side then very delicately, extract the dagger from her back. Blood gushes out and I choke on a sob at seeing it come from my mate.

Painful moments pass and my hope starts to diminish. My vision starts to go dark around the edges and it is getting tougher to breathe.

It was not enough. She was too far gone.

The others have the same thought, that or my thoughts are spread through the pack link, because all at once we drop our heads solemnly.

A gasp spears the silence and the body in my arms jerks like a lightning bolt has hit it. A rush of feeling enters my body, nearly overwhelming me and I feel the bond solidify and strengthen. The healing energy cuts off. My eyes shoot to Jessie's face and her bright brown eyes are open, staring right back.

"Moonfire?" I say, choking on a sob.

The others' heads pop up and they look at Jessie. When they see what I see, Elias whoops loudly and raises the Chalice to his lips to give it a long kiss.

Janie and Danika yip happily and lick Jessie's face.

Jessie groans so I shove the wolves away and help her sit up.

"How are you feeling, my love?" I search her face and down her body to see if this is real and if she has any injuries. When I find nothing wrong, I look back into her eyes, waiting for a response.

"What—" She frowns and looks around. "I was stabbed."

She tries to look at her back and when that doesn't work she reaches back with a hand to touch the spot where a dagger had once been. Finding nothing there, not even a bloody hole she asks in a breathy voice, "How?"

Elias holds out the Chalice. "Welcome to the immortals club."

Jessie gasps and looks to me. "Does that mean— Does that mean I am...a werewolf now?"

Elias and I chuckle.

When our laughs subside I hug her close again. "No, you are not turned. That would have killed you if I tried. You are just going to live a very long life." I give her a stern frown. "But you will have to stay away from silver from now on."

She nods, a slow smile spreading over her lips. "No silver, got it."

She looks around at the dead bodies and finally at the mutilated carcass of her former boss. A pang of sadness spears her heart, and therefore mine.

"Now what?" She asks.

I lean down until she is only an inch away. Our breaths mingle and my lips tingle although I haven't pressed them to hers yet. "Now we go home."

Then I kiss my mate.

Epilogue

Jessie

Immortal.

Not a word I ever thought I would use to describe myself.

I reach back and touch the spot where a dagger had been impaled in my body. It is so strange not to feel anything there, not even a sore muscle. I am pretty sure I was dead, or as close to it as one could be without the soul actually leaving the body. Yet, I felt a pull deep in my bones to wake up and an electric tingle zipped through my entire body. Finally, the mate bond pulled me the rest of the way out of the dark depths and I opened my eyes to see North crying over me.

My heart aches remembering that first sight upon wakening.

A hand reaches out and squeezes mine.

I look up into golden-green, sympathetic eyes.

He must have felt my emotions.

I smile and squeeze his hand back, then take a deep breath and face forward.

"Ready?" North asks.

I press my lips together in a determined line and give him a single nod showing a confident exterior look. However, inside my belly is twisting with nerves and my hands are starting to shake. North steps closer until I am pressed into his side.

"It's only my Father, you have nothing to worry about."

Just as he says this to me, the door to the large manor house opens and three forms rush out.

Easton, Wesley, and Sutton. Or as they call themselves: East, West, and South. Each brother nicknamed after the compass point they are in charge of in the world. North told me how his Father hated those nicknames and I am a little excited to see that annoyance in person. That being the only thing I am excited about for this visit.

South does not stop when he reaches us. Instead, he yanks me away from North's side and picks me up to give me a bear hug. I groan at the tight squeeze and tap his back to put me down.

South laughs and sets me down after a couple more moments of hugging.

"You are going to kill me with those hugs," I say hunched over, wheezing to get air back in my lungs.

South laughs and smacks me on the back in a friendly manner but his werewolf strength sends me flying forward. "You're immortal now, that won't kill you anytime soon."

North catches me and growls over my shoulder at his brother. "That doesn't stop it from hurting," he says in a low, dangerous voice.

South holds up his hands, palms outward, in surrender and backs away.

East and West approach much more calmly and each give me a gentle hug.

I smile up at the brothers, glad they are all here to show support for what I am about to face.

"Norden," a voice booms from the doorway.

I jump, startled by the sound and we turn as one to face the new arrival.

An older man with thick, wavy, dark hair and a commanding air stands with his hands in his expensive looking suit pants. He is not wearing a matching suit jacket, but he has the sleeves of his white button shirt rolled halfway up his forearms. His skin is tan as if he has spent plenty of hours in the sun. His jaw is hidden behind a dark beard with matching mustache and his eyes are as green as North's. From this distance, I cannot see if his eyes also have golden rings like North's but I am too nervous to move forward and check.

His eyes move to me next and tighten in disapproval.

"Father," North says in greeting, pulling his attention away from me.

Without saying another word, the King of wolf shifters turns and walks inside the manor, expecting us to follow.

I look to North and bite my lip worriedly. He throws an arm around my shoulders and tugs me toward the building. "Don't worry, I am right here."

"Yeah, we won't let him mess with you," South says from my other side.

Right. I have four Alphas on my side plus intensive training as an assassin. I don't have anything to be worried about. The words do little to comfort me.

Inside, the hall opens up into a large greeting area. A chandelier hangs above us and down the hall are plenty of archways that lead deeper into the home. On the right is a staircase leading up further into the house. Off to the left is a sitting room in which North steers me and two people are already seated on a floral love seat. A tea tray is set out on a table in front of the couple but neither look interested in drinking any.

The King does not rise or say a word when we enter, but the woman next to him does not hesitate to come over and greet each of her sons with a hug and kiss. I take a moment to study her. She obviously has a different sort of character to her husband. Where he is cold and aloof she is warm and friendly. She is about the same height as the King but her hair is the same golden color as North and Sutton's and her eyes are brown. She looks older but there are no wrinkles anywhere on her skin. She is wearing a green jumpsuit of fine, expensive material.

Lastly, she turns to me and looks me up and down with a genuinely happy smile. When she is done with her perusal she looks to North with a satisfied grin and winks at him. My cheeks heat and I shoot North a wide-eyed look.

North is smiling at us, pleased with his mother's approval.

Suddenly I am wrapped up in a hug and I tense, unsure what I should do. Do I hug the Queen back or stay still? I end up patting her back with one hand, a half hug, and she finally pulls back but her hands grip my shoulders refusing to let go completely.

"It is so lovely to meet you, Jessie. You can call me Aida. Come, come."

She guides me to a couch across from the love seat and gestures for me to sit down before moving back to her spot next to her husband. North and South take seats on either side of me while East and West take the two chairs flanking the couch.

"Tea, dear?" Aida asks, her hand on the teapot.

I shake my head, too nervous to be able to hold a cup of hot liquid, so she raises her eyebrows in silent question as she looks to the others in the room.

Only East nods and she pours a cup for herself and him. All the while the King stares at North and me, an unreadable expression on his face. Silence fills the room, pressing in on me.

I decide to make the first move and clear my throat. "It is nice to meet you both, Aida and…" North never told me his father's name, so I leave it open for the man himself to fill in.

"Call me King Alpha," he says.

North snorts and shakes his head but does not offer a different suggestion.

I nod slowly. "Ok, well nice to meet you Aida and…King Alpha?" My statement turns into a question by the time I am done speaking. It feels odd to call him King or Alpha considering I am not part of the pack.

"Why are we here?" North jumps in when the silence starts to grow.

"Norden, you know we want to meet your mate. If it was up to you, we would never meet her," Aida says with a chuckle, but her voice is tight and she glances at her husband warningly.

He ignores her look and leans forward with a fake smile. "Yes, it is…interesting to meet your mate. An assassin. Who tried to kill you twice already." His smile tightens and his eyes flash wolf yellow before going back to green. "And someone you gave immortality to without consulting your King first."

North's emotions slam into me, rage being in the forefront. "She would have died," he says tightly.

The King sits back and arches a brow. "Whatever way it happened, she has drunk from the Chalice without being pack. She is not tied to us in any way—"

"You mean other than being my mate?" North adds sarcastically.

The King continues, ignoring his comment, "—and the rules of the packs will not bend for anyone."

"What are you getting at?" West asks, a dangerous note entering his tone.

The King looks to all of us before settling on Norden and speaking like I am not even there. "She must become a wolf. She must go through the change…"

Finally, the King Alpha looks at me and a slow predatory smile spreads across his face. "…or she dies."

My head snaps to Norden as his does to me. His eyes are full of rage and I feel it burn inside me as well as a sense of protectiveness from his wolf. I know he will do whatever it takes to protect me, even from his Father. But his father is King Alpha and his Alpha power is surely much stronger than any of the brothers. They might not get a choice in the end.

Dread settles in my belly.

I am immortal but that doesn't matter. I must become a wolf…or die.

Note from the Author

Ways to help Independent authors (without paying anything!):

--Rate and review the book on Amazon and Goodreads

--Follow them on social networks

--Post about the book

--Recommend to friends, family, and even strangers.

Your support means everything and would be much appreciated.

Acknowledgements

I am so glad this book is finally done. My motivation has been at a low point throughout the year and it has been a struggle to juggle work and writing.

Thankfully I have an amazing support system with Victoria Gillette who is always asking about my works in progress and loves being the first to read anything I write and with Harrison Lambeth, my hubby, who has recently been doing a variation of the 'are we there yet' phrase by saying 'is your book done yet' nearly every day.

I also want to show my appreciation here for those who read and love my books. I write for you and your support and words of love for my stories makes me happy and wanting to do more.

Here is a big shout out to the amazing Sheila Rougé (Ouroboros Design) for the cover design. Brilliant as always. I hope to work more with them in the future.

About the Author

Katie Dunn grew up in the hot part of Arizona where she graduated NAU and became a teacher. She got a taste of the author life after her first YA contemporary fantasy novel Ancient Elements. Finding out she loved writing just as much as reading, teaching, and traveling, she sat down and wrote the first installment of the YA fantasy adventure Skor Stone trilogy: Pirates from Under and YA contemporary fantasy novel Myth Blessed. She has a notebook full of other ideas and will slowly be adding more stories to her author library.

You can check out more about Katie Dunn's books and works in progress at Kdunnauthor.com or social media platforms under Kdunnauthor.